GWYNNETH EVER AFTER

By Linda Poitevin

Unlikely Meetings

He took a couple of steps away, then swung back to face her again. "You wouldn't like to get a cup of coffee, would you?"

"I beg your pardon?" She stared at him. She knew she was being rude, but she couldn't help it. She was too stunned to be polite.

"Coffee," he repeated, the thread of amusement back again. "Hot, black…I'm sure you'll recognize it when you see it."

"I-I-" Gwyn stammered. The bus, dinner for the kids…oh, heck, why not? What was another half hour added on to how late she'd already be? Even if he turned out not to be the real Gareth Connor, she'd have one heck of a tale to go along with Sandy's gift. She took her keys out of the ignition, picked up her uncooperative shoulder bag, and exited the car.

"Coffee would be nice," she said, and held out her hand to him. "I'm Gwyn Jacobs."

"Gareth Connor," he replied, accepting her handshake.

Gwyn's heart gave a mighty thud, knocking most of the air from her lungs. All right, so women like her did sit beside famous actors in obscure Ottawa theaters. She collected herself, withdrew her hand, and said with what she considered remarkable aplomb, "I thought I recognized you."

Praise for Gwynneth Ever After

"An intriguing, fast and fun read, Gwynneth Ever After sparkles with Poitevin's fresh voice." – *Joan Swan, USA Today Bestselling Author*

"GWYNNETH EVER AFTER is double-chocolate cake" — *The Romance Reviews*

"Endlessly fun and charming! Gwynnth Ever After is the ultimate Cinderella tale complete with toddlers, single parenthood, and paparazzi." – *Carolyn Crane, author of The Disillusionists*

"…endearing characters, full of warmth and depth, in a beautifully compelling story so deftly told it made me feel like I was coming home to old friends." –*Romantic Reads and Such*

"I laughed, I cried, I cringed and by the end of the story, I definitely wanted more." –*Unconventional Book Reviews*

"…a descriptive flair that makes even the normal and small moments special." – *The Pleasure of My Good Regard*

"I had a hard time putting the book down, in fact I didn't, I stayed up all night just so I could finish it." — *Dandelion Wine Book Blog*

GWYNNETH EVER AFTER
(Previously published as A Fairy Tale For Gwyn)
Published by Michem Publishing
Copyright 2013 by Linda Poitevin
Cover art by Kanaxa

For more information, address: Michem Publishing,
P.O. Box 146
203 Chemin Aylmer
Gatineau, QC Canada
J8H 1E5

ISBN: 9780991995813

For Pat, my very own Prince Charming

Acknowledgments

Bringing a book to print publication on one's own is a longer and more involved process than I ever imagined—but it can be made infinitely easier with the support of enthusiastic readers. For giving me such support, a huge and heartfelt thank you goes out to my Facebook followers and the Wattpad reading community. Your encouragement gave me the push I needed, and I am so very pleased to finally put this book in your hands. I hope you enjoy!

CHAPTER 1

Gwyn Jacobs stuffed sketchpad and charcoal pencils into her shoulder bag, and then, satisfied she had everything she needed, she turned to her babysitter.

"There," she said, pulling on black leather gloves. "I think I'm organized. Any questions?"

Her neighbor's eighteen-year-old daughter, Kirsten, eyed the black bag. "Are you sure they'll let you do that?"

"What?"

"Sketch during the play. It just seems…I don't know…rude, I guess."

"I arranged for a private box." Gwyn tucked a stray auburn curl behind her ear with one hand and waved away Kirsten's concerns with the other. "Besides, even if the other seat happens to occupied, which isn't likely on a Sunday, how distracting can a piece of paper and a pencil be?"

She slung the bag over her shoulder and, using her gloved fingers, ticked off a list of instructions. "Lunch is in the fridge, they can have fruit and cookies for a snack, and I'll keep my cell phone on vibrate in case you need me. Oh, and Katie will be home sometime around two from the birthday party, so if you go to the park, you'll need to be back in time for her. I should be home around four thirty."

She called a final farewell to Maggie and Nicholas, parked in the adjacent living room in front of their favorite computer game, then pulled open the front door and stepped onto the porch. A gust of wind whipped her coat around her legs. Eyeing the gloomy November sky, she looked over her shoulder at Kristen.

"And make sure—"

"Raincoats," Kristen said, making shooing motions. "They'll wear them, I promise. Now stop worrying and go have fun!"

Gwyn stashed her shoulder bag behind the driver's seat and checked her watch. Late, of course. When was she ever on time for anything? She sighed and slid in behind the steering wheel. Even if she hit every light green along the way, she'd be lucky to make it in time for the curtain.

A few fat raindrops spattered against the windshield and she muttered an imprecation under her breath. Great. First a long-winded conversation with a client, then a desperate sprint to the department store for a birthday gift for Katie to take to the party she'd forgotten, then a juice incident in the living room, and now rain. Everyone from the kids to the weather gods appeared to be conspiring against her last-ditch effort to get Sandy's birthday present under way.

The rain fell faster, pinging against the car's metal shell. With another sigh, she switched on first the windshield wipers and then the headlights.

She arrived at the theater and dashed in as the lobby lights flickered on and off in a warning to patrons to take their seats. An usher met her at the top of the sweeping staircase and guided her to a small, private box. He murmured to her to enjoy the show, then disappeared behind the crimson velvet drape that dropped across the doorway. In a tangle of coat, gloves, scarf, and bag, she plopped into a seat.

A sideways glance told her the other seat was occupied after all. Her heart sank a little. So much for the hope of not disturbing anyone else with her sketching, though given the day so far, she supposed she should have expected as much.

The house lights flickered again, prompting her to sort herself out. She tried to do so with as little fuss as possible but still managed to whack her seat companion on the knee with her bag—twice—before dropping her gloves at his feet. Then, when she dived down to retrieve the errant items, her pencils spilled onto the floor with a clatter and her coat slid off her lap onto her feet.

Pausing, Gwyn closed her eyes and took a slow, deep breath. If she continued like this, she'd knock apart the theater before the curtain rose. Or else get herself kicked out.

She opened her eyes again. With all the calm she could muster, she picked up her coat, stuffed gloves and scarf into one sleeve, and shoved the bundle under her seat, hoping to God as she did that the floor had been swept sometime in the last decade. Turning to retrieve her pencils, she blinked as they came into focus under her nose, held out to her by her neighbor.

"Are you always this organized?" a deep male voice asked, a faint accent—British?—and a definite thread of amusement running through it.

Wrinkling her nose, Gwyn reached to accept the pencils from her seat companion. A lighthearted comment about not getting out often sat enough on the tip of her tongue, but it died there as she raised her eyes to the face beyond the hand. It couldn't be. No way. A look-alike, maybe, but not the genuine article, because things like this just didn't happen in real life.

Women like her simply didn't sit down in a faded, yesteryear Ottawa theater and find themselves staring into the eyes of a Hollywood star.

She realized her companion waited for her response, one heavy black eyebrow raised. The lights began to dim. Snapping her mouth closed, she hoped against hope the encroaching dark would hide the blush scorching her cheeks. And then, because eloquence failed no matter how hard she tried, she fell back on automatic and very dull manners.

"Sorry," she muttered, and subsided into her seat.

Sorry? She thought she had an honest-to-God, real-live famous actor in the seat next to her, and all she could find to say was *sorry*? Whatever happened to *wow, you look just like Gareth Connor*—or something even more straightforward, like *aren't you*—? Heck, even if the man weren't the actor himself, he was the spitting image...and he was sharing her box!

She missed the first act entirely.

When Gareth—or whoever he was—began applauding, she jumped in her seat and took a full ten seconds before following suit. Then, as the stage curtain descended and the lights brightened, she risked a sideways peek from under her lashes. The man slumped sideways in his seat, leaning against the armrest furthest from her and studying his program.

He wore a thick fisherman's knit sweater, its snowy color accenting dark and undeniably familiar good looks. Her mouth went dry. She swallowed hard, then let her eyes take in other details.

Same trademark thick, wavy hair brushing his shoulders. Same high cheekbones. Same heavy eyebrows. Same mouth that thousands of women in the developed world fantasized about...

She gave herself a mental shake.

But definitely the wrong odds.

Gareth Connor lived, she presumed, either in Wales, his country of origin, or in Hollywood, where he made his films. The chances of his being in the Canterbury Theater in west-end Ottawa on a Sunday afternoon in November—and sharing her box, to top it off...

It simply wasn't possible.

After what had to have been the longest intermission in all of history, and certainly the most awkward, uncomfortable silence Gwyn had ever experienced, the overhead lights dimmed again. Reminding herself she'd come to the theater for a reason other than adolescent gawking, she withdrew her sketchbook from her bag. Between school activities, Halloween costumes, and client deadlines, it had taken her the better part of a month to make time for this project in the first place. With Sandy's birthday only a couple of weeks away, it had become a now-or-never kind of thing. So. She'd just ignore who's-his-face next to her, pretend she was in complete control, and—

The curtain lifted. Focusing on the stage construction, she put pencil to paper and, by the glow of the exit sign over the curtained doorway, began to work.

It wasn't easy. Every time the Gareth look-alike shifted in his seat, her heart gave an absurd little jump, and her pencil quite maddeningly followed suit. Halfway through the third act, however, she had a reasonable sketch of the stage, and her concentration had returned.

By the time the overhead lights came on at the end of the play, she was so absorbed in adding last-minute details that she'd quite forgotten about the man seated next to her. Right up until she heard his voice beside her ear.

"You're very talented."

Gwyn's charcoal pencil tip skidded across the page. She swore under her breath.

Her seatmate did the same. "Damn. I'm sorry, I didn't mean to startle you." He picked up the eraser from the armrest and handed it to her.

"That's all right. It's repairable." She scrubbed away the error and then held up the sketchpad. To her critical eye, her earlier lack of focus was painfully obvious. She sighed. At least it was a start, however, and she still had time to improve on it before taking it in for framing.

"I think it's very good. But do you always come to plays so you can ignore the actors and draw pictures?" A glint of laughter in his dark eyes belied the seriousness of his voice.

Gwyn smiled back. "Only when I've sat through so many rehearsals I think I know everyone's lines by heart. I helped with the set design."

"And today you sketched it because—?"

"It's a birthday present for my best friend. She wrote and directed the play—it's her first. I wanted to do something for her as a keepsake, but for all the times I've sat here and stared at that blasted stage, do you think I could remember a single detail when I tried to do this at home?"

Her companion chuckled. "Well, it was worth the effort. I'm sure she'll love it."

"Thank you. Here, let me get my things out of your way."

She reached down, only to have history—to her everlasting mortification—repeat itself. The bag tipped, and an assortment of charcoal pencils scattered for a second time at their feet. Gwyn sat, frozen. Then she ventured a peek at her neighbor.

"I don't suppose you'll believe me if I say that I'm not usually this clumsy, will you?"

He met her gaze with a solemnity that lost something in the twitching of his lips. "Not a chance," he replied.

"I didn't think so." She started to lean over, but a hand on her arm stopped her. Her heart skipped two full beats.

"Maybe I should do the honors."

He gathered the pencils with quick efficiency and handed them over once again. Then he waited for her to replace everything in her bag, refusing her offer to move out of his way so he could leave.

"I think we'll get everything sealed up where it can't escape first," he said.

When she had her drawing tools packed and the zipper done up on her bag, he retrieved her coat, removed her gloves and scarf, and shook everything out. Gwyn slid her arms into the lined, navy-blue wool garment he held for her.

"Thank you," she said. "For your patience as well as your help. I hope I didn't distract you too much."

Her seat companion opened his mouth as though to say something, paused, and smiled. "It was for a good cause. I hope your friend likes her gift."

With a smile and a brief incline of his head, he stepped through the velvet curtains into the hallway beyond and disappeared. Gwyn stared after him, still wondering, shoulders tingling from the touch of warm, strong hands as he'd settled her coat into place.

CHAPTER 2

Gareth Connor fished the car keys from his coat pocket as he stepped out of the theater and into the cold Canadian November. That had been quite the experience in there—rather like tangling with a small tornado, albeit far more pleasant. Shaking his head at his own lingering smile, he turned up the collar on his wool coat and skirted a puddle on the sidewalk.

He'd almost introduced himself, but after her initial start of recognition, she'd seemed content to withdraw into her own little world. It had actually been quite a novelty for him, sitting beside a stranger who hadn't behaved as if they were best friends. His smile turned rueful. For that reason alone, he should have introduced himself. A woman who didn't fall all over him was downright refreshing.

And a woman who didn't fall all over him *and* who looked as good as she had...

He'd ended up ignoring much of the play in favor of watching her work, barely visible in the dim light of their shared box. Her hair had fascinated him. A wild tangle of spirals that she'd tried—and failed—to tame with a clip. Until the full set of house lights had come on at the end of the play, he'd had to guess at its auburn color. He'd been strangely satisfied to find his guess accurate. Not because he was right, but because auburn suited her so well. Rich, untamed auburn.

And blue eyes. Laughing blue eyes that crinkled at the corners when she wrinkled her nose at her finished sketch.

And skin the color of—

A sudden, icy blast of wind sliced through thoughts he had no business having. Rounding the corner of the theater to the parking lot, he pulled out a pair of gloves and tugged them on, putting the woman out of his mind. As intriguing as the encounter might have been, he had other concerns right now.

A raindrop splashed onto his cheek and he put up his hand to wipe it away. God, what a time of year to be visiting this part of Canada. Trust Catherine to move all the way across the Atlantic to this. Sometimes he wondered if her choice hadn't been just a little bit spiteful...

He shrugged off the thought. None of that mattered anymore. He was here now, they were both adults, and he had too much at stake to start analyzing motives or leveling accusations. Far, far too much at stake.

Very soon, they would talk, he and his ex. They would talk, and they would settle this once and for all. And then...then he would see. Just as he wouldn't analyze motives, neither would he jinx the outcome with too many expectations.

Patience, Connor. You've waited this long, you can last a few more days.

Long strides brought him to a blue sedan, one of a handful of cars left in the lot. He inserted a key in the lock, then paused. A few spaces away, headlights glowed faintly from a car that held no occupant. His mind returned to spilled pencils and auburn hair. Another smile tugged.

What were the chances?

Gwyn saw her car's dying headlights the instant she entered the parking lot. Her heart dropped to her rapidly chilling toes. *Oh, no. No, no, no.*

She couldn't have.

But she had, and the faint click when she twisted the key in the ignition, unaccompanied by even the tiniest turn of the engine, confirmed it. She groaned, swore vehemently, and groaned again. Her breath fogged in the chill.

She folded her arms across the steering wheel and rested her head against them. She pictured the overdue auto-club membership form nestled in the 'to-do' basket on her desk at home. A groan escaped her. Maybe she'd rename the receptacle the 'too-late' basket when she got home. *If* she got home.

And it was a big *if*.

With significant payments from three clients sitting in the same *too late* basket, she'd temporarily maxed out her credit card and bottomed out her checking account. A tow truck to give her a boost would cost a fortune that didn't exist in an obtainable form just now. Ditto a cab to take her home.

Heck, she'd even arranged to pay Kirsten with a check, on condition that her babysitter not cash it until after Gwyn made it to the bank tomorrow.

She squeezed her eyes shut and tried to think calmly through her options. Sandy always went out for drinks with the cast after a performance, and she didn't own a cell phone, so she'd be no help. Alex and Elaine, Kirsten's parents, were away for the weekend, and—

A tap on her window made her turn her head. She stared in disbelief at her former seatmate. His mouth tipped upward at one corner and he motioned for her to roll down the window.

"Problems?" he asked.

She bit her lip, loathe to admit her idiocy. Then she sighed. "I left the lights on," she said. "You wouldn't happen to have any booster cables, would you?"

He shook his head. "I'm afraid not. I have a cell phone, though."

She held up her own. "So do I, thanks."

"Have you called a truck?"

"No. I'll just catch a bus home and have my neighbor drive me over to collect the car tomorrow." At least she had that much money with her. She hoped.

"Are you sure?"

"Positive."

Yeah, right. Absolutely certain she wanted to spend the next three hours trying to travel the short distance across the Ottawa River to the Aylmer sector of Gatineau on the buses' roundabout Sunday routes. Oh well, at least it would give her ample time to reflect on how much of a ditz this incredibly good-looking man must think she was.

She mustered a weak smile. "Thanks anyway."

"You're welcome. Goodnight." He took a couple of steps away, then swung back to face her again. "You wouldn't like to get a cup of coffee, would you?"

"I beg your pardon?" She stared at him. She knew she was being rude, but she couldn't help it. She was too stunned to be polite.

"Coffee," he repeated, the thread of amusement back again. "Hot, black…I'm sure you'll recognize it when you see it."

"I-I-" Gwyn stammered. The bus, dinner for the kids…oh, heck, why not? What was another half hour added on to how late she'd already be? Even if he turned out not to be the real Gareth Connor, she'd have one heck of a tale to go along with Sandy's gift. She took her keys out of the ignition, picked up her uncooperative shoulder bag, and exited the car.

"Coffee would be nice," she said, and held out her hand to him. "I'm Gwyn Jacobs."

"Gareth Connor," he replied, accepting her handshake.

Gwyn's heart gave a mighty thud, knocking most of the air from her lungs. All right, so women like her *did* sit beside famous actors in obscure Ottawa theaters. She collected herself, withdrew her hand, and said with what she considered remarkable aplomb, "I thought I recognized you."

"I wasn't sure if you did or not."

"I think it was more a case of not believing my own eyes," she said, her voice wry. "Canterbury Theater in Ottawa is a little out of the way for you, I'd think."

He smiled and shrugged without giving a direct reply. "There's a bistro across the street. Shall we?"

She held up her cell phone. "Give me two seconds to call my babysitter first. I need to let her know I'll be late."

Gareth Connor's eyes flickered at the word *babysitter*, but he said nothing, merely moving a few steps off to wait for her.

Gwyn made a quick call to ask Kirsten to reheat yesterday's leftover macaroni and cheese casserole for dinner—and to assure her she'd make it home sometime before the kids went to bed. Then, ending the connection, she took a deep breath and joined her coffee companion, the real live Gareth Connor, on the sidewalk.

CHAPTER 3

The warmth of the bistro wrapped around Gwyn the instant they stepped through the door, making her realize how cold the late afternoon had become. Shivering, she pulled her chin into her scarf. A few tables away, a waitress looked up, did a visible double-take, and nearly dropped a coffee cup into an equally startled customer's lap. Excitement murmured through the room.

Gwyn glanced sideways at Gareth, but he seemed oblivious to the sudden stir in the tiny restaurant.

"There's a table over there," he said, nodding toward the window.

His hand settled into the small of her back, guiding her through the bistro, past the whispers and stares marking their progress. At the table, she peeled off her gloves and tucked them into a pocket, then unbuttoned her coat. Gareth moved to slide it from her shoulders.

"Not yet, thanks," she said. "I think I'll warm up first."

Gareth shed his own coat, hung it on the back of his chair and joined her at the table, which promptly shrank ten sizes. Facing her companion across the blue-and-white checked tablecloth, Gwyn tucked her hands into her lap and tried for a casual air.

When she couldn't think of a single thing to say, however, she felt pretty sure her attempt failed miserably.

The silence at their table stretched. Just as it reached excruciating on the awkward scale, the waitress arrived with two cardboard menus and a steaming coffee pot.

"Just coffee for me, thanks," Gwyn murmured.

"Are you sure?" Gareth asked. "If your kids are eating dinner without you..."

"I'm fine, thanks." Far too many butterflies resided in her belly to allow the addition of food. Coffee alone could be a challenge.

The waitress took her time filling their cups and retrieving their menus. She made no effort to conceal her blatant appraisal of Gareth, excitement warring with disbelief in her eyes. Gwyn ducked her head to hide a smile. She knew exactly how the poor girl felt.

At last the waitress departed, still looking undecided about Gareth's identity. Gwyn regarded her companion.

"Is it always like this when you go somewhere?"

Gareth shrugged. "Sometimes it's worse," he said. "You get used to it."

Gwyn reached for the chrome-and-glass sugar dispenser and sprinkled a rough teaspoon's worth into her coffee. She searched for a conversation topic.

"So, what in the world are you doing in Ottawa, Mr. Connor?"

Not overly clever as an opening, but better than another silence.

"Gareth," he replied. "And I'm hiding."

"Oh?" She smiled at the frank admission. "From anyone in particular?"

Gareth shook his head. "More like everyone in general. I have a cousin here, and when I needed a holiday, he suggested I visit him. Apparently you Canadians are very respectful of people's privacy. Remarkably unobtrusive, he called you."

"When we're not hitting you with shoulder bags and dropping pencils at your feet, you mean."

He chuckled, a rich, warm sound that blended well with the cozy bistro surroundings and made Gwyn's breath hitch a little.

"Something like that," he agreed.

"How long are you here for?"

"A week or two. I'm—" He hesitated, then shrugged. "It depends."

"You picked a heck of a time of year to visit."

Gareth stirred a teaspoon of sugar and some cream into his own coffee. "It's not that bad. You're about three weeks closer to winter than we are at home, but otherwise the weather is similar."

"You have the same indecisive weather gods in Wales? Lucky you." Gwyn grimaced. "So far we've been scraping ice off the windshields one day and going without our jackets the next. But I shouldn't complain too much. We might even have a green Christmas this year."

"That's a good thing?"

"It depends."

"On?"

"On whether you're speaking to my kids or the person who has to shovel the driveway." She flashed him a grin. "If I had my way, it would snow on Christmas Eve and melt on

Boxing Day. Although I suppose it could snow now," she added thoughtfully, "if it would stick to the lawns and stay off the roads and sidewalks."

Gareth laughed. "You don't dream big, do you?"

"Me? Never." She wrapped her hands around her own mug and lifted it to her lips, pausing to inhale the pungent aroma before taking a sip. Hot and faintly bitter, the dark liquid chased away the last of her chill. She set down the cup again and shrugged out of her coat.

"Do you do set design for a lot of plays at the theater?" Gareth asked, nodding out the window towards the building on the other side of the street.

"Not really—I just have trouble saying no to someone with a good story." Gwyn picked up her mug again. "Sandy's my best friend and I wanted to help out. The only people I know who actually frequent that place are the ones trying to have it preserved as a historical monument of some kind."

"I take it you don't think the theater is worth preserving?"

"Hardly. Don't get me wrong, I love heritage buildings. My own house is well over a hundred years old. But I don't believe in saving a place just because it was built a specific number of years ago. The Canterbury was an eyesore when it went up, and it remains one now."

"What about its architectural style?"

She snorted. "Styles, plural. Whoever designed the place drew on about seven different ones that should never have been combined."

"You wouldn't by any chance be an architect, would you?"

"Am I that obvious? Sorry about that." A sudden possibility occurred to her and she scrunched up her nose. "Crap. Let me guess. Your cousin is the head of the preservation committee and you're in Ottawa to act as a spokesperson, aren't you?"

Gareth shook his head, teeth gleaming against tanned skin. "You don't have to apologize, and no, I'm not here for the sake of the building."

"The play, then?" Gwyn raised a skeptical eyebrow. "I love Sandy dearly, and I'm thrilled her play ran as long as it did, but there's no way you were there because of word-of-mouth."

"Would you believe Sunday afternoon boredom? Sean—my cousin—is a cop. He's working today and I got tired of looking at his apartment walls, so I went for a drive. When I saw the marquee, I decided to give it a try. I asked for a private box and ended up sitting beside you."

"Where you were too busy picking up my pencils to be bored anymore."

"Exactly." Gareth's dark eyes danced. "You were very entertaining."

"I can imagine." She took another swallow of coffee. "Has your cousin lived here long?"

"All his life, but he spent summers in Wales with my family until he started university. We're the only boys in the family, so he's always been more of a kid brother than a cousin."

"That must have been nice for you."

"Not when I was fourteen and he wanted to follow me everywhere, but I appreciated it once I grew up. What about you? Does your family live here?"

"My parents both died a few years ago. I have a sister down in the States and a brother who's working in South America somewhere. We're not what you'd call close."

"That has to be tough for you, with kids of your own."

"It has its moments," she admitted, "but for the most part the kids and I manage pretty well. I have an amazing sitter, whom they love, and a great bunch of friends who help out when I need it."

Leaning back in his chair, he raised his hands and locked them behind his head. His sweater pulled tight across his chest. Gwyn tried hard not to notice, but she couldn't help but wonder just how well developed pectorals had to be before they became visible under—

"How many do you have?" Gareth asked. "Kids, I mean, not friends."

"Excuse me," a voice interrupted, "but aren't you Gareth Connor?"

Gwyn pulled her gaze from the chest she wasn't staring at. The waitress had returned, blushing fiery red, shredding a paper napkin and gritting her teeth with fierce determination. Two other servers huddled open-mouthed by the cash register, watching the proceedings, and several restaurant patrons eavesdropped with no sign of embarrassment.

Gareth turned his attention to the young woman beside their table. "I am," he said. "And you are—?"

"St-St-Stephanie. Stephanie Williams. My friends call me Steff."

"I'm pleased to meet you, Steff," he said, his eyes crinkling at the corners.

Gwyn regarded Stephanie Williams with faint alarm. The poor girl looked like she might explode without any warning at all. Her knees actually buckled when Gareth reached to shake her hand.

The waitress shot her a quick look. "I don't mean to interrupt or anything," she stammered, "but would you—could I—?"

She gave up trying to speak and shoved the napkin toward Gareth. He took the remains of what looked to have been worried half to death by a terrier and smoothed it out on the tabletop.

"Do you have a pen?" he asked.

Stephanie plucked a pen from her apron pocket with shaking fingers. Gareth scrawled something across the tattered paper and then handed pen and napkin back to the waitress. The girl fled without so much as a thank you.

"Sorry about that," he said, turning his attention back to Gwyn. "Where were we?"

"Does that happen often?" she asked, genuinely curious.

"Something else you get used to. You were going to tell me about your kids."

"Pardon?"

"Your kids," he reminded her. "How many do you have?"

"Oh. Three. Katie is seven, and Maggie and Nicholas are four."

"Twins?" One dark eyebrow ascended.

She nodded and ran a finger around the rim of her coffee cup. That would make him wonder what he'd got himself into. First she was a klutz, and now she was a klutz with three young children. She hid a smile. The poor man had to be regretting his coffee invitation in a major way by now.

"They must keep you busy."

"And then some," she agreed. She glanced at her watch. The waitress' intrusion had jarred her back to reality. As nice as this interlude had been...well, all good fantasies had to come to an end. She may as well put the poor man out of his misery, and at the same time catch an early enough bus to get home by the bedtime hour she'd promised Kirsten.

"I should get going, Mr. Con–"

"Gareth," he reminded her. He made no move to leave.

"Gareth," she repeated, managing with great effort not to stumble over the name. She slid her coat up onto her shoulders and began pulling on one of her gloves. "I'm sure you have other plans, and I—"

"Actually, I don't."

Gwyn's movements faltered. She'd just given the man the easiest out he could ask for. Surely he recognized that. She finished tugging her glove over her fingers and peeked up through her lashes at him.

Gareth regarded her. "Forgive my bluntness, but are you married?"

"M-mar—no, I'm not." She shook her head, trying to keep pace with the conversation's sudden change in direction.

"Then have dinner with me."

The second glove slid from suddenly nerveless fingers. Her mind ground to a standstill. She stared at him, incapable of response. Gareth's mouth twitched and humor lit his dark gaze.

"Well? Is that a yes or a no?"

"It's an 'I'm stunned,'" Gwyn replied honestly. Coffee was one thing, but dinner?

He tipped back his head and laughed, drawing the admiring gazes of the waitresses and several other women in the bistro. "You are refreshingly blunt, Gwyn Jacobs. What is Gwyn short for, anyway? Gwyneth? Gwyndolyn? Guinevere?"

"Gwynneth," she said. "With two n's."

"It suits you. Now, Gwynneth with two n's, why are you stunned?" He sat forward, folded his arms, and leaned on the table.

She frowned. "Why do you want to have dinner with me?"

He raised an eyebrow. "The usual reasons. I enjoy your company."

"You don't know me well enough to enjoy my company," she pointed out.

"Then I'd like to get to know you better."

"Mr.—Gar—" She stopped, drew a steadying breath, and continued. "Gareth, I'm a thirty-five-year-old mother of three—which, incidentally, is enough to make most men run screaming—and you could have dinner with just about any woman in this city. Why me?"

Gareth considered her question for a minute before he spoke. "Because I'm not most men. And you're not just any woman."

Temptation was great. No, it was enormous.

But so was reality.

"Thank you, but I have to get home to my kids." *Be strong, Gwyn, it's for the best.*

"Tomorrow night, then." He rested his chin in one hand and gave her a coaxing grin. "Sean starts nightshift and I'll be bored out of my skull by myself. Won't you take pity on a stranger in your town?"

She twisted her fingers in her lap, her ungloved hand clinging to the gloved one for dear life. Lord, she'd thought the man potent in his movie roles. His lethally charming onscreen presence had nothing on the real thing.

"I thought you came here to hide from people," she reminded him.

"I'll settle for keeping a low profile. Well?"

"I can't tomorrow night. The kids have Jiu Jitsu practice."

"When do they finish?"

"Six. But I have a deadline—"

"Work tonight, while you're not having dinner with me."

She couldn't help laughing. "You're very persistent, did you know that?"

"Mm. My mother calls it stubborn. I like persistent better. Well? Do we have a date?"

A date. The very word sent a quiver through her belly. She didn't date, she reminded herself. She even had an entire list of reasons for not doing so. Unfortunately, her stalled brain couldn't recall any of them at this particular moment. She tried to think of something—anything—that would make a plausible excuse. She looked into lazy dark eyes. *Thank you very much, Gareth,* she coached herself, *but...*

"We have a date."

"Good. Come on, I'll run you home."

"You don't have to do that, I'm fine with the bus..." Gwyn's voice trailed off as Gareth rose and came around to pull out her chair and retrieve her fallen glove.

"I gave in on the dinner thing, now it's your turn to be gracious," he said easily.

Still in a state of shock at her treacherous acceptance of a date, it wasn't until she was seated in his car and he'd slid in beside her that she frowned.

"Wait a minute, you didn't give in on the dinner thing. I did."

"I wondered when you'd catch that." Gareth turned the key in the ignition and put the car into gear. He glanced over his shoulder to check for traffic, then slanted her a quick smile as he pulled away from the curb. "If it's any consolation, though, you were very gracious."

CHAPTER 4

Gareth slid his belt through its final loop, buckled it, and reached for the sport coat he'd dropped on the end of his bed. His cousin appeared in the bedroom doorway, leaning against the frame.

"Meeting Catherine?" Sean asked. "I thought she hadn't returned your calls yet."

"She hasn't." Gareth shrugged into the sport coat.

"Oh?"

"I have a date."

"Ah. What happened to keeping a low profile while you're in town?"

"I can't stay cooped up in your apartment the whole time I'm here," Gareth pointed out. "I've already been seen at the airport anyway. And at lunch with you today."

"True, but there's a difference between being seen in town and flaunting some new acquisition on your arm. Not to mention the risk she'll talk to the press. They always do."

"Gwyn isn't a new acquisition and she's not the kind to talk to the press."

"And you know this for a fact, do you? After knowing her for how long, exactly?"

Gareth turned to face the uniformed man in the doorway, eyeing him with exasperation. "Don't you have someone to arrest or something?"

"I'm not on duty yet. And you're changing the subject."

"Very observant. Did they teach you that in detective school?"

Sean ignored the jibe. "How long have you known her?"

"None of your business."

"Did you meet her on the plane?"

Gareth glowered at Sean. Then he shook his head. He'd practically grown up with his cousin, and he knew that look—the one that said Sean wasn't about to let the matter drop. "If you must know, I met her at a play."

"She's an actress?" Sean rolled his eyes. "Oh, that's even better, because it's not like she won't take the first opportunity she can to put herself into the spotlight with you."

"She's not an actress, she's an architect."

"A what?"

"An architect. We shared a box at a play on Sunday and had coffee afterward. She's a very nice woman, and she's not looking for any spotlights. Satisfied?"

Sean's gaze narrowed further. "*A very nice woman*?" he echoed. "I don't think I've ever heard you describe any female that way."

"Sean," Gareth grated, beginning to lose patience.

"Nice," Sean repeated, as if tasting the word. "*Nice?*"

"Would you get lost, please?"

"What exactly *is* nice, anyway?" Now his cousin's eyes danced with undisguised amusement. "Define it for me."

"Kiss off," Gareth retorted. He picked up his wallet from the bureau and slid it into his pocket, then retrieved his keys from the nightstand.

Sean's gaze turned serious. "Just remember what's at stake here, cuz. The way you told it, Catherine was pretty clear on the publicity issue."

"I know what's at stake, and this is a dinner date, nothing more. Now get off my case and tell me where I can take Gwyn that's reasonably quiet."

"No way," Kirsten said.

"Way." Gwyn smoothed lipstick over her lips. She replaced the cap on the tube and dropped it into her purse, then plucked a tissue from the box on the bathroom counter, trying hard to stifle her jangling nerves.

From the moment she'd risen this morning, the day's events had seemed consistently beyond her control. Elaine, Kirsten's mom, hadn't been able to drive her over to her disabled vehicle until well after lunch, and then Gwyn had waited almost two hours for the auto-club tow truck. That put her in rush-hour traffic on the return home, made her late to pick up the kids from school, and gave them just enough time to drop school bags at home, grab a snack, and race off to Jiu Jitsu.

They'd walked back in the door twenty minutes ago, and she'd left the kids at the table with warmed up spaghetti while she'd raced to get dressed for her date with Gareth.

All in all, she'd had none of the time needed to prepare, either physically or mentally.

Especially mentally.

"The real thing," her babysitter said. "The actual Gareth Connor."

She met Kristen's eyes in the mirror. "In the flesh."

"You're making this up."

Gwyn finished blotting her lipstick and tossed the tissue into the garbage. "No, sweetie, I'm not. This is real, true, and completely on the level."

"You're going out with Gareth Connor. You. Gwyn Jacobs. From Nowhere, Canada."

"Just for the record, you're not helping my nerves any."

"*Your* nerves? I'm more worried about my own," Kirsten retorted. "I think I'm going to pass out."

Brush in hand, Gwyn shot her babysitter a severe look. "You most certainly will not. And no squealing or giggling either. Save it until we're gone. And remember you promised not to tell anyone." Thank God she'd had the foresight to extract that vow from Kirsten before she'd told her Gareth's name.

"Not a soul," she emphasized. "Gareth doesn't want the entire world to know he's in Ottawa, and I don't want to be responsible for ruining his holiday."

"Mommy!" Katie's voice called from the living room at the front of the house. "Someone's at the door!"

Kirsten clutched her heart with both hands and leaned against the doorframe in a dramatic pose. "I'm definitely going to faint."

"Go and open the door," Gwyn said, hoping to heaven that Kirsten didn't notice her own trembling hand. She'd never hear the end of it. "I'll be there in a minute."

Hand fluttering against her breast and broad grin on her face, her babysitter departed down the stairs.

Gwyn sagged against the counter and stared at her reflection. The sheer panic she saw in her own eyes reached out from the mirror and gripped her belly. What in God's name was she doing? Dinner with Gareth Connor—*the* Gareth Connor. He, a famous actor from Wales. She, a struggling, single mother-slash-architect in Gatineau, Quebec. Kirsten was right—they didn't even travel in the same universe, let alone the same circles.

She should never have agreed to this.

Nicholas let out a howl of rage in the living room below, and she winced, then smiled wryly at the mirror. Gareth wanted to get to know her better, did he? Well, this ought to do the trick. With a sigh, she switched off the light and headed towards the dispute.

By the time she arrived at the scene, however, order had been restored. Not by Kirsten, who appeared to be starstruck in the worst way, sitting pink-faced and speechless in the corner chair, but by Gareth himself, who crouched beside Nicholas and Maggie, calmly divvying up a pile of building blocks between them.

He glanced up at her arrival, his eyes warming as they met hers. "I'll be with you in a minute," he said. "I have some unfinished business here."

Gwyn nodded. She wouldn't have been able to speak if she'd tried. The sight of him crouched beside her two blond offspring had knocked the wind right out of her. This wasn't just any man in her home, after all. It was Gareth Connor. Hollywood mega star and object of feminine fantasies around the world. Eye candy in the extreme. He should have looked entirely out of his element on the floor of her living room. Out of place in her home.

She had no idea know what to make of discovering the exact opposite to be true.

"There," Gareth said. "That's twenty-three each, with one left over." He held the remaining block up for examination, then tucked it into his coat pocket. "Now I can build one, too."

Maggie giggled. Nicholas roared.

"Cannot!" he declared. "You have to have more than one for a real castle."

Gareth looked surprised. "No! Do I really? Well, how many do I need?"

"Lots," Nicholas advised.

"Seventy-fifteen," Maggie volunteered. "At least."

"You can share with me," Nicholas offered. "Then we can build a really big castle."

"I don't think your mum would like that."

Pretending to frown, he glanced at Gwyn, his eyes dancing, and another shock of surprise went through her. He was enjoying himself. Not just a little, but a lot.

"I'm supposed to take her out for supper, remember?" he added, returning his attention to her son.

"Oh, yeah." Nicholas nodded. "You'd better do it soon. She gets grumpy if she's hungry."

Gareth smothered a laugh. "Does she indeed? Thank you for the advice, Nicholas. I'll make sure I remember that. And now, what do you suppose I should do with this?" He withdrew the block from his pocket.

Maggie giggled again, and Gwyn rolled her eyes. Heaven help her, the man appeared to have the same effect no matter what age the female.

"Maybe they could build a castle together," a new voice piped up as Katie abandoned her television show and moved in for a closer look. "Instead of sharing with you, Nicholas could share with Maggie. I could help, if they want."

The latter was delivered in an offhand way, so it wouldn't betray Katie's interest in an activity she considered beneath her.

Gareth widened his eyes and looked slowly from Nicholas to Maggie and back again. "Your sister," he advised them in a stage whisper, "is very, very smart. Don't you think?"

Wide-eyed themselves, the twins nodded. With great care, Gareth reached out and set his block in Katie's hand.

"There. When your castle is done, Katie can put on the last block," he said. "And make sure you leave it up for your mum to see when she comes home, all right?"

More nods. Gareth braced his hands on his knees and pushed himself upright. He turned to Gwyn.

"Now," he announced, "I'm ready."

Tongue-in-cheek, Gwyn said, "You're sure about that? If you'd rather stay and build castles…"

Gareth walked past her to the closet. He took out the same navy wool coat she'd worn to the theater, helping her slide it on over her simple, crimson wool dress. "And have you turn grumpy on me? I think not."

Amid a flurry of hugs and kisses goodnight, Gwyn delivered last-minute bedtime instructions to Kirsten, who still hadn't found her voice, and then the door closed behind them.

The air outside was sharp, but not unpleasantly so, and the night sky crystal-clear. She paused at the edge of the porch, forgetting her nerves in a moment of spontaneous delight as she gazed up through the gigantic, winter-bare maple on her front lawn at the stars suspended against black velvet.

"What a gorgeous night!" she exclaimed. Then she shot an apologetic glance at Gareth. "Don't mind me. I don't get out after dark very much."

"It is beautiful," he agreed, tipping back his own head. "You can even see all of Orion tonight."

Gwyn paused again, halfway down the steps. "You know the constellations?" She peered through the branches, but had no idea what to look for.

"Some. I used to know more when I was a kid. I wanted to be an astronomer when I grew up."

She couldn't resist. "So you became a star instead of studying them?"

Lame as the pun was, he chuckled. "You could say that, I suppose. Did you find Orion?"

"I think that would depend on what I'm looking for."

"Look for his belt first. Three stars in a diagonal line. Over there." Gareth came to stand behind her, his breath stirring her hair, and pointed past the maple tree, toward the south. "Hold up your hand to block the glare from the street lamp. See it? Then up from there, you'll see others forming an arc. That's his shield. And the really bright one at the top is the tip of his sword."

"I'm not sure." Right. Like she could see anything through the haze of sudden oxygen deprivation. She shifted away a little. "Oh, wait. I found it!"

She smiled at her own delight, her discomfort dissipating. "Thank you."

"You're welcome. Now, I don't know about you, but I'm starving."

"I passed that level a while back. Without becoming grumpy, I might add."

They continued down the walkway to Gareth's car in the driveway. He unlocked her door and held it open for her. "I asked Sean to recommend a place and he suggested *L'orée du Ruisseau.* Do you know it?"

Gwyn stumbled. She wasn't sure she could cope with the idea of dinner with this man to begin with. But at L'orée du Ruisseau? An image of the restaurant loomed in her mind, tucked beside a stream in the hardwood forest of Gatineau Park. She'd only been once, years before for Sandy's thirtieth birthday, but she remembered the ambience all too well. Cozy, casually understated, and way too intimate for dinner with a man she wasn't likely to see again.

Maybe she could suggest something else, instead. Such as her kids' favorite fast-food place.

She raised her gaze to Gareth, who waited for her answer. "I do know it," she admitted.

"And?"

"It's beautiful."

CHAPTER 5

Gwyn toyed with her knife as their server presented the wine for Gareth's approval, then poured it into their glasses. They'd been seated with quiet efficiency in a corner at the back of the restaurant, away from the curious eyes that followed their progress between the tables. The stares and whispers hadn't yet diminished, but they seemed less intrusive when screened by strategically placed greenery and soft classical music.

Schooling herself to ignore the unfamiliar attention, she flexed the fingers of her other hand under the table. At least in a setting such as this, they wouldn't likely be interrupted by an autograph-seeker.

"To spilled pencils and new friends," Gareth said, lifting his glass. He smiled over the rim as the waiter departed.

"To spilled pencils," Gwyn countered, touching her glass to his, "and new friends who are willing to forget them."

They both sipped their wine, and then Gareth set his glass down and leaned back in his chair. Dressed tonight in a tailored sport jacket, snowy white shirt, and dark slacks, he exuded refinement—and a devastating masculinity that sent a frisson of unfamiliar awareness down Gwyn's spine. She took another mouthful of wine.

"How did the lesson go tonight?" Gareth asked.

Normal conversation. Good. She could handle that.

"Jiu Jitsu?" she responded. "It went well. Maggie and Nicholas actually participated for a change. They usually end up rolling around on the mats in the corner."

"White belts?"

Gwyn nodded. She rested her elbow on the table and settled her chin into her hand. "For another year or so."

"What about Katie?"

"She tests for her orange belt next month."

"Good for her. Was this something they wanted to do, or was it your idea?"

"My idea, but they enjoy it. Jiu Jitsu and swimming lessons are non-negotiable. I plan on worrying as little as possible when they're out of my sight."

"Wise mother. They're nice kids, by the way."

"Thank you. I think so, too."

"How do you think the castle-building went?"

"I imagine it degenerated fairly fast. They were tired." Gwyn glanced at her watch. "They'll be asleep by now. You handled that very well, by the way. The dispute, I mean."

Gareth inclined his head. "Thank you. I thought I should step in before blows were exchanged. Your babysitter sure didn't say much."

Her lips twitched. "Just be glad she didn't follow through on her threat to faint."

Gareth looked startled. "Oh."

"You even had Maggie giggling, and she's usually hiding behind any available object when she meets someone new. Do you have that effect on all women?"

Mischief glinted in his eyes. "I don't know," he said. "Do I?"

Gwyn choked on her wine. Mouth quirking at one corner, Gareth handed her his linen napkin.

"*Madame*," their waiter murmured beside her. Glancing up, she saw him waiting with salad plates in hand. She handed Gareth's napkin back to him and sat back. The waiter set their salads down, bade them *bon appetit*, and left again.

"You haven't answered my question," Gareth reminded her, his deep voice reaching across the table to send a shiver down her spine.

Heat rose in her cheeks, but Gwyn raised her chin a notch and met his eyes square on. "And I'm not going to, either."

He chuckled, and then, to her immense relief, turned the conversation away from anything quite so personal, seeming determined to put her at ease. Over the course of appetizers and dinner, and then dessert and coffee, they discovered a mutual affinity for Bach and Enya, a passion for the outdoors, an abhorrence of politics, and a dozen other things in common.

As if by some silent, mutual agreement, not once did either of them volunteer or ask for information that might cause the slightest discomfort. It was the first time a man seemed more interested in getting to know her than in the details of her failed marriage, and it was an extraordinary experience.

In fact, the entire evening was extraordinary.

They laughed until Gwyn's ribs hurt, argued until one or the other of them rolled their eyes and gave in out of sheer exasperation, and shared silences that contained not a single awkward moment. Through it all, Gwyn felt herself sinking slowly into an ocean she knew better than to swim in.

When her internal warning bells became too loud, she tried to tune them out by telling herself that it was just one evening—a single night of fantasy out of an entire lifetime of reality—and she'd more than earned it. When a part of her remained unconvinced, she simply ignored it.

At last, Gareth consulted his watch with an air of reluctance. "I hate to call it a night, but it's getting late, and I imagine you have to be up with your kids in the morning."

Gwyn glanced at her own watch, and her eyes widened in horror at the one-thirty time showing on its face. "It can't possibly be that late," she muttered, giving her wrist a shake.

"I think it is," Gareth whispered. "And I'd venture a guess that we're not welcome to linger any longer."

She followed his gaze around the dining room, finding the place empty but for themselves and an employee laying out fresh linens and tableware for the next night. "I think you might be right," she said, rising from her chair. "I can't believe we stayed so long."

"I'm a little surprised myself," he admitted. "I don't remember the last time I enjoyed myself so much. Thank you."

"You bought me dinner," she reminded him, following him from the dining room to the front door and the coat check. "I should be thanking you."

"Only if you enjoyed it as much as I did." The light note in Gareth's voice seemed to contradict the intensity of his eyes, and Gwyn felt her breath catch a little.

A single night of fantasy or not, she'd be wise not to get too carried away.

"I did," she told him.

"Then you're welcome. Now let's get you home so you can catch a few hours before you have to get up again." He took her coat from the hanger and held it out to her. She slipped her arms in and let him settle it across her shoulders.

"If I need to, I'll sneak in a nap while the kids are at school in the morning. I don't have to pick up Nicholas and Maggie until eleven-thirty, so I have a couple of hours to myself."

"You met your deadline, I take it?"

"I did. At three-thirty this morning—or yesterday morning, I suppose."

"Two late nights in a row? You'll be dead tomorrow."

"Probably, but it was worth it." Realizing how her words might be taken, she added hastily, "So I could take a bit of a break, I mean."

"Of course." Gareth held the door open for her. "Do you work from home a lot?"

"All the time." She stepped past him onto the porch and waited for him to close the door and join her. "I'm self-employed. It makes things a little interesting financially now and then, but I like setting my own schedule around the kids. Katie is in school full-time, and Nicholas and Maggie go into a junior kindergarten for the morning, so I work while they're gone and then again for a few hours after everyone goes to bed."

"Not always until three-thirty, I hope." Gareth offered her his arm when they reached the uneven stone path at the bottom of the stairs.

Gwyn tucked her hand through the crook of his elbow with a naturalness that surprised her. "Only once in awhile. I'm too old for a steady diet of that." She shivered in the night air.

"Cold?"

"A bit, but I don't mind."

She stumbled on the loose gravel and Gareth caught hold of her hand to steady her.

"Are you all right?"

"Fine, thanks." She slowed her steps as they moved toward the unlit far corner of the parking lot, and Gareth followed suit. As her eyes adjusted to the increasing dark, she glanced up at the sky and glimpsed again the stars overhead. Without the glare of streetlamps to interfere, thousands more pinpricks of light studded the deep night.

"Oh," she breathed. "There are so many of them."

"Makes you realize how much we miss with all our city lights, doesn't it?" Keeping his grip on her hand, Gareth drew her into the center of the parking lot, away from the trees overhanging the perimeter, their tangled branches obscuring part of the sky even in their leafless state.

"Look over there," he said. His chest brushed against her back, solid and comfortable and a whole lot of other things that she tried very hard not to think about. He rested one of his hands on her shoulder and lifted the other to point upwards. Fighting the sudden urge to nestle into the potent male strength behind her, Gwyn made herself focus on his words.

"Just to the left of the Big Dipper, and a little bit up. See the long string of stars curving up and then back down again? That's Draco. And there's Ursa Minor, the Little Bear. You can see the Little Dipper inside it, with Polaris at the end of its handle. Up and to the right of that is Cassiopeia..."

Twenty minutes later, a thoroughly enchanted Gwyn shivered until her teeth clacked together. "I hate to leave," she said. "But I'm not dressed for this."

Gareth released her shoulders and stepped away. "Your teeth are chattering," he said. "I'm sorry."

"Don't be. That was my first-ever astronomy lesson. I loved it. Thank you."

"You're welcome."

"Of course, you realize that I'll have forgotten ninety per cent of it by tomorrow." She paused as Gareth shrugged out of his coat. "What are you doing? Oh, no, Gareth, don't. I'm fine, really."

"I'm not shivering," he pointed out. "You need it more than I do."

Stepping in front of her, he reached around to lay his coat across her shoulders, wrapping her in warmth. His warmth. A faint male scent drifted upward from the fabric, tilting her world another degree away from reality.

Gwyn's insides turned liquid.

Gareth placed his hand under her elbow. "Come on, let's get you into the car where it's warmer."

Only after he'd seated her, tucked his coat over her legs, and slammed the door shut, did Gwyn remember to breathe.

CHAPTER 6

Gareth raised his head and cracked one eye open to peer at the clock. He turned a disbelieving gaze on his cousin, who was seated in the armchair beside the bed, grinning and using a booted foot to prod him in the ribs.

"Morning," Sean said cheerfully.

Remaining on his stomach, Gareth buried his face in the pillow and growled, "It's six a.m."

"I know. I have court this morning, so they let me off early."

"I don't care if you're flying to Mars. It's still six a.m., and you'd better have one hell of a reason for waking me at this hour."

"I'll be gone again before you roll out of bed. I wanted to know how your date went."

"You've got to be kidding."

"Nope. Quite serious, actually. So? How was it?"

"Goodbye, Sean."

Sean grunted. "I figured as much, when I found you here."

Gareth puzzled over the statement for a second, then decided sleep had made his brain fuzzy. He raised his head again, along with one eyebrow. "What?"

"Well, if it had been any good, you'd have been at her place."

This time Gareth let out a pained groan as his head dropped. He rolled onto his back, away from Sean's booted toe, and covered his eyes with his arm. "She has three kids, Sean. It could have been the most earth-shattering date in the world and I wouldn't have stayed at her place."

It may well have been the most earth-shattering date in the world, but that was beside the point.

Silence met his response. Sean cleared his throat. "*How* many kids?"

"Three."

"Just how old is this Gwen, anyway?"

"Gwyn," Gareth corrected. "And she's thirty-five. Not that it's any of your business."

More silence. Longer this time. Gareth pictured his eternal-bachelor-type cousin digesting his words and hid a wry smile. Maybe now he'd shut up and go away.

No such luck. Sean's boot gave him another, even less gentle shove in the ribcage.

"You're dating a thirty-five-year-old woman with three kids? Are you out of your mind?"

"Not that I'm aware of, no."

"You've never dated anyone over the age of thirty in your life. Hell, you're famous enough that you'll probably never have to."

Gareth sighed. "Is that supposed to be some kind of compliment?"

Sean ignored him. "Do you have any idea of the complications involved with someone like that?"

"Someone like what?" Gareth peered at his cousin from under his forearm.

"Middle-aged, kids, desperate—" Sean broke off, waving his hands in the air. "You know."

"She's seven years younger than I am, and two years younger than you. I'm pretty sure she still has a little life left in her," Gareth retorted, annoyance creeping into his voice. A memory sidled into his mind of Gwyn's slender form in the body-hugging red dress she'd worn the night before. "And trust me, she's a long way from needing to feel desperate."

Sean gaped at him. "You like her."

"Of course I like her. I wouldn't have taken her out for dinner if I didn't like her."

"No. I mean, you *like* her. Enough to get involved with her."

"I'm not getting involved with anyone," Gareth disagreed. "I have enough on my plate right now."

"You sure as hell do." Sean dropped his foot from the bed and stood. "And you'd be doing yourself a significant favor by remembering that."

Unbuttoning his uniform shirt, he strolled toward the open door, pausing in the opening to look back. "So are you going to see her again?"

"I don't know. Maybe."

Sean shook his head. "You really are out of your mind," he said. "Oh, and before I forget, someone named Angela left a message last night, too. Way to collect 'em, cuz."

Gareth opened his mouth to correct his cousin, but Sean had already disappeared. Chasing after him to tell him Angela was nothing more than his agent seemed like way too much effort. Especially when he could employ his energy so much more pleasantly on other thoughts. He crossed his arms under his head and smiled at the ceiling.

Thoughts of certain "nice" single mothers, for instance.

"What do you mean, you can't tell me until my birthday?" Sandy followed Gwyn into the kitchen, her voice pitched higher than normal in confusion. "That's two weeks away. And what the heck does my birthday have to do with your mystery date, anyway?"

Gwyn sighed. "Give it up, Sandy. I'm not telling you."

Sandy crossed her arms, bright blue eyes snapping beneath her shocking, red-dyed bangs. "Let me get this straight. I call last night to chat; Kirsten tells me you're out with a man, dissolves into giggles and refuses to tell me another thing; I drive myself crazy with curiosity all blessed night; and now you won't tell me anything, either?"

So Kirsten had refused to divulge any information, had she? That was a good sign. Gwyn removed the last tray of peanut-butter cookies from the oven and switched off the temperature setting.

"In a nutshell, yes."

"God damn it, Gwynneth—"

"Language, Masters."

"Fine. Then gosh darn it, Gwyn—"

Gwyn giggled. Sandy was the only person in the world who could reduce her to giggles, but Gwyn still wasn't about to ruin her friend's birthday surprise by admitting Gareth's identity, which would inevitably lead to an explanation of how she'd met him. She set the cookie tray on a wire rack and threw the blue plaid oven mitt at her friend.

"Would you please give it a rest? Don't you have to go back to work soon?"

"Not for another half-hour," said her friend, who had dropped by unannounced during her lunch break. "And I won't give it a rest, because I'm hoping if I bug you long enough, you'll tell me."

"If you bug me long enough," Gwyn corrected, "I'll throw you out of my house. With no cookies."

The phone on the counter by the fridge rang. Gwyn reached for it, turning back in time to smack Sandy's fingers as her friend reached for the cookie tray. "Go away! Hello?"

"Is that me or one of your kids you'd like to go away?" Gareth's deep voice asked in her ear.

Gwyn reached for the counter to steady herself. "It's you." She realized what she'd said, and added hastily, "I didn't mean it's you I'd like to go away, I meant—"

"I know what you meant," he replied with a rumble of amusement. "Did I call at a bad time?"

"No! No, not at all. I was just trying to fend off a cookie thief. My friend Sandy is over."

Said thief raised an eyebrow, leaned on the center island with chin in hand, and listened without shame. Gwyn glared and turned her back on her.

"Did you manage to take a nap this morning?" Gareth asked.

"No, I ended up meeting with a client instead. But I'm fine. I wasn't nearly as tired as I thought I'd be."

Actually, she suspected she'd been functioning on pure adrenaline all day, because after Gareth had said goodnight to her on her front porch—in a moment tense with unexplored potential—she'd barely slept at all. But she didn't see the need to admit so.

"What about you? Were you tired?"

"Only because Sean woke me up when he got in at six from work. He wanted to hear about my date."

She tried not to ask, but her voice seemed beyond her control. "What did you tell him?"

"That it was none of his business."

"Funny, I was just telling Sandy pretty much the same thing."

"You know what would drive them really nuts, don't you?"

"What?"

"A second date."

Now her voice simply disappeared.

After a moment, Gareth asked, "Are you still there?"

"I'm here," she croaked.

"I want to see you again, Gwyn."

How did he do that? How did his voice reach through the phone line to make her feel as though he'd just picked up where he'd left off on her porch last night, when his lips had brushed the back of her hand in a gesture of gallantry she'd never experienced? As though her world had gone fuzzy for a moment, then come back into focus in a place she'd never been before?

"I know it's a school night," Gareth continued, "and that you probably have work to do, but–"

She interrupted before her nerve failed—and before her better sense kicked in. "You're welcome to join us for dinner, if you'd like."

Silence met her invitation. She swallowed hard and put a hand to her hot face. Dear Lord, what was she thinking? You didn't invite a man like Gareth Connor over to share a tossed-together weekday dinner with three kids and their frazzled, hopelessly gauche—

"I'd love to."

He would?

Innate honesty prompted her to warn, "It's nothing fancy."

"Will you have any cookies left?"

She smiled. "I'll try to keep some away from Sandy."

"What time?"

"We eat early. Five o'clock."

"Can I bring anything? Dessert?"

"If you'd like."

"I'll see you at five."

Gwyn stared at the receiver in her hand for a long moment after it went dead, then she replaced it in its cradle and turned to Sandy. Her friend stared at her across the kitchen island, slack-jawed.

"Excuse me, but did I just hear you right?" Sandy squeaked. "Did you just invite a man into your home for dinner with you and the kids? You, Gwynneth Jacobs? With the iron-clad rule about never involving your children with your dates—what ridiculously few you've had?"

Gwyn ignored the jab. "The kids like him."

"They've already *met* him?" Sandy's mouth flapped a few times before she pulled herself together. "Gwyn, in the last four years, I can count on no hands the number of times you've introduced your kids to a new man in your life. Hell, I can count on *no* hands the number of times you've introduced them to any man in your life who isn't permanently attached to another woman."

"This is different."

"I can see that."

"Ga—" Gwyn caught back the rest of Gareth's name, recovered from her near slip, and said, "He's only in Canada for a couple of weeks. It's not like anything will happen."

Both of Sandy's eyebrows shot up, disappearing under her bangs. "I have news for you, my friend. If you've let him cross your threshold, something already has."

CHAPTER 7

"Sleep well, sweetie," Gwyn said softly, closing Katie's door behind her. She paused for a moment in the hallway, fighting the temptation to stop off in her bathroom to repair the ravages of the day before she went back downstairs to join Gareth.

And have him think you're coming on to him? Do you really want to do that?

Well...honestly?

She pulled a face at herself in the hall mirror. No makeup, she told herself. No special efforts. He's good company...

And incredibly attractive.

...and there might be a tiny spark of something there...

Understatement of the millennium, Gwynneth—you saw how he looked at you over dinner.

...but no way did she want it to go further.

Her inner voice snorted.

Gwyn gripped the handrail so tightly her fingers ached. This was getting her nowhere. She was a big girl—lord, she was a grown woman, the single mother of three, a successful architect...she could handle this. So she'd broken a rule or two, bringing Gareth into her home and her kids' lives. It didn't mean anything, regardless of what Sandy said. It just happened to work out that way.

She took a deep breath and, through sheer force of will, set her foot on the first step of the descent.

She'd go downstairs, offer him a coffee, and go about her usual routine. By the time she'd tidied the kitchen and made Katie's lunch for tomorrow, he'd be ready to leave. It was simple. Really.

There was nothing to it.

She stepped off the stairs into the main floor hallway and made her way to the kitchen at the back of the house. Gareth turned at her arrival, his denim shirtsleeves rolled up to his elbows. Wiping his hands dry on a tea towel, he smiled.

"All tucked in?" he asked.

Gwyn nodded. She stared at her kitchen. "You shouldn't have done this," she said, waving a hand to encompass the room. "I didn't expect you to."

"You made the dinner," he pointed out. "The least I could do was clean up. I hope you don't mind."

Mind? Common sense said that she shouldn't, of course. After all, the kitchen surrounding him gleamed. Dishes had disappeared from the counters, and pots and pans had been washed, dried, and put away, all in the same night. That never happened.

And now—she twisted her hands together—now she had nothing left to keep her busy. Nothing to put between her and the man standing a scant few feet away, looking far more at ease in her home than she herself felt at the moment. She dug her fingernails into her palms.

"Thank you," she said.

"You're welcome."

Gareth threaded the tea towel he held through the fridge door handle. What would Gwyn do if she knew the real reason he'd cleaned her kitchen for her? If she knew he would have mucked out a barn if he'd had to, just to keep himself busy? Just to keep from dwelling on the tantalizing knowledge that when she came downstairs, they would be alone. The two of them. No kids. No interruptions. No distractions.

He watched her slender, ringless fingers pluck at her long navy skirt. She cleared her throat.

"Would you like some coffee?" she asked.

The slight tremor in her voice told him she, too, had felt the tension kick up a notch between them.

"I'm fine, thanks."

He should leave. He'd decided he would, while he'd been submerged up to his elbows in soapy water, listening to her steps overhead. Decided that his cousin, in spite of being nosey, had been right. He had too much at stake right now to risk an involvement, and involvement with Gwyn Jacobs would be all too easy. Something about her—her ease, her naturalness -

He brought his thoughts up short. The silence between them grew uncomfortable. *Just say it, Connor. Say thanks for dinner, but I really should be going. Say it's been nice meeting you, but—*

He nodded towards the dining room, separated from the kitchen by French doors. "Is that where you work? May I see?"

Gwyn looked surprised at the sudden request, but not as surprised as Gareth felt. That wasn't anything near what he'd intended to say. Still, he supposed it wouldn't hurt to have a quick look around—for the sake of politeness, of course—before he left.

He followed her to the French doors. She opened them and flicked on a light switch, then stood aside. Gareth stepped past her and paused in the doorway, hands tucked into jeans pockets, surveying the room.

Books were stacked across nearly every surface, rolls of papers sat in the corners and filled boxes underneath tables, and he couldn't see so much as a square inch of either desk or tabletop under the clutter strewn across them. Given the order he'd seen in the rest of her house and the obvious routine of her family, the utter chaos startled him.

He looked down at her. "I suppose you're going to tell me that this is organized," he said, making no effort to hide a grin.

"Of course it is."

A roll of papers, unbalanced by the draft from the open door, slid off the long worktable along one wall and dropped to the floor with a hollow thud.

Gwyn's lips twitched. "Sort of," she added. "I know where most things are, anyway."

Gareth crossed the room, stooped, and picked up the roll. "May I?" he asked, holding it up. She shrugged and he set the papers on the table as he unrolled them. "Is this something you're working on right now?"

"Just finished, actually. It's a house for a client in Montreal."

He twisted his head one way and then the other, studying the top blueprint. "It looks like it's written in a foreign language," he said at last. "You actually know what all this stuff is?"

She nodded.

"How long have you been doing this?"

"Almost ten years. I worked for a firm in Ottawa before I had Katie, and I've worked from home ever since."

"Is it all computerized?" He flipped through the sheets one by one.

"Most of it, yes. I still do my preliminary sketches by hand because I think more creatively with a pencil than I do with a mouse, but I use CAD for drawing up the actual plans."

"CAD?"

"Computer-aided design."

"So you do the designs and then have someone print them for you?"

Gwyn shook her head. "I have my own plotter." She pointed across the room at a machine sitting on a table of its own. "It's a kind of specialized printer."

Gareth re-rolled the house plans, set them back where they'd started out, and strolled across to examine the plotter. "It looks expensive."

"Think second mortgage," Gwyn said dryly. "I bought it three years ago and it cost me a fortune, but it was worth every penny."

Gareth straightened. "Aren't you afraid your kids will total it?" he asked over his shoulder.

"This room is off limits on pain of lifetime exile to a bedroom. No one is allowed to so much as sneeze in here." Gwyn wandered over to join him as he studied the paper taped to the table. "That's a veterinary clinic I'm working on for a client in Buckingham, about a half-hour from here."

"You don't specialize, then?"

"In houses, yes. But I designed Dr. Maurier's house for him a couple of years ago, and he asked me to take on this, too. Normally I'd say no to a commercial building, but Jean-Paul can be very charming when he wants something."

Gareth's gut twisted at the thought of her finding another man charming. *Be polite,* he reminded himself. *And then leave.* He re-rolled the papers.

"How many projects do you have going at once?"

"As many as I can juggle without dropping too many balls. I don't like to take on more than three or four at a time, but a lot depends on the deadlines. And I don't like to take on just one at a time, because the income is too staggered that way."

Gwyn reached past him for a sketchbook. Her hair brushed against his shoulder and a strand remained clinging to the denim of his shirtsleeve. Gareth clenched his jaw.

"Right now I have this clinic," she nodded at the partial drawing on the board, "plus a townhome infill project and this." She flipped open the book and handed it to him.

He studied it, admiring the detail and the obvious complexity. She really was very good. "It's huge. What is it, an apartment building?"

"A single family dwelling, believe it or not. Thirteen thousand square feet. Anyone who builds something that big has way too much money, in my opinion, but—" She stopped suddenly and wrinkled her nose. "Please tell me I didn't just insult you."

Gareth set the pad on the work table. "Three-bedroom flat in London," he said. "Big, but not nearly that big."

"Thank heaven."

"Some of my best friends would fall into the too-much category, however," he added, tongue-in-cheek.

"Oh."

He decided that the tinge of color in her cheeks suited her. And that he ought to find something else to think about. He pointed to a framed sketch hanging over the desk. "What's that?"

"It's the addition on this place. The sitting room off the kitchen."

He stepped forward to have a closer look at the sketch. "I'll be damned. So it is." He studied it for a long moment, eyes narrowed and head tilted to one side. Then he grinned at her. "Now I need to have a proper look at the room itself."

And then he'd leave.

Really.

CHAPTER 8

He'd noticed the room during dinner, of course. Only a few feet from the kitchen table and elegantly designed even to his untrained eye, it would have been hard to miss. Until he stepped down into it, however, he hadn't even begun to appreciate it.

Calm permeated every corner, giving the space the air of a retreat. It presented a study in harmony and balance, from the soothing shades of moss green on the walls and ceiling to the Palladian windows that soared from floor to twelve-foot ceiling around the perimeter. Narrow strips of wall broke the expanse of glass, just wide enough to pull back the drapes without sacrificing the view, and a set of French doors opened onto a wide stone terrace visible in the shadowed night outside.

A woodstove, unlit at the moment, sat in one corner. A huge wooden trunk served as coffee table. Dark leather couch and chairs were oversized and overstuffed. There was probably too much furniture for the size of the room, but far from feeling cluttered, the entire space invited a person to come in and stay a while. To be at home.

Much the way its designer did.

He realized Gwyn waited for him to speak.

He cleared his throat, working past the *home* thought. "So when you sketched that picture and drew up the plans, this is what you envisioned?"

She nodded, and her satisfied gaze wandered the room.

"Exactly this," she said. "I'd sat inside this space a thousand times before I ever hired a contractor."

"Then I'll say it again. You're very talented."

She gave him a pleased smile. "Thank you. I'm glad you like it. Are you sure you don't want coffee or tea? I can plug the kettle in while I make Katie's lunch for tomorrow."

A clock in another room chimed a distant eight o'clock. Gareth glanced at his own watch for confirmation of the time and looked askance at her.

"I'm not intruding? You said you work in the evenings."

"Nothing that can't wait until tomorrow. I may even be a little ahead of schedule at the moment, though I'll probably jinx myself by saying so. You're welcome to stay for awhile."

He thought of the cluttered work desk and knew she lied. Knew, too, that he would accept even as he went through the entire list of reasons he shouldn't. It wasn't a real involvement, he told himself, just a brief interlude. A moment of peace in a currently insane life. Surely not even the jaded Sean would begrudge him that.

"All right. Coffee would be nice, then."

And it was. Very nice.

At first, Gwyn wasn't sure about the wisdom of her invitation. While she made Katie's lunch and tried very hard to keep the flutters in her belly to a minimum, her gaze wandered again and again in Gareth's direction as he flipped through her music collection.

He'd left his hair loose tonight. It gave him an unruly, untamed air, in sharp contrast to the sleek, pulled-back look of the night before. In fact, everything about him was different. And as mouth-parchingly handsome as he'd looked in his sport-jacket-and-slacks dinner attire, jeans and an untucked denim shirt were proving a hundred times more dangerous.

Gwyn swallowed and pressed the lid of the plastic sandwich box into place.

His appearance was only the beginning. Far more unsettling was the comfortable way he'd fit into the family dynamic. From the moment he'd walked in the front door, he'd been so natural with the kids, so at ease with tuna casserole and bagged salad.

And he'd cleaned her kitchen.

How many real men cleaned a woman's kitchen on their second date?

That, she decided, was the true problem. She stuffed a handful of baby carrots and some celery sticks into a plastic container and pressed on the lid. Gareth Connor *wasn't* real. He was a fantasy come into life for a brief time, and that was all. She tucked the various containers into Katie's lunch box: veggies, sandwich, yogurt, grapes.

Heck, this evening hadn't even been a real date.

The rich, gravelly voice of Louis Armstrong drifted into the kitchen. Glancing over, she saw Gareth straighten up from the CD player. He turned, caught her eye, and smiled.

A fantasy, she reminded herself. Only a fantasy.

"What a wonderful world," sang Louis.

They sat at opposite ends of the couch. Gwyn facing Gareth with both her feet tucked up under her, he half-turned toward her with his arm stretched along the back. Conversation that had seemed easy the night before became positively comfortable now.

He asked more questions about her work, about where she'd trained and why she'd chosen architecture; listened to stories of her family with an attentiveness that had her revealing details she'd long ago forgotten.

He described growing up with two younger sisters in Cardiff, Wales, and moving away to London when he was fifteen in a dismally unsuccessful attempt to break into the theater. He told her about returning to school and emerging older and wiser several years later with no particular degree but a determination to try the stage a second time.

He had her in stitches with his descriptions of his first roles, and in awe of the entire movie world with his tales of what life was really like on the set.

And once again, with a perception that was almost uncanny, he steered clear of territory that might be too personal. He was funny, he was warm, he was fascinating...

...and fantasy or no fantasy, Gwyn was in serious trouble.

She'd suspected it all evening, of course, but she managed to more or less ignore the possibility—right up until the clock in the living room chimed midnight and Gareth smiled his regret.

"I think that's my cue to be going," he said.

She had to quite literally bite her tongue to stop herself from asking him to stay. Controlling her impulse for the moment, she made a show of looking at her watch.

"Time really flies, doesn't it?" she murmured. She hated herself for the inanity of the remark but needed to say something to fill the sudden silence that threatened.

Gareth's lips twitched. "Indeed it does." He rose from the couch and raised his hands over his head in a stretch. "Thank you again for dinner, and for coffee. I hope I didn't keep you from anything too important."

Gwyn didn't think much could be more important than watching a thin denim shirt strain across a broad chest, but neither did she think it wise to say so. She simply smiled and shook her head.

"Nothing at all," she said, hoping he wouldn't hear the slight strangulation in her voice. She uncoiled her feet from beneath her and leaned forward to put her mug on the trunk. When she straightened up, she found Gareth's hand extended to her.

She hesitated, exhaling shakily. Then she put her hand in his and let him pull her to her feet, inches away from the broad shoulders she'd just admired. Along with all the rest of him.

No amount of reasoning with herself could make her raise her gaze to his. Long seconds ticked by, alive with electric expectation. Gareth cleared his throat.

"I should go," he said, his voice husky.

A tremor twisted through Gwyn's belly.

She stared at a button at eye level on his shirt. The one that marked the beginning of an open vee and exposed a glimpse of dark, curling hairs. "I know."

"Gwyn—"

She inhaled sharply at the rough sound of her name. Gareth's fingers tightened for an instant on her own, then began a slow slide up her arm to her shoulder, around to the nape of her neck. She closed her eyes. A strand of hair, not her own, brushed her cheek.

"Mommy, my head hurts."

It took a moment for the whimper to penetrate. Another moment for the world to steady itself enough that she could step away from Gareth's hand and not fall over.

Maggie stood by the end of the couch, rubbing her eyes and swaying on her feet. Gwyn's heart sank as a single glance took in her daughter's abnormally flushed cheeks. Crouching down, she held out her hands.

"Come here, sweetie."

Gareth guided the little girl past his own feet until she'd reached Gwyn, then he sat on the edge of the couch.

"Is she all right?"

Gwyn swept a damp lock of hair away from Maggie's forehead and folded her daughter into her arms where she nestled listlessly, her hot face pressed into the crook of Gwyn's neck. "She has a fever," she replied.

"Is it serious?"

"I doubt it. It could be the start of a cold, or it could disappear by morning. We'll have to wait and see."

"Can you give her something?"

Gwyn shook her head. "Not just yet. I'd rather let it run its course as long as she's not too uncomfortable. I'll bring her into bed with me for the night—"

A sudden flash in Gareth's expression swept away the remainder of her words. Whatever it was disappeared again so quickly, she felt sure she'd imagined it. She grimaced.

Inspired by her own frustration, no doubt.

"Can I do anything for you before I go?" Gareth asked.

"Thanks, but we're fine."

"Shall I see myself out, or do you have to lock the door?"

"I have to lock." With Maggie cradled in her arms, Gwyn rose to her feet and led the way through the house to the front door. She waited while Gareth put on shoes and coat, then she attempted a smile, not quite certain how to behave after what had almost happened.

Gareth took away the guesswork, along with her breath.

First he stroked Maggie's head and, his voice soft, said, "Feel better soon, Maggie."

Then he stepped close to Gwyn, tipped up her chin, and brushed his lips across hers, feather-light. "I'll call tomorrow," he said. "To see how Maggie is."

Then he left.

CHAPTER 9

"Well?" Sandy's voice demanded the instant Gwyn put the telephone receiver to her ear. "How did it go?"

"Hello to you, too," said Gwyn. "And I'm fine. Thank you for asking."

"Yeah, yeah, whatever. Now how did it go?"

Gwyn grinned and tucked the receiver against her shoulder so her hands were free. She continued slicing mango into a bowl of fruit salad for Maggie.

"You know what you are, don't you, Sandra Masters? Nosey."

"Gwyn!"

Gwyn relented. "It went fine."

A small silence ensued on the other end of the line. "That's it? You invite a man into your home for the first time ever, and that's all you're going to tell me? 'It went fine'?"

"There's nothing else to tell. He had dinner with us and stayed for coffee. That was all."

Right, Gwyn, but if it hadn't been for Maggie...

Gwyn's insides did a brief series of back flips. She paused in her slicing, afraid of doing damage to herself.

As if she'd read her mind, Sandy said, "Oh, my."

"Oh, my, what?"

"You have it bad."

"What? All I said was—"

"It's not what you say that counts, Gwynneth, it's what you *don't* say. And you know it. You've told me everything about any other date you've ever had. What you ate, what you did—"

"We ate tuna casserole and chocolate-fudge-ripple ice cream, and he cleaned the kitchen while I put the kids to bed. Then he asked to see my work, and then we had coffee. Is that better?"

Gwen rinsed her hands in the sink and reached for the kitchen towel hanging on the fridge door. An image of Gareth wiping his hands on the same fabric popped into her mind. She took a clean one from the drawer.

"He cleaned your kitchen?" Sandy echoed. "Did you ask him to?"

"Of course not!"

"Hell, I haven't even met him and *I'm* in love with him," her friend muttered. "So when are you seeing him again?"

"I don't know if I am."

"Mommy!" a pathetic whine came from the sitting room, where she'd left Maggie dozing on the couch.

"Was that my little Magpie?" Sandy asked, distracted at last from her third-degree routine. "What's she doing home?"

"She has a fever. I was up most of the night with her." Gwyn carried the bowl of fruit to her daughter. Maggie lay where she'd left her, cuddled under the duvet brought down from her bed. The flush of fever had gone from her cheeks, replaced by a pallor that made the normally robust four-year-old look tiny and fragile.

A single pink spot stood out on one cheek.

Gwyn's heart dropped.

"Oh, no," she muttered.

"What?" Sandy asked.

Gwyn jumped. She'd forgotten she even held the telephone.

"You're not going to believe this," she told Sandy. She perched on the edge of the couch beside her daughter, dropped a kiss on the hot little forehead, and smoothed back damp hair.

"What?" Sandy asked again, her voice impatient.

Gwyn tugged Maggie's pajama top out of the way. Tiny pink dots covered the little belly. Gwyn's heart plummeted even further, coming to rest somewhere in the region of her knees. She groaned.

"Spots," she informed Sandy.

"Spots?"

"Chicken pox."

"You're kidding."

"Oh, believe me, I wish I was." Pulling a face at Maggie, Gwyn leaned over to rub noses with her. She turned her attention back to her friend. "I have to go, Sand. I need to locate the calamine lotion and then pick up Nicholas. I guess I'll see you again when we're spot-free."

Sandy, who had never had chicken pox, groaned. "I'd forgotten about that. I can't even help out."

"Don't worry about it. It's temporary, and I've been through it before with Katie, so at least I know what to expect. I'm sure we'll manage."

"Call me later. At least I can commiserate with you."

Gwyn laughed, said goodbye, and regarded her daughter ruefully. "Well, munchkin," she said. "That'll teach me to brag about being ahead of schedule, won't it?"

Gareth slammed the telephone receiver into its cradle. His curse echoed off Sean's beige living room walls and rang in his own ears. Damn it to hell, but that woman could be frustrating. His fingers tightened on the hapless instrument still in his grasp. Only with an effort did he refrain from ripping the phone cord from its jack and throwing the whole damned thing through the glass balcony door.

After all this time, *knowing* he was coming here, knowing what it meant to him—bloody hell, how *could* she?

He threw the phone onto a chair. Watched it bounce apart. Scowled at the faint dial tone.

He should have seen it coming. He paced the width of the black and white area rug between leather couch and balcony doors. After the sixteen years of hell she'd put him through, knowing how her mind worked, he should have expected her to throw some kind of curve at him.

But even if he had—this? How could he have expected this?

He stopped beside the expanse of glass overlooking the Ottawa River, ten stories below and across the Western Parkway, slate gray in its reflection of a sullen November sky. He closed his eyes, picturing the sixteen wrapped packages that filled a second suitcase in his bedroom. One for each birthday he'd missed. Waiting, as he had, for a date that had just been ripped away from him.

Damn Catherine's vicious hide. He wouldn't let her get away with this.

He turned and snatched up the telephone again, stabbing the re-dial button with his thumb. He listened to the ringing and steeled himself for Catherine's melodic, slightly husky greeting.

"It's me," he announced without preamble. "We had a deal. I'm here for ten more days. I don't care how you do it, but you have exactly five of those to get her home. After that, so help me God, I'll cut you out of the picture and do this my way, Catherine. You know I will. Call me when you know her arrival date."

He hung up again without waiting for her response. She wouldn't like it, but she'd cooperate. She'd wait until the last possible minute, not wanting to believe he'd called her bluff, but in the end, she'd do it. She'd bring Amy home because she knew she couldn't stand in his way any longer, and because she couldn't bear the thought of not controlling their daughter's first meeting with her father.

Leaning against the sliding doors, he ran his free hand over the back of his neck, rubbing at the tension there. Typical. A three-minute conversation with his ex-wife had him tied in absolute knots. The complete antithesis to how he felt after a conversation with Gwyn—

His hand stilled at the sudden intrusion of Gwyn in his thoughts. Then he resumed his massage. Who was he trying to kid? Gwyn Jacobs hadn't been more than a few seconds away from his thoughts all morning. Or most of the night, for that matter.

In fact, after only two dates, the woman occupied entirely too much of his mind. Not a good thing when he'd meant what he'd told Sean about not getting involved.

His gaze wandered to the wall clock hanging over the dining room table. Two-thirty. The afternoon stretched before him. He could phone his agent, he supposed. Knowing Angela, she'd have worked herself into a complete lather because he hadn't returned her calls yet. He'd probably catch her at lunch, but she'd be waiting to hear from him—

And Gwyn would be waiting for her oldest to get home from school...

Hell, there he went again. He sighed. His timing couldn't have been worse if he'd tried. The first time in nearly forever he'd felt more than a passing interest in a woman, and here he sat, embroiled in circumstances that precluded involvement of any kind. It just bloody figured.

His mouth twisted. No liaisons. Nothing that might draw attention to his presence in Ottawa or make people wonder why he was here. Catherine's instructions had been clear, and he'd had no qualms about agreeing to them at the time, especially given the stakes. It wasn't every day that a man got to meet his grown-up daughter for the first time in sixteen years, and he would have promised the stars if he'd thought it would smooth the way to that meeting.

Recognizing the past tense of his thoughts, he brought himself up short. He still *would* promise the stars. Even now. Because as much as he enjoyed Gwyn's company—and as much unexplored potential as there might be between them—he wouldn't jeopardize his reunion with Amy. Not for anything.

His gaze slid to the phone he hadn't put down yet. He thought of his promise to call and see how Maggie was doing. One phone call to check on a little girl. How dangerous could that be?

CHAPTER 10

Gwyn had installed an increasingly uncomfortable Maggie in an oatmeal bath while Nicholas wandered between the bathroom and the television, looking lost and forlorn.

"How come I can't take a bath with Maggie?" he asked for the fourteenth time, pausing in Gwyn's bedroom doorway where she folded laundry on the bed.

"Maggie doesn't want company today, sweetheart," Gwyn explained, also for the fourteenth time. She listened for the tell-tale splashes signaling Maggie's continued presence in the tub. Then she picked another t-shirt out of the basket. "She's not feeling well, and she just wants to be alone for a little while. You can have a bath with her another day."

"When's Katie coming home?"

It was only the tenth time for that question.

Gwyn ruffled her son's hair. "Soon, love. Can you go see if Maggie's all right for me?"

Nicholas scuffed out of the room, head hanging. Gwyn rubbed a hand over gritty eyes. Lord, this week was shaping up to be a long one. And if Nicholas came down with—

The phone rang, intruding on her self-pity. She reached across her bed for the receiver. "Hello?"

"How's your patient doing?" Gareth asked.

The sound of his voice triggered the now familiar twisting sensation in her stomach. She ignored it.

"Remember how I said I'd probably jinxed myself?" she replied.

"It's serious?"

"Just miserable. She has chicken pox."

"You're kidding."

"Oh, believe me, I wish I was. Unfortunately, I'm quite serious." Gwyn carried the cordless phone to the door of her room so she could peek into the bathroom. Maggie still sat in the tub, squeezing the oatmeal-filled sock and watching the milky liquid trickle out. Nicholas stood in the hallway outside the bathroom door, slumped against the wall and looking for all the world like he hadn't a friend on the planet. A sudden thought occurred to Gwyn. "Gareth..."

"Yes?"

"Please tell me you've had them."

"Chicken pox? Relax. Sean and I both had them in the middle of the summer when he was two and I was seven. I remember being really ticked with him for giving them to me—I couldn't go swimming for an entire week."

"Thank God. I would've felt awful if you'd caught them from the kids now."

"So are Nicholas and Katie next in line?"

"Only Nicholas. Katie had them three years ago."

"How long will all this take?"

"That depends on when Nicholas gets them. At worst, four to six days for Maggie's to crust over, then up to three weeks' incubation for Nicholas. Plus the week after the rash starts when he's still contagious, of course. So that's what, just over a month?"

Gwyn's heart sank as she made the calculations aloud. Lord, she hadn't stopped to total it up like that. Even if she worked during the three-week incubation, she'd lose almost two full weeks away from her desk. How in the world would she manage?

As if plugged in to her thoughts, Gareth asked, "What are you going to do about work? Is your babysitter available during the day for you?"

"She's in university." Running a hand through her hair, she sank down onto the bed. Was this what it was like to have your life flash before your eyes?

"As far as work goes, I can put some of it on hold," she said, thinking aloud. "The townhome developer might squawk a bit, but once Maggie's over the worst of it I can work in the evenings and while she naps."

"What time does Katie get off school?"

She blinked at the sudden change in subject. "In about a half-hour, why?"

"I'll be there in twenty minutes."

"What?" Startled, Gwyn nearly dropped the telephone.

"You can argue with me then."

"But—" The line went dead, clicked, then resumed its steady dial tone. Lowering the receiver, she stared at the pile of laundry beside her.

Twenty minutes later she was still trying to come up with an argument.

"I can't ask you to do this," she said weakly, watching Gareth hang his coat beside hers in the closet. Maggie lay against her shoulder, little arms clinging to her neck.

"You didn't ask," Gareth pointed out. "I offered." He touched Maggie's hand gently. "Hey, kiddo, how are you doing?"

Maggie shrugged, but she didn't turn away as Gwyn expected. In fact, for the first time all day she seemed to take an interest in something other than imitating a burr. She even gave Gareth a small smile.

Gwyn raised her eyebrow. "I haven't been able to coax one of those out of her all day," she commented.

"It must be that effect I have on women," Gareth drawled. He held his hands out to Maggie. "How about it, Magpie, shall we let Mummy go fetch Katie?"

"Hey, that's what Auntie Sandy calls Maggie!" Nicholas exclaimed from his seat on the bottom stair.

"Does she? Then I think I like Auntie Sandy already."

Nicholas giggled. Gareth returned his attention to Maggie, who eyed his hands but hadn't yet moved to accept the change of venue. He turned back to the closet and reached into his coat pocket, pulling out a package of washable markers.

"Know what these are for?"

Maggie shook her head.

"They're for playing dot-to-dot." He leaned in closer and added in a whisper, "On you!"

In a quick aside to Gwyn, he said, "A colleague had a son with chicken pox once. I thought her idea was very creative."

Maggie's eyes widened. Nicholas bounced off the stair and into the hall, tugging at Gareth's pant leg.

"Can I play too?" he demanded.

"Maggie?" Gareth asked.

After a small hesitation, Maggie nodded her blonde curls. She held her arms out to Gareth. "We can all play," she said. "Me first, then Nich'las. You have to be last 'cause you're bigger."

Gareth settled Maggie on his hip and handed the markers to Nicholas to carry. "There," he said to Gwyn. "You're free. Now go fetch your eldest."

She would have objected again, but a sudden shrill intruded. Gareth reached for the cell phone in the holder clipped to his belt. He glanced at the display, then flipped the mouthpiece open, shrugging an apology in her direction and effectively ending her argument.

"Hey, Sean."

His cousin's name. With a shake of her head, Gwyn reached into the closet for her coat. In the three brief days she'd known Gareth Connor, she had yet to win so much as the smallest victory in a discussion. Stubborn, he'd said his mother called him. She was beginning to think the woman was a master of understatement. She slid her arms into her coat and reached for her scarf.

She tried not to eavesdrop, but even with Gareth carrying Maggie into the living room and pitching his voice low, his words still reached her. So did his anger.

"I don't give a—" he paused, then finished coldly, "I don't care what her message said. And I don't care how many times she's called. I've said everything I intend to for the moment, and she can go hang if she thinks she can sweet talk her way out of this one. What? No, I don't want you to give her my cell phone number, just don't answer. Let your machine screen the calls."

Gwyn glanced from the front entry into the living room. In stark contrast to the chill in his voice, Gareth grinned and reached out to lightly tap Maggie's nose as he set her on the sofa. He patted the cushion beside Maggie in silent invitation, and Nicholas clambered up as well.

"Your concern is touching," he informed his cousin, "but it's none of your business."

Gwyn left, the word *she* still ringing in her ears.

CHAPTER 11

Peering over the wire rim of her glasses, Gwyn looked out through the French doors of her office into the kitchen. Maggie and Nicholas both sat on the counter before Gareth, and the three of them appeared to be consulting over something. Nicholas nodded. Maggie shook her head. Gareth looked thoughtful. He spoke again and both blonde heads nodded vigorously.

All three turned to Katie, who also nodded, looking pleased. Muffled giggles reached Gwyn through the French doors. Curiosity got the better of her. She pushed away from her desk and crossed her office to open the door.

"Am I allowed in on the fun?" she asked.

Gareth glanced at her, his grin filled with mischief. "We were just deciding on dinner," he said.

"French fries!" Nicholas shouted.

Gwyn pursed her lips, trying to look severe. "You're spoiling them. Fast food is for weekends."

"And for chicken pops?" Maggie asked hopefully.

Gwyn caved with a laugh. "All right," she said. "For chicken pops, too. But only on the first day. You need good food in your tummy to help you get better."

"Wanna see the effelant on my tummy?" Maggie held up her pajama top proudly. Gwyn walked over to the island and admired the colorful creation on her daughter's spotted, round little belly.

"It's beautiful, sweetie. Very elephantish." She looked up to find Gareth regarding her strangely.

"What?" she asked.

"I'm not sure. Yes, I am. The glasses. I knew there was something different. I didn't know you wore them."

"Only for close work. A sign of my advancing age."

"You didn't have them at the theater when you were sketching."

And she didn't know he'd paid that much attention.

"I was afraid to take them out of my bag," she admitted. "In case I annoyed you any more than I already had."

"You didn't annoy me."

She frowned. "You told me I did."

"No, I agreed that you'd distracted me." He quirked an eyebrow in a gesture of wicked amusement. "That's entirely different."

He lifted Nicholas down from the counter. "Nicholas and I are going to get dinner. What would you like?"

"I'll get my purse."

"Don't worry about it. My treat."

"You've done enough already today," Gwyn objected. "You're not paying for my kids' dinner too."

Gareth rolled his eyes. "If you tell me one more time that I've done enough today, I will throw something at you," he threatened, to the great amusement of her children. "Now, what do you want to eat?"

Taking in the somewhat steely expression in his dark eyes, she bit back another objection. "Nothing, thanks. I'll make something later."

"Are you sure?"

She nodded.

"We'll be back in a few minutes, then. And I like them, by the way."

"What?"

"Your glasses. They suit you. You look very—" he paused, and his gaze traveled over her calf-length wool skirt and snug-fitting, long sleeved tee-shirt, both in shades of charcoal gray. Then he shot a quick, sidelong look at her three children and cleared his throat. "Refined," he finished.

Taking Nicholas, he departed, leaving Gwyn with the distinct, breathless impression that had they been alone, he might have chosen a far different adjective.

Maggie's good humor and willingness to be entertained by Gareth ended shortly after dinner. At the sound of a tap at her door, Gwyn looked up from the computer to find him standing in the doorway, her tearful daughter in arms.

"Has she had enough?" Gwyn asked.

"I think so. She's pretty itchy and uncomfortable."

Gwyn slid her glasses off and placed them beside her keyboard. Rising, she reached over to switch off her desk lamp.

"It sounds like it's time for another bath. What do you think, sweetie?" She took Maggie from Gareth. "Poor baby, it's lousy, isn't it?"

She kissed the top of her daughter's head, stroking her back as she followed Gareth into the kitchen office. Maggie snuggled miserably against her.

Gareth frowned. "Is she all right? Do you want to take her to a doctor or something?"

Gwyn smiled at his concern. "She's fine, I promise. The first few days are bad, until all the spots appear and crust over. Nights are always the worst." Gwyn glanced down at the bundle in her arms. "I don't imagine either one of us will sleep much again tonight, will we, love?" she murmured.

"Can I get Nicholas ready for bed for you?" Gareth asked.

Gwyn shook her head. "I can manage. Whether you want to hear it or not, you *have* done enough today. I don't even know where to begin thanking you."

"I'm glad I could help out."

Gareth stretched out a hand. Gwyn's heart stuttered, then sheepishly resumed its normal beat when strong fingers swept a lock of hair back not from her face, but from her daughter's. She closed her eyes against a disappointment she had no right to feel. Gentle fingers tilted her chin upwards. Her eyes flew open again to meet Gareth's.

"You look completely done in," he said, his voice gruff. "Let me stay and get Nicholas ready for you. I assume Katie can get herself ready?"

"Yes, but—"

"You're going to be up most of the night, remember? You may as well take advantage of me while you can."

At his choice of words, Gwyn's eyes flashed up to meet his, but the expression there seemed quite benign. Feeling as if Maggie's 'effelant' had migrated to her stomach, along with a great many of its friends, she asked, "Are you sure?"

"Of course. You get Maggie into a tub, and Nicholas can show me the routine."

"All right. Thank you." She meant it from the bottom of her heart, and his smile told her he knew that.

"You're welcome."

Gwyn paused in the kitchen doorway. "Oh, and Gareth?"

He turned.

"He gets one story," she said. "Not three. And yes, he has to brush his teeth, and no, he can't sleep in his clothes so he can be ready early in the morning to watch cartoons."

"Are you telling me your son is a con artist?"

"Yes."

He chuckled. "Gotcha. Do you want me to get Katie moving, too?"

"Tell her she has fifteen more minutes."

CHAPTER 12

Gwyn sat on the closed toilet seat, watching Maggie swim "like a mermaid" in the bathtub. Chin propped in hand and elbow resting on knee, she listened to the sounds drifting to her from down the hallway. It felt so odd, sitting here while someone else tended her child--

No, that wasn't quite true. Many times Sandy or another friend had pitched in with the kids' evening routine, and she'd listened to them without this strange hollowness beneath her ribs. No, this was different.

Maggie drew her attention to her swimming attempts, and Gwyn dutifully watched and praised. But her attention soon wandered again, drawn by the voices from Nicholas' room. The high-pitched giggles and shrieks of her little boy mingled with the deep tenor belonging to Gareth.

She sucked in a quick breath. That was it. Nicholas had never had a man ready him for bed before. Sandy's husband, Rob, had played ball with him in the back yard or taken him fishing on occasion, but he'd never participated in the more intimate family routines. No man ever had. Gwyn's dates had been rare at best, had never amounted to anything approaching serious, and had never, ever touched her children's lives.

Nicholas laughed again. Gwyn's heart constricted.

Katie came in to brush her teeth, pausing to give her an enormous hug.

Gwyn returned the gesture in surprise. "What was that for?"

"You looked sad," Katie said. "I wanted to make you happy."

"I'm not sad, sweetie," Gwyn denied, with a tiny laugh. "I have you and Maggie and Nicholas. How could I possibly be sad? But thank you for the hug anyway."

...you and Maggie and Nicholas...

But never any man. She'd been so busy protecting her children that she'd never stopped to consider that she might have deprived them, too. Until now.

"Right, here's another one for teeth," Gareth said, making an appearance in the bathroom doorway with a giggling, pajama'd Nicholas slung over his shoulder. "Where shall I dump him?"

"In the baftub!" Maggie shouted, joining in her brother's laughter.

Gareth glanced at Gwyn. "I see the oatmeal bath is working magic," he observed.

He swung Nicholas off his shoulder and set him on a stool beside Katie, who handed him his toothbrush.

Gwyn pulled herself together, tucking her thoughts away until she could take them out and examine them again later. When it was safe to do so. When Gareth was gone.

"It generally does, as long as they remain in it. And as long as the spots are in the right places. Poor Katie had most of hers on her face. Those were a little hard to soak in a tub." She grimaced at the memory.

"Don't most kids get this at the same time as their siblings?" Gareth asked. "Weren't the twins born yet?"

"Yes, but they were only a few months old, and they managed to avoid it. At the time, it was a blessing. It was my first year on my own. I'm not sure I could have handled all three." Gwyn tapped Nicholas on the shoulder and held out her hand for his toothbrush. He handed it over obediently and opened his mouth for her to continue the brushing job.

She looked up at a quiet Gareth and found his dark brows almost converged over his nose.

"What?" she asked.

He shook his head, the frown clearing. "Nothing," he said.

But he somehow managed to convey the impression of the exact opposite.

Gwyn went back to brushing Nicholas' teeth, acutely aware of Gareth's eyes following her every movement. Katie finished her own teeth, dropped her brush into the holder on the counter, and sidled past Gwyn. She paused to drop a kiss on top of Maggie's head.

"'Night, Mags. Hope you're better soon." She looked hopefully at Gwyn. "Can you still read me a story, Mommy?"

"Of course, sweetie. We'll read the next chapter." Gwyn watched her trot off with a wide, happy grin, then glanced at Gareth.

"*Harry Potter*," she explained. "Sandy gave it to her for her birthday and we're almost done. All right, bud," she said to Nicholas. "You're done. Rinse and spit, then have a drink. A small one."

Nicholas complied, then turned to Gareth. "Ready!" he announced, sliding his small hand into the man's. "We can read the Grinch."

Gareth looked doubtful. "Isn't it a bit early for Christmas stories?"

Gwyn laughed. "Are you kidding? We read that one year round. You ought to try it on a sticky July afternoon." She leveled a severe look at her son and reminded him, "One story, Nicholas. And no hassling Gareth."

Gwyn dried off Maggie to the accompaniment of Gareth's deep voice drifting in from the twins' room. She slathered her daughter's spots with calamine lotion, then dressed her in fresh pajamas. Together, they tiptoed into the bedroom, finding Katie drawn there as well, and settled onto Maggie's bed to listen to the rest of the story, brought to magical life in a way that Gwyn had never achieved.

The story ended, and Gareth looked up at them all from the rocking chair, his eyes twinkling. "What's this, a whole audience?"

"We couldn't help ourselves," Gwyn said. "That was marvelous."

"You were even better than Auntie Sandy," Katie told him.

"High praise indeed," Gwyn said. "Sandy has been the world's best storyteller around here for years."

Gareth chuckled. "My agent will be pleased to know I'm making a reputation for myself." He looked down at Nicholas, nestled into the crook of his arm, and handed him the book. "I think this makes it your bedtime, my friend."

Nicholas took the book and slid off Gareth's lap. He cast a sly, pleading glance at Gwyn. "Just one more?" he asked.

Gwyn raised an eyebrow. With a defeated sigh, her son crossed the room to replace the book on the shelf. Minutes later, both he and Maggie were tucked into bed, and Gwyn began the final kiss-and-hug routine.

Or what used to be the final one.

Tonight, as she leaned over Maggie, her daughter whispered a request in her ear. Gwyn smiled past a lump in her throat.

"I'll ask," she said. She looked over at Gareth, waiting in the doorway. "Maggie would like to know if she could please have a kiss and a hug from you, too."

Gratified surprise flickered across Gareth's expression and he detached himself from the door post.

"I would be honored," he said. He duly delivered a kiss-hug to first Maggie, and then at Nicholas' demand, to him as well, before joining Gwyn at the door again.

She pulled the door partway closed, reminded Maggie to call her if she woke up, and turned to find Gareth leaning against the wall, his arms crossed over his chest. Her heart skipped a beat, then, when she met his dark gaze, it skipped several more. Visions of their parting scene the night before danced through her head. She smoothed damp palms against her skirt.

"How long do you think she'll sleep?" Gareth asked, breaking the spell as he nodded towards Maggie's door.

"If I'm lucky? An hour or two. I'll just keep giving her baths as she needs them, and then bring her into bed with me when I come up later."

"You're going to be tired tomorrow."

"Nothing I haven't been before, I can assure you," she said dryly. "Parenthood and exhaustion are synonymous, didn't you know?"

A shuttered expression crossed Gareth's eyes, so fast it was gone before she really had time to register it. He changed the subject. "How are Nicholas and Katie getting to school in the morning?"

"My neighbor is chauffeuring Nicholas to and from kindergarten for me, and Katie's friend's mother will pick her up on their way."

"Good." He nodded, seeming satisfied that she'd covered all the bases. "Are you ready for a cup of tea or something?"

The *or something* held distinct appeal, but Gwyn managed to hold her tongue. "I'd love a cup of tea, but are you sure you have time? I don't want to keep you if you have other plans."

"Are you trying to get rid of me?"

Heat crept across Gwyn's cheeks. "Of course not. I just thought—I meant—"

"You tuck Katie in. I'll put on the kettle."

She was only too happy to make her escape.

CHAPTER 13

Gareth watched a wisp of steam drift from the kettle. On the counter beside the stove, a tray stood ready. He sent it a baleful glance. Sugar, milk, spoons, teapot...and one cup.

One, because he still held the other in a death grip while common sense wrestled romantic fancy.

One, because no matter how much he wanted to stay, he shouldn't. Should never have come here in the first place. He rubbed his stubbled jaw with one hand and scowled at the offending mug he held in the other.

What in the hell did he think he was playing at here, anyway? Why couldn't he just be sensible and walk away? Breaking promises to Catherine, keeping secrets from Gwyn...

He raked his hand through his hair.

It wasn't as if he hadn't met attractive, sexy, intriguing women before, because he had. Many of them. Some had been mistakes from the very start; some had made a deeper impression than others...

A metallic hiss vibrated through the copper kettle on the stove, and steam wisped from its spout.

But none had been like Gwyn.

None had surprised him with a quirky honesty as enchanting as it was refreshing. None had made him, with a simple note of weariness in her voice, want to drop his own life so that he could make hers a little easier. None had made all his complications fade away with nothing more than her smile.

And none had ever made him stand in a kitchen debating the addition of a second cup to a tea tray.

He hefted the cup in his hand. *Well, Connor? You know you want to...and you know you shouldn't. What's it going to be?*

Things would be so much simpler if he could just be honest with Gwyn. If he'd hadn't given his word to Catherine to keep Amy a secret until Amy herself decided to make their relationship public. But with so much at stake, he would not—*could not*—break the first promise, however indirectly made, he'd ever given his daughter. Not for anyone.

So, did he put this second cup on the tray, continue to deceive Gwyn for the moment, see where this spark led, and hope that she understood when she eventually found out? Or did he turn around, walk away, keep his promises intact, and, for the rest of his life, wonder *what if*?

Gareth sighed. Bloody hell. When he put it like that...

He set the cup on the tray.

For the second evening in a row, Gwyn's belly twisted into knots as she descended the stairs. She couldn't remember the last time she'd felt so distracted. Lord, she'd stumbled so many times over reading to Katie that her poor daughter had finally heaved an exasperated sigh, taken the book out of her hands, and told her they'd continue tomorrow.

But not even the resulting guilt had stilled Gwyn's thoughts of Gareth.

He waited for her in the sitting room. A tea tray sat on the wooden trunk, her CD of Bach's violin concertos played quietly in the background, and Gwyn's stomach did three complete flips before she even stepped down into the room.

He looked up from a magazine as she walked around the trunk to join him on the couch. "Break time?"

"Until the next round," Gwyn agreed. She motioned at the tray. "Thank you for making the tea."

"You're welcome. I won't stay long. I know you have work to do tonight."

"Not nearly as much as I'd have if you hadn't taken over the kids." She perched on the edge of the couch, her hands alternately pleating and smoothing the fabric of her skirt. "You're very good with them, you know."

"And they're very good kids," he returned lightly. He leaned forward and lifted the teapot from the tray. He poured a little into one of the mugs. "Strong enough for you?"

Gwyn nodded. He filled her cup, added the bit of milk she requested, and passed it to her. Stirring it, she watched him pour his own. Curiosity finally got the better of her.

"Do you have any of your own?"

Gareth raised a dark eyebrow. "Any what?"

"Kids. You're so natural with them, I thought maybe..." she trailed off.

Gareth's hand hovered over his cup for an instant, holding a teaspoonful of sugar. Then he dumped the white crystals into the milky liquid and stirred. "I've never considered myself much in the way of father material," he said brusquely.

Surprise made her speak honestly and without thinking. "Are you kidding? You'd be wonderful!" Then it occurred to her how her words might sound, coming from a single mother. Her face heated. "That is—I mean—"

Gareth slanted her a crooked, reassuring smile. "I know what you mean. And thank you."

The strains of Bach floated into the awkward silence between them. Gwyn rested her elbows on her knees and cradled her cup in her hands.

"Can I ask you something?" Gareth's voice sounded studiously casual.

Gwyn stilled. So they'd come to the personal things at last, had they? She sipped her tea. Well, she supposed she'd started it.

"Of course."

"Where is he now?"

She didn't pretend not to understand. "Somewhere on the planet, one would presume," she said, her voice devoid of expression.

"He doesn't see the kids?"

"Jack isn't what *anyone* would consider much in the way of father material."

"What happened?"

Gwyn sent him a sidelong glance.

"You don't really want to hear the sordid details of my life, do you?" she asked, in a dry attempt at levity.

Gareth's eyes flicked to meet hers, brooding and intense. "Humor me."

She held his gaze a moment, then looked down into her cup again. "Jack decided he couldn't handle the responsibilities of being a father. He went out to get milk one night, a week after Nicholas and Maggie were born, and called three days later to tell me he wouldn't be coming home again."

Gareth frowned. "You must have had problems before that."

She snorted softly. "To this day, I can't remember the slightest warning sign. We had the usual arguments, but I thought things were pretty normal. He was thrilled when Katie was born—took her everywhere with him. And when we found out I was expecting twins, he called everyone he knew to tell them the news. Apparently once they were born, however, he panicked. He said he could handle one child, maybe even two. But three—especially with twins—were more than he could deal with." She took another swallow of tea and tried again to lighten the conversation. "See? I told you you didn't want to hear the details."

"Does he ever ask to see them?"

"He did once, about a year after he left. My lawyer notified him I was seeking sole custody. The next day he turned up on the doorstep with his new girlfriend. She wanted to see the kids for herself before they decided whether or not he should sign the papers."

Gareth muttered a harsh expletive. Gwyn shot him a wicked grin.

"Not to worry," she said. "Nicholas had the flu that day. He threw up all over the girlfriend's designer suit the minute she picked him up. Two days later, Jack signed over custody."

A muscle flexed in Gareth's jaw. "It must have been hard on the kids."

The comment sounded harsher than she might have expected, as if it had been torn from him against his will, and Gwyn sent him a curious look.

"Maggie and Nicholas never knew him," she pointed out. "But it was hard on Katie. It was three years before she stopped asking when he was coming home." She paused, feeling her throat constrict. She hadn't been down this road in a long time, she reflected, and for good reason.

"Katie thought she'd done something wrong—something to make Daddy angry. She cried herself to sleep for months. I think I could have ripped him apart on those nights."

She swallowed the lump that accompanied the memories. *Stop*, she told herself. *You've said too much already.*

But Gareth's questions hadn't finished.

"What if he wants to come back into their lives one day?" He turned to look at her, his eyebrows a single dark slash above his flat gaze. "Will you let him?"

A question she'd asked herself many, many times. And one she'd been so very, very glad she hadn't yet had to answer.

She thought of her daughter's tiny body shaking with sobs. The times she'd had to leave her little girl to weep alone at night while she'd tended the needs of newborn twins. Tears blurred her vision, threatened to overflow. She blinked them away, appalled at her weakness.

"Any man who can do what Jack did to Katie doesn't deserve a second chance," she said, her voice steady. Cold. "He walked away from his own kids and never looked back. Never called, never dropped by to see them. It was as if he forgot they ever existed."

Despite her rapid blinking efforts, a tear escaped and slid down her cheek. She swiped it away with the back of one hand. "So to be honest, I don't know if I'd let him. I don't know if I could."

Long seconds ticked by. Then Gareth reached to set his cup on the trunk with careful deliberateness.

"It's late," he said. "I'll see myself out."

A hollow spot formed beneath Gwyn's ribs. That was it? No comment, no nothing? She watched him rise.

He paused as he reached the kitchen, looking back but not meeting her gaze. "Don't forget to lock the door behind me."

She stared after him, listening to the retreat of his footsteps, the opening of the door, the finality of its closing again. So. The fantasy had come to an end, wreathed in the flames of reality. She closed her eyes. Damn. She'd known this would happen if things turned too personal.

She just hadn't expected it to sting quite so much.

<h1 style="text-align:center">CHAPTER 14</h1>

Gareth flicked open the newspaper and ignored the half-naked blonde parading through Sean's living room on route to the kitchen. It was her fifth trip in twenty minutes. In spite of the fact Sean slept soundly just down the hall, she'd made no secret of her interest in Gareth—or her availability if he returned the interest.

Which he did not.

Christ, what was she, half his age? He snapped the newspaper again, staring at it without reading. He needed a coffee, but he didn't dare emerge from behind his flimsy protection. He also needed a shower and a shave, but he didn't trust Sean's friend not to pick the lock and join him. Five more minutes, he told himself. Five more minutes and then—

A door opened down the hallway. Finally.

Gareth peeked over the top edge of the paper. Sean saluted him lazily, tugging a tee-shirt over his tousled head as he wandered into the living room. He dropped into a chair opposite and lifted his bare feet onto the coffee table.

"Morning. You got in late."

"I'm surprised you noticed."

The blonde returned from the kitchen. Leaning over the back of Sean's chair, she wrapped her arms around him, exposing more than Gareth cared to see. He went back to staring at his paper. A muffled giggle reached him, then soft steps padded down the hallway.

"She's gone," said Sean.

Gareth dropped the paper onto his lap and rubbed both hands over his face. "Please tell me Bunny isn't a regular here," he muttered.

"Her name is Carolyn, you know I avoid regular, and when did you stop appreciating a beautiful woman?"

"Maybe when she started looking the same age as my daughter?" He ignored Sean's glower. "I need a coffee."

Sean snorted. "You look more like you need a stiff drink. Did you get any sleep last night?"

"Not much."

"Your non-involvement with the single mother getting to you?"

Gareth glared at his cousin. "No. If you must know, I was thinking about Amy."

"Oh?"

"Something Gwyn said—" Gareth broke off and sighed. "It messed up her oldest daughter pretty badly when her husband left."

Sean linked his hands behind his head and regarded him in silence. "You're worried the same thing happened to Amy," he said at last, his voice quiet.

Gareth turned his head to stare out the window at the gray morning. "Katie asked about her dad for three years after he left. Gwyn still doesn't think she understands."

"How old is Katie?"

"Seven."

"And when her dad left?"

"Three."

"It's hardly the same thing," Sean pointed out. "You weren't that much in the picture to begin with, and by the time Catherine remarried, Amy probably didn't even notice you were gone."

Gareth forced a breath past the knife embedded in his chest. "Thanks a lot."

"You know what I mean. Besides, you weren't the one who left, remember? Catherine did that."

"But I let her go, Sean—I gave up any right I had to her. How the hell do I explain that?"

Sean rose to his feet, stretched, and headed for the kitchen. "Be honest," he suggested over his shoulder. "She's eighteen now, remember? I imagine she understands life a little better than your girlfriend's seven-year-old daughter does."

Pausing in the doorway, he gave Gareth a sly grin. "And speaking of being honest, was it really only Amy who kept you awake all night?"

Gareth thought of the pain he'd seen in Gwyn's eyes the night before—pain he'd caused with his questions but hadn't been able to ease because he'd been too wrapped up in his own guilt.

The knife in his chest twisted and slid in a little deeper.

"No," he said. "It wasn't just Amy."

Gwyn was having a bad day.

It started at midnight when Maggie crawled into bed with her, followed by a feverish Nicholas an hour later. At three a.m.,

Gwyn ran a bath for Maggie, and after one look at Nicholas, added him to the same tub. A second bath for both followed at four forty-five, and a third at six thirty.

Things had gone downhill from there.

Nicholas and Maggie squabbled endlessly. Having run out of calamine lotion, Gwyn had resorted to baking soda paste, not nearly as effective, until Sandy could take her lunch break and run by the drugstore for more of the precious pink liquid. By noon, she'd dealt with no fewer than three telemarketers—the last of whom would no doubt reconsider being quite so perky in future—and a client who wanted major structural changes made to his already completed plans.

Just as she finished arguing about everything from when she could do the work to whether or not she would bill him extra, frantic cries for "Mommy!" made her drop the phone on the desk and bolt from her office. The sound of running water penetrated as she tripped halfway up the stairs, scraping the entire length of one shinbone. She ran faster.

Limping and cursing, she hobbled into the bathroom to find the tub near to overflowing and Nicholas gamely trying to turn off the tap. Gwyn dived over him and shut off the water. Closing her eyes and clinging to the tap, she took a moment to breathe.

And to remember she was a mother, her children were merely sick, and they didn't deserve to be locked up until they were thirty.

She turned to her pathetically spotted, crestfallen little boy, trying to muster what calm she could. "What were you doing, Nicky?"

"Helping," he said in a small voice. His bottom lip quivered. "Maggie was itchy, and you were on the phone, so I was making her a bath."

"I see."

"I put porridge in it like you." He held out the large oatmeal tin he'd concealed behind his back.

Gwyn took the container, hefted it in her hand, and then gave it a shake. She eyed the murky bathtub water.

"All of it?" she asked. She wasn't sure she wanted to hear the answer, even though the empty tin spoke for itself. "Did you wrap it in a cloth?"

Nicholas shook his head. A tear fell from his lashes onto his rash-roughened cheek.

Maggie produced the rubber plug from the bathtub from behind her back. She held it out to Gwyn.

"The water was icky," she said. "So I pulled the plug."

Gwyn stared at the plug in her hand, then at the near-to-overflowing, sludge-filled tub.

She closed her eyes.

Her shin throbbed.

The doorbell rang.

Sandy. Thank God.

With Nicholas and Maggie trailing after her, Gwyn limped downstairs. She halted the twins at the foot of the stairs, reminding them that Auntie Sandy didn't need to catch their chicken "pops," and then opened the door.

Gareth stood on the porch, one hand braced against the door frame, hair neatly pulled back once more, eyes hidden behind sunglasses as black as his leather jacket. Gwyn's mouth turned into the Sahara.

"Hi," he said.

Her mouth flapped in response. Mortification settled over her like an itchy sweater, and her fingers tightened around the door, resisting the impulse to slam it shut. She wasn't ready to face him. Not after the scene in her sitting room last night. A scene that had played over and over again in her mind ever since: her poor-wronged-woman performance of a lifetime, and the way she'd come within seconds of bawling all over a Hollywood mega star.

Followed by that star's abrupt departure.

Heat flooded her face. The more she thought about it, the more painful it became.

"I dropped by to see how things were going." He looked down at the two faces peering past her legs, and the corners of his mouth curved up. "You appear to be fighting a losing battle."

She swallowed several times before risking her voice. "I'm trying to look on the bright side," she said, forcing a lightness she didn't feel. "At this rate, we'll be back to normal in a week."

"True." Gareth stared at the porch floor. "Gwyn, about last night—I'm sorry I left like that. So abruptly, I mean."

Gwyn blinked at him. Wait a minute. She'd all but come apart at the seams and he was apologizing to *her*? Gareth peered over the top of his sunglasses, his heavy brows drawn together. She knew he was waiting for her to reply, but shock had robbed her of speech.

He sighed, lifting his chin and becoming invisible behind the dark lenses again. "I know I should explain—"

"You don't owe me any explanations," she interrupted. She'd intended to articulate her own apology, but the stiffness she heard in her own voice made her cringe anew. She looked away from the gaze she could feel but not see. Why couldn't he have called instead of coming over? At this level of embarrassment, *I'm sorry* would be a great deal easier over the phone rather than face to face.

Gareth straightened and shoved his hands into his jacket pockets. Hell, this wasn't going at all well, and he couldn't blame her a bit. First he'd run out on her, and now he was botching his apology. If only he could just tell her—

"Gwyn, there are things about me—things you should know, but—" He paused as a car horn tooted behind him. He glanced over his shoulder at a red sports car that had pulled up by the curb in front of the house. "Are you expecting someone?"

"I ran out of calamine lotion this morning. Sandy said she'd bring some by on her lunch hour. That's her."

Nicholas edged past his mother's leg, but Gwyn caught him back. "Oh, no, you don't. Auntie Sandy hasn't had chicken pox. She doesn't need to catch them from you, my spotted little monster." She glanced at Gareth. "Can you watch the kids for a second while I run out to her car?"

"You have no shoes. I'll go."

"No! It's fine, thanks. I'll just slip these on." Gwyn snatched up a pair of muddy clogs and slipped them onto her feet.

"I'd like to meet her."

"No, you wouldn't." Gareth laughed, not sure what else to do. "Gwyn—"

"I'll be back in a minute." Gwyn rushed out the door past him, down the steps, and across the lawn to the waiting car.

Gareth frowned after her. What was that all about? A desire to protect his privacy? Given that she'd already introduced him to her babysitter, he doubted it. And besides, she'd looked embarrassed. Ashamed, almost.

He struggled with a foreign sense of offense. He'd never had anyone want to keep him a secret before.

He realized Nicholas had ventured out onto the cold wooden floor to stand beside him, accompanied by Maggie. Both children waved madly at the red car's occupant, and Nicholas was inching his way toward the stairs.

"Nice try, buddy, but I don't think so," Gareth said. He placed a hand atop each blond head and turned them in an about-face. "If you come down with pneumonia on top of everything else, your mother will have my head. Back inside."

"What's new—new—" Nicholas grappled with the unfamiliar word but trudged obediently back into the house.

"Pneumonia," Gareth repeated. Casting a last glance at Gwyn, who leaned through the open passenger window of the sports car, he closed the front door and turned to answer Nicholas' question.

CHAPTER 15

Gwyn took the plastic bag Sandy held out to her and shivered in the chill November wind, wishing she'd thought to grab a jacket, too.

"Thanks so much for bringing this over, Sandy, you're a real life saver. I don't know what I'd have done if I'd had to get it myself. Can you imagine the looks if I paraded my two spotted kids through the drugstore? You know, they should sell this stuff in gallon tubs. I'm sure that's how much I'll go through."

"Gwyn." Sandy stared at her.

Gwyn stared back. A wave of heat rose in her face.

"You're babbling."

Gwyn dropped her head onto her forearms against the car door. "You noticed."

"It was pretty hard not to. Such uncharacteristic behavior wouldn't have anything to do with the man who was standing on your front porch just now, would it? The one you so obviously didn't want me to meet?"

The man who *was* standing on her porch? She snuck a quick glance at her house and her heart sank. Great. Gareth had stepped inside with the kids—eliminating any chance of politely not inviting him in. She held back a weary sigh. She was in no shape to cope with Gareth Connor today. She had enough trouble dealing with that magnetism on a good day. She couldn't imagine doing so when she felt like this.

"I didn't say I don't want you to meet him," she said. Despite her denial, however, she avoided her friend's gaze and, after several seconds of stony silence from the car's interior, she caved. "Fine. I don't want you to meet him."

"I'm trying very hard not to have my feelings trashed here, Jacobs," Sandy said. "But you're making it pretty difficult."

"I told you I'd fill you in on your birthday, remember?"

"Bull. My birthday has nothing to do with you babbling—or with keeping secrets from me. You owe me an explanation."

Gwyn floundered. "I don't know. I guess it just seems so unreal."

"What, are you afraid he'll disappear if he crosses paths with the rest of your life?"

"I guess. Maybe. I don't know." She did know, actually, but she wasn't about to confess the truth. Sandy might be her best friend in the entire world, but she was also a hard-core realist who didn't believe in pulling her punches. Gwyn didn't think she could handle hearing what an idiot Sandy thought she was by indulging in this little fantasy. Much better to extricate herself first...and to recover.

"I'll give you a week," Sandy announced. She started the car. "Maggie and Nicky won't be contagious then, and you can have Rob and me over for dinner. But no birthday stuff. I've decided I'm in denial."

"When are you not in denial about your age?"

"True. Oh, before I forget, I know you have lots of kids' movies, but I thought you might be able to use some adult entertainment, too. Your favorites," she added with a wink, handing another plastic bag to Gwyn. "I borrowed them from someone at the office, so there's no rush to return them."

Gwyn peeked into the plastic bag. Three Gareth Connor DVDs in full-color cases. She held back a bubble of laughter—hysterical, no doubt—through sheer force of will. Clutching the bag in stiff fingers, she summoned a smile that felt more like a grimace, and stood back to wave as Sandy pulled out onto the street. Then she started back up the walkway to her house—and the man inside it.

The front hallway stood empty, but voices coming from upstairs simplified her search. She found her children perched on the counter in the bathroom, watching Gareth, who was up to his elbows in the murky bath water. He grinned at her over his shoulder as he hauled out a handful of what looked like lumpy, gray glue and dumped it into the bucket by his side.

"I'm not sure I'm making any progress," he said. "For every handful I pull out, it seems two more take its place."

He leaned back over the tub, shirt straining across his shoulders and jeans across his—she sucked in a swift, strangled breath. Gareth looked over his shoulder again.

"Are you all right?"

Gwyn started to shake her head, stopped herself, put a hand to her hot cheek, and made herself nod instead. "Yes, I'm fine. But I should be doing that. You're getting soaked."

On the counter, Nicholas and Maggie giggled, and she sent them a look that quelled them instantly.

Gareth pulled another oatmeal glob from the water. "Did your friend have the lotion for you?"

Here it came. But she *had* behaved rather strangely when he'd offered to go out to Sandy's car, so she supposed he had a right to ask why. She just had no idea how she'd answer. She braced herself. "Yes."

"Good."

That was it? She blinked in surprise. He wasn't going to ask difficult questions? A sudden thought occurred to her, warming her cheeks all over again. Maybe he just wanted to avoid any deeper involvement—and after last night's display, who could blame him? The glob plopped into the bucket.

"I'll run out for more oats when I'm done with this," he continued. "Or I can sit with the kids if you need to get other things as well. You might enjoy the break."

"I can't ask you to—"

"You didn't ask, remember? I offered."

And that was supposed to make her feel better about having a movie star remove cold porridge from her plumbing?

For the second time in the space of a few minutes, she bit back a somewhat hysterical giggle. Lord, between unruly hormones and sleep deprivation, she was losing it. Maggie and Nicholas had better let her get some sleep tonight, or—

Gareth sat back on his heels and raised an eyebrow. "What's so funny?" he asked.

"Nothing." The corners of her mouth twitched.

Gareth's eyebrow rose another notch.

"It's not really funny," she allowed, "just bizarre. The whole idea of having you here—cleaning up after my kids, babysitting, eating tuna casserole and cold chicken nuggets...I know you've offered to do all these things, Gareth, but it just seems—well, it seems—" She waved her hands, searching for the right words. "I'm sorry, but you can't possibly have expected any of this."

She thought he'd laugh with her, or at least chuckle. Instead, his expression took on a brooding intensity that robbed her of breath. It seemed an eternity before he finally responded, a small smile playing about his mouth.

"I didn't expect it," he agreed. "But didn't anyone ever tell you? Some of the best things in life are the ones we don't expect."

Through a haze of fluttery, unfamiliar confusion, Gwyn registered Maggie's and Nicholas' avid interest in the conversation. A little unsteadily, she crossed the bathroom to where they still sat on the counter and lifted down first one, then the other.

"All right, you two, go find something to do while Gareth finishes repairing the damage you caused, all right? And stay out of trouble this time. You can watch TV or read a book, but that's all. Stay out of Katie's room, stay out of the kitchen, and stay out of my office. Clear?"

"Can we do dot-to-dots on our tummies again?" Nicholas asked.

Gwyn agreed, and the two of them thundered down the stairs. Behind her, Gareth chuckled.

"I seem to have created monsters," he said, for all the world like the last few moments had never happened. "I hope it doesn't become a problem."

Gwyn made a monumental effort to follow his lead, but her smile felt too unsteady to qualify as bright. "As long as they confine their new dot-to-dot skills to the chicken pox on themselves and don't undertake to include walls or furniture, I should be fine." She motioned toward the tub. "Can I do something? It's not fair that you're doing all the work when my kids made the mess."

"For the third time, it's not a problem. I'm sure you have other things you need to do, so let me handle this for you."

"But—"

Gareth frowned at her. "Are you always this stubborn about accepting help?"

"No, but—"

"Then go away and stop bothering me."

She hovered in the doorway for another few seconds, until Gareth sat back on his heels and sent her a positively ferocious look. Deciding prudence might be the better part of valor under the circumstances, she turned on her heel and left.

CHAPTER 16

Staring after Gwyn, Gareth scratched absently at his jaw line. A blob of congealed oats stuck to the stubble that had formed since his morning shave. He grimaced, swiping at the spot again with the back of his wrist, but he only succeeded in making a worse mess.

Scowling, he returned to fishing oatmeal from the bathtub's drain. Grayish goop oozed between his fingers as he plopped it into the bucket.

Gwyn looked exhausted. Being up with the kids all night would have something to do with it, but he was certain his own behavior had also played a role. Asking questions that had triggered her tears and then leaving her alone to deal with her upset hadn't just been unchivalrous, it had been downright wrong. Guilt shafted between his ribs.

She'd deserved better from him. Deserved to be held and comforted, but he'd been too busy picking out the shrapnel of harsh words, directed at another man, from his own soul.

Too busy wrestling with an image of his own daughter weeping for a father she thought didn't care.

He slapped another handful of ooze into the bucket.

Logic told him Sean was right about Amy being different from Katie, and about his own situation being different from what Gwyn had described. Guilt, however, hadn't turned out to be terribly logical so far.

Then again, neither was anything else in his life right now.

Promises he'd made to an ex-wife who meant nothing to him, but who held the key to the heart of a daughter he hadn't seen since her second birthday...a comfort level with Gwyn's family that surpassed how he felt with his own kin...an attraction to Gwyn herself that rocked him to his core...

More oatmeal spattered into the bucket.

He could still walk away. *Should* walk away. The way he'd handled last night proved he wasn't ready to take on anything major in his life right now. He had Amy to think about, and sixteen years of lost time to make up for. It was the worst possible time for a romantic involvement, especially one of the proportions promised by Gwyn.

Gwyn of the warm, quick humor and guileless honesty; of the bottomless, summer's-lake blue eyes and wild auburn hair; of the cluttered life and formidable strength; of the many, many layers that would take a lifetime to uncover...

Oh, yes. He should definitely walk away.

He'd be a fool if he didn't.

And perhaps a greater fool if he did.

Gwyn peeked into the living room at Nicholas and Maggie, absorbed for the moment in a cartoon, then continued down the hallway to the kitchen, where she set about restoring order to at least one part of her life. She cleared and scrubbed, washed and dried, and had a long, serious, and well-overdue discussion with herself.

Or at least, she tried.

Unfortunately, the memory of Gareth's departure the night before kept getting in the way. How he'd stood up in the wake of her meltdown, walking out in a silence that had spoken volumes about his level of discomfort.

Gwyn threw the dishcloth into the sudsy water, sending a spray of bubbles across the counter. Why, oh why, had she opened up the whole personal arena last night? Things had been going so well until then...

Liar, said her little voice.

Fine. Things had at least been under control until then. They'd been friendly, but not involved...

Her little voice made a rude noise.

And now he was back. She stared at her reflection in the dark glass of the wall oven, studying the haphazard ponytail atop her head, the dark circles under her eyes, the face she hadn't even had time to wash, let alone apply makeup to. He was back, apologizing to her for his abrupt departure, and rolling up his sleeves to get involved in her family once more.

And she didn't know why, and she didn't know what to do about it, and she was scared half to death.

She really needed to get a grip on herself.

Abandoning her kitchen-cleaning efforts, she grabbed the wicker laundry basket from the table. The clean scent of freshly washed and dried fabric rose from it, a note of normality in a life that had otherwise completely strayed from its chosen course. A life she needed to put back on track. Today.

Balancing the basket on her hip, she scooped up a stack of Katie's books with her free arm and marched down the hallway. Maggie and Nicholas were still in the living room, oblivious to her presence. They sat on the couch, their two blonde heads—Maggie's hair long and curly like her own, and Nicholas' short and straight like his father's—side by side.

A sudden pang shot through her. They'd missed out on so much, not having a father in their lives. Having Gareth come into their home had highlighted a need that none of them—including her—had even known they had.

And now, having highlighted that need, and having begun to fill it...

The pang turned to a knife, carving her heart in two, underscoring the need to return life to normal. Now. Before any more damage was done. If Gareth had been just an ordinary man, then maybe—

But he wasn't. And she had no business risking her children's hearts in order to indulge her own personal fantasy. Gareth Connor no more belonged in her life than she did in his. Regardless of how kind and gentle he was with her children or how much of a spark existed between the two of them, in just over a week he would leave their world and return to his own.

It was up to her to make sure her children weren't destroyed a second time by that leaving.

Determination fueling her stride, Gwyn climbed the stairs. She reached the top hallway as Gareth emerged from the bathroom to the accompaniment of a gurgle from the bathtub.

"Done," he said triumphantly. He hefted a bucket of congealed *ick* in his hand, his soaked shirt molded to the lean six-pack beneath it.

Gwyn tore her eyes from the clinging fabric—and her imagination from what lay beneath. Clutching at her resolve with both hands, she set the books she carried onto the folded clothes and shifted the basket to her other hip. She'd come up here for a reason. An important one.

"Thank you," she said. "I'm sorry if I sounded ungrateful earlier. I really do appreciate your help. Not just today, but all of it. I don't know what I'd have done without you this last couple of days."

Gareth raised a quizzical eyebrow. "You sound like a kid who's been coached in what to say to some cantankerous old uncle. You don't have to apologize, Gwyn."

"I just don't want you to think I'm not grateful."

"I never thought that, but I'm not looking for gratitude, either. I'm enjoying myself."

"Entertaining my sick kids and cleaning out my bathtub?" she asked dryly.

His smile made her toes dig into the hall carpet-runner. He shook his head. "No, being with you."

Before Gwyn could do more than draw a startled breath at his unexpected—and confounding—honesty, he dropped a towel onto the floor near the top of the stairs and set the bucket on it.

"I've missed out on the family thing, remember?" he added. "It's nice to be a part of yours for a while."

Oh. No, wait. That was why she'd come up here. To tell him he couldn't—

"And besides, I have ulterior motives. You wouldn't happen to have something dry I could borrow, would you?"

She stared at him, panic licking through her. "P-pardon?"

He plucked at his soaking, oatmeal-smeared shirt. "Something dry."

"No. Not that." She shook her head. "I meant pardon about the other thing. What ulterior motives?"

Gareth undid the top button on his shirt. "Sorry, that's a secret."

She shifted the basket again, holding it between them, gripping it with traitorous hands that urged her to toss it aside and take over Gareth's tantalizing task. The temperature in the hallway shot upward, flushing her cheeks with heat and turning her mouth dry.

"A s-s-secret?"

Lord, 's' was a hard sound to make with her tongue cleaved to the roof of her mouth. She forced her gaze to remain on his face instead of following the path of his hands. He released another button. Then a third. Then a fourth. The heat in her cheeks spread, snaking a slow, traitorous path to other parts of her anatomy. Any resolve she'd had when she'd climbed the stairs became a fleeting memory.

His half-smile knowing, teasing, wicked, Gareth undid the final button.

"Mm," he said, "but I'll give you a hint. It hinges on kids recovering and turning their mother free again."

He slid the shirt from his shoulders.

Gwyn inhaled sharply and forgot all about not staring. She'd known the man was achingly gorgeous—after seeing him all those times on the big screen, how could she not? But the screen had never done him full justice. It couldn't, not when he was so much more in person.

So much more.

Her gaze traced the broad slope of his shoulders, muscled, defined, offering a woman's head a sanctuary like none she'd ever known. His chest...deep, powerful, inviting her touch and promising—

Gareth cleared his throat. Gwyn's gaze flew up to meet the smolder of his. As if he'd heard her every thought, felt every frantic beat of her heart.

"A dry shirt?" he reminded her huskily.

She fled.

CHAPTER 17

The last of the dishwater disappeared down the drain, leaving only soap suds in its wake. Turning on the tap to rinse them away, Gareth looked over to the sitting room, where Gwyn, Maggie and Nicholas had nestled together for a story after dinner. Exhaustion had claimed the trio about an hour ago, and they all slept soundly, oblivious to his rattlings in the kitchen.

He turned off the water again, shaking his head at the sheer domesticity of the whole situation. If anyone had told him a week ago he'd be helping out with dishes and plumbing and sick kids, he would have laughed outright at both messenger and idea. So how did something that should have been ludicrous turn out to feel so right?

A noise from the sitting room drew his attention and he glanced over to see Nicholas squirm in his sleep. Without waking, Gwyn reached for the little boy, drawing him further into her warmth, and he relaxed once more.

A hollow formed beneath Gareth's ribcage. He really had missed out, hadn't he? He'd suspected it all along, of course. Hell, he'd regretted handing over Amy to Catherine almost before the ink had dried. But he'd never had it driven home like this. Never really stopped—or dared—to think about the thousand little things he'd missed sharing with his daughter: the stories, the hugs, the fleeting moments of innocence and trust.His mouth tightened.

He'd been *such* an idiot.

He draped the dish cloth over the faucet and wiped his hands against the seat of his jeans. Enough. Katie had gone upstairs to put on pajamas and brush her teeth, so he had time to phone Sean. He wasn't holding his breath that Catherine would have called with anything but more complaints, but hey, miracles happened.

His cousin answered on the fifth ring.

"Yeah."

"Did I interrupt something?" He didn't think Bunny looked the type to stick around this long, but you never knew.

"No, I just got tired of running for the telephone so I could pretend to be your answering service."

"Ah. I take it Catherine called, then?"

"I've been writing the messages on sticky notes. Another hundred or so and I'm thinking I'll have enough to wallpaper the living room."

Gareth pinched the bridge of his nose, closing his eyes. "Should I apologize?"

Sean sighed. "Nah. It's not your fault. But for your sake, I sure as hell hope Amy doesn't turn out to be a case of *like mother, like daughter.* Oh, and before I forget, Angela called again, too. She said it was urgent. You keeping secrets, cuz?"

"Now that you mention it, yes, but Angela's not one of them. She's my agent. She thinks everything is urgent."

"She left a number."

"I have it, thanks. What about Catherine? What was the message from her?"

"Let's see. 'Call me. Tell him I called. Call me. Why hasn't he called me? Call me as soon as possible.' Do you want me to continue?"

"That's okay. I think I've got the message."

"No pun intended, right? Tell me again why can't I give her your cell number?"

Gareth looked into the sitting room at the peaceful, slumbering trio. *Because that part of my life doesn't belong here. Because I haven't decided yet if I belong here. Because Gwyn deserves better from me than to drag Catherine into her home.*

"Because I asked you not to."

A pause. Then Sean drawled, "Right. So how is she, anyway?"

"Who?"

"The one you can't tell about Catherine and Amy. Gwen, or Gwyn, or whatever."

"Gwyn," Gareth said. "And she's fine. She's sleeping right now. Two of her kids are down with chicken pox and she didn't have a very good night."

Silence.

"Two of her kids have chicken pox, and so you're just there helping out," Sean finally replied.

"Is that so hard to believe?"

"On your holiday."

"It's not really a holiday, and until Amy gets back, there's not a lot else for me to do anyway."

"So you thought you'd step in and play daddy to someone else's kids for a few days for what—fun?"

Gareth paused in polishing his fingerprints from the chrome faucet. Annoyance stirred in him. "It's not like that."

His cousin grunted. "Uh huh. And I suppose when Amy gets back and you have something to fill your time, you're just going to walk away, right?"

"Her kids are sick, and she could use a hand. Is that a crime?"

"That depends on whether or not they're used to having strange men walk in and out of their lives," Sean observed.

A hard note underlined his voice, born of personal experience. Sean hadn't spent his childhood summers with Gareth's family in England because of a warm, sunny childhood here. With divorced parents and a mother who had been rather free with her "friendships," those few brief weeks every summer had been the only stability in his cousin's life for years.

"I haven't asked," he said.

"Don't you think you should? With the amount of time you're spending at that house—like every waking hour—someone's going to get attached to you pretty soon. Or you to them."

"I'm a big boy, Sean. I think I know the risks."

"Then you're a bloody fool, because you have no idea what the risks are. What the hell is it that's so bloody attractive about this woman, anyway?"

A thousand things. Everything. Gareth cleared his throat.

"She's pretty." *Make that beautiful...*

"So are a million other women."

"She's smart, she's sweet." *And sexy as hell...*

"I repeat, so are a million other women," Sean growled.

"She's not like a million other women, Sean. She's different."

Sean snorted.

Gareth pulled his gaze from Gwyn and scowled at the phone. His cousin's rocky-childhood excuse only went so far. "Are you *trying* to irritate me?" he demanded. "Because if so, you're succeeding."

"I'm trying to get you to see reason," Sean said wearily. "You want to hear my theory on what you find so attractive about her?"

Gareth had strong ideas regarding what Sean should do with his *theory*, but a tug on his shirtsleeve distracted him before he could speak them.

"Gareth?" a sad little voice asked.

Gareth glanced down, took one look at Katie's tear-stained face, and promptly hung up on both cousin and theory. He crouched down to the little girl's level, taking her hands in his. "Katie, sweetheart, what's wrong?"

"Will Maggie and Nicholas be finished their chicken pox tomorrow?"

He hid a smile. "I don't think so, love. Why?"

Her head drooped and fresh tears flowed in the wake of the others. "Nothing."

Gareth circled her tiny waist with his hands, straightened up, and lifted her onto the stool beside the island counter. "It must be something," he said. "People don't cry for nothing."

He plucked a tissue from the box on top of the refrigerator and dried her tears. "If you tell me, maybe I can help."

Katie snuffled. "It's job day tomorrow."

He tried, but drew a blank. "Job day?" he asked.

"Mommy's supposed to come and tell my class about her job. All the other parents are going to be there."

Ah. Of course. "Well, maybe mummy can come another day," he suggested. "Maggie and Nicholas will only be sick for a few more days and..." He trailed off as fresh tears flooded Katie's eyes.

"But tomorrow's the only day," she wailed. "Madame Morin won't let her come another day!"

Gareth heard Gwyn stir in the sitting room. Hastily, he lifted Katie down and steered her out of the kitchen, grabbing the tissue box on his way. When they reached the stairs at the other end of the hallway, far enough not to wake the others, he settled Katie on the small landing and himself a step below her. "Right," he said. "Now we can talk. Are you sure tomorrow's the only day? Maybe Madame Morin will make an exception for mummy if she knows—"

Katie shook her head. "She said that if the mommies and daddies couldn't come tomorrow then they'd have to come next year, but it's already next year and Mommy promised!"

It's already next year?

"Was mummy supposed to come to job day last year?" he hazarded.

Katie gave a miserable nod. Her chin quivered. "Maggie was sick last year too. And Mommy said this year she'd come. She promised!"

Yes, he'd gotten that. Gareth propped his chin in one hand, his elbow resting on his knee, and regarded the distraught little girl. He wracked his brain for a solution.

"Could someone else come instead?" he suggested. "What about Auntie Sandy?"

"She came last year!" Katie buried her face against her knees, the epitome of abject misery. Her small frame shook with sobs.

"Mommy promised!" came the repeated mumble.

Gareth patted the little girl's back. He could think of few occasions when he'd felt more helpless. He considered offering to look after the twins while Gwyn went to the school, but he somehow didn't think any of them would take to that idea at this stage of illness. "Someone else, then. What about—"

Katie's head lifted. "Could you come?" she asked.

Gareth's mouth flapped. He stared into blue eyes, identical to her mother's, swimming in a sea of tears. Hope stared back.

So did innocent trust.

He held back a sigh. He couldn't go, of course. A visit to a classroom hardly fell into the low-profile category demanded by Catherine or promised to Amy.

Mindful of his young companion's fragility, he formed his refusal with great care. He might even have uttered it, if Katie's soft, sweet voice hadn't added, "Please?"

The word stopped him in his tracks. He stared down at the little girl, thinking of how she had cried herself to sleep all those nights over a missing father, of how hard Gwyn had worked to comfort her, be there for her, heal her. He thought of how he himself had been an absentee father, theoretically causing the same havoc in his own child's life. His jaw tightened.

No more.

He had it within his grasp to begin making amends. Here. Now. Catherine and the media be hanged.

As for Amy—well, surely she would understand. Reaching out to ruffle Katie's blond head, he smiled. "I would be honored to come," he said.

CHAPTER 18

Gwyn came awake with a start as the warmth nestled against her side lifted away. Blinking away a blur of exhaustion, she looked up at Maggie, snuggled into strong, male arms. Gareth's dark gaze met hers over the little blond head. He smiled.

"You all fell asleep," he whispered. "Nicholas and Katie are both tucked in. I just came back for Maggie."

"I'll do it," she offered automatically, moving to rise from the sofa. A hand on top of her head halted her mid-way. She looked up at Gareth again. "Or not?" she hazarded.

"Or not," he agreed. "I'll be back in a minute."

She remained on the couch while he was gone, entirely too comfortable to move. He'd placed a blanket over her at some point, and she snuggled into its warmth, drifting in the state of semi-consciousness that came with sleep deprivation. A few minutes later, she heard him rummaging around in the kitchen, and then his steps across the creaky, tiled floor and into the sitting room. Rousing herself, she opened her eyes and stared at the steaming cup of tea he held out to her.

"Are you awake enough to hold it, or is it safer on the table?" he asked.

She took the cup. "Thank you."

He sat down beside her. "Did the sleep help at all?"

The mere mention of the word had her yawning. She covered her mouth with her free hand and turned rueful eyes on him. "I suspect it will take more than a fifteen-minute nap to make up for what I've missed."

A smile quirked one corner of his mouth, pulling his deep laugh lines into play. "Two hours, actually."

She stared. "No."

"You all nodded off during the story. It was a toss-up as to who went first, to be honest. Katie helped me clean the kitchen, then did her homework. I tucked her in at eight. We didn't have the heart to wake you."

"I'm so sorry—"

"Why? You needed it."

"Well, yes, but—"

"Gwyn. You needed it."

She swallowed further objection and asked instead, "Was Katie okay going to bed on her own?"

"She was fine. It was actually her idea." Gareth leaned back and stretched his arm out along the back of the couch. "You really do have great kids, you know."

She raised an eyebrow and smiled into her tea, trying hard to ignore the warmth radiating from his hand as it rested behind her neck. "In spite of the oatmeal incident?"

He chuckled. "In spite of that," he agreed. "By the way, Katie asked me to remind you that tomorrow is job day."

Horror enveloped Gwyn. Katie had been so upset when she hadn't made it last year—the poor baby would be crushed if it happened again.

"Damn!" she groaned, letting her head drop against the couch cushion behind her and hastily raising it again when she connected with gentle fingers instead. "I completely forgot. Katie will never forgive me."

Gareth cleared his throat. "Actually, she might. If you let me go instead."

Her heart thudded to a standstill. "You?"

"I didn't think you'd mind. She was pretty upset. I suggested someone else could go, and she asked me." He shook his head and sighed, looking bemused. "Is there a secret to refusing tear-filled blue eyes?"

A soft warmth unfurled deep inside Gwyn's chest at the idea of Gareth comforting her daughter. The greater implications, however, made her go cold. Tomorrow was intended as a parent thing. No way should Gareth be going in her stead, and the fact that asking him had been Katie's idea set off all kinds of alarm bells.

She'd been right to worry this afternoon. Her kids—all of them—were showing serious signs of attachment to this man.

Not good.

"I'm not sure you should do that," she said.

Gareth said nothing for a moment. Then, "May I ask why?"

"You've been around here a lot the last few days, and the kids really like you."

"And that's a bad thing because...?"

"You'll be leaving to go home soon."

He frowned, his dark brows meeting over his nose. "You must have had other...friends who have moved away before."

As careful as his words were, Gwyn heard the unspoken question underlying them. She balanced her cup on her knee with one hand. With the other, she plucked at the bits of fluff pilled on the blanket. She really, really didn't want to get into this.

"I don't believe in having a series of men parading in and out of my kids' lives," she said quietly.

Gareth rubbed a hand across his eyes, and then down his jaw. He stared across the room. "We're not just talking about Katie's class tomorrow, are we?" he asked, his voice gruff.

Gwyn twisted a handful of blanket. "No."

"Because it's best for the kids?"

She nodded, unable to meet his gaze.

"And what about for you?"

"I-I think it might be best for me, too."

"And what about what's happened between us? Do we just ignore that? Pretend it's nothing?"

A little of her tea slopped over the cup and soaked through the blanket, setting her knee on fire. She peeked up at him. "I have three children to think about, Gareth."

A tiny muscle worked in Gareth's jaw line as he stared at his own tea. "I know you're worried about your kids," he said finally, "and I know that there are no guarantees that this will work out, but—"

"Please don't."

Eyes darkened by frustration rose to meet hers. "Don't what?"

"Don't..." Gwyn waved her hand vaguely. "This. All of this." *And please don't make me spell it out for you.*

Gareth took a long time to reply. When he did, his voice was rough. "I hadn't counted on this happening any more than you had, Gwyn, but now that it has, I'm not sure I want to ignore it."

"We live five thousand miles apart."

"In an age of technology," he said dryly. "Cell phones, air travel, Skype?"

Gwyn lifted her chin in a show of determination that couldn't have been further from the truth. She knew she was doing the right thing—but if he pushed the issue, she knew just as well that she would fold like a house of cards.

"Neither of us is that naïve," she said. "It isn't just the miles, it's our entire lives. Everything about us is different. Too different."

"You've given this a lot of thought, haven't you?"

She looked away. Nodded. "Yes."

"You know that whatever happened between you and me, I'd never just walk out on them."

"Their own father walked out on them," she reminded him. "I'm not saying you would—only that I'm not willing to risk it. I can't do that to them again. Or to me. "

A flash of something akin to pain flashed through Gareth's eyes and twisted his mouth. Again she had the fleeting impression that he held something back from her, but she didn't dwell on it. Didn't dare. Instead, sensing victory, she pressed home her advantage, laying her hand atop his, steeling herself against the jolt that ran between them. Outside, the November wind tapped a bare maple branch against the window.

"I'm too old to believe in fairy tales, Gareth," she said quietly. "And my kids are too young to have to stop believing in them."

"What about Katie's class tomorrow?"

"I'll explain you can't go."

"You'd disappoint her like that?"

She glared at him. "That's not fair."

"You're right. I'm sorry." He sighed. "What about letting me sit with Maggie and Nicholas while you go, then? Do you think they'd stay with me?"

"I think it's better if I find someone else."

His mouth tightened into a grim line. "He really did a number on you, didn't he?"

Her throat constricted. She didn't need to ask who he meant any more than he needed a response.

Pushing to his feet, Gareth set his mug on the tea tray. "I'll leave you my cell phone number. If you can't find anyone for tomorrow, call. I'll look after the kids for you—as a friend, with no strings attached."

Gwyn trailed into the kitchen behind him and watched him scrawl a phone number on the dry-erase board stuck to the side of the fridge. Neither of them spoke. She because she couldn't force words past the lump in her throat, and he for reasons she felt sure she didn't want to know.

Gareth returned the dry-erase marker to the drawer beside the fridge, underscoring the comfort level he'd attained in her home. Gwyn's lips went tight. She'd definitely made the right decision about this.

Hadn't she?

She rubbed her hand over her chest, surprised to find her heart still beating there. She'd been certain it had been swallowed up by the same hollow ache that made the simple act of breathing so painful. Gareth closed the drawer.

Following him down the hallway to the front entrance, she let her gaze rove the breadth of his shoulders, the lean length of his body. The ache in her center moved deeper. Doubt assailed her.

Dear God, what was she doing? She'd spent four years protecting herself and her kids from another Jack—and those same four years denying herself things she'd very nearly forgotten until now. Why couldn't she—just this once—go with the flow? Live for the moment? Do what she so desperately wanted to do?

Other women had relationships with men, and their children survived—lord, she could even make sure her kids had no more involvement in any of this. It could be between just her and Gareth. A harmless fling.

She bit back a groan.

Except that was the problem. No fling with him would ever be harmless. It couldn't be, because harmless and Gareth didn't go together. Devastating, yes. Earth-shattering, probably. Reality-altering, definitely. But never harmless.

Gareth took his leather coat from the closet. He turned to face her, his expression filled with purpose.

Gwyn swallowed hard.

Take control. Take control now, before he—

She stuck out her hand into the space separating them, mortified to see it shake wildly, too terrified to remove it.

"Goodbye," she said, her voice thick and unrecognizable even to her own ears. "And thank you again for everything. I enjoyed meeting you."

Her insides cringed. Dear lord, could she have chosen less adequate words?

A wickedly lazy smile curved Gareth's lips. "A handshake?" He raised his gaze to hers and shook his head. "I don't think so, Gwynneth with two n's."

Gwyn backed away, coming up short against the wall by the living room doorway. He wouldn't. He couldn't. Not now...

But Gareth's pursuit was measured.

Unfaltering.

Relentless.

It brought him to within a scant few inches of her, where he stopped. He braced his left hand against the wall by her head, then lifted his right hand, still gripping his coat, and did the same on the other side. Before Gwyn could draw the breath she so desperately needed, his head descended.

His mouth fastened on hers with a jolt that traveled her entire length, at once both hard and gentle. Coaxing, demanding, promising...delivering. When Gwyn's own lips parted under the mind-spinning assault, he wasted not an instant in taking full advantage. His tongue slid against hers, tangled with it, and took complete, uncontested ownership.

Not once did his hands move to caress her.

Not once did his body touch hers.

But he imprinted himself on her as indelibly as if he had possessed her in every way imaginable.

At last, his breathing unsteady, he drew back. One at a time, he dropped his hands to his sides and stepped away. He slid his arms into his jacket and shrugged it up onto his shoulders.

"I'll go now," he said, his voice thick, "but just for the record, I haven't agreed."

"A-agreed?" Gwyn whispered. Of its own accord, her trembling hand found its way to her mouth. Her fingertips brushed against lips that felt as if they belonged to someone else, because surely hers wouldn't have responded with such abandon...

"Not to see you again." Giving her a slow half-smile that focused her on his mouth all over again, Gareth pulled open her front door and disappeared into the night.

CHAPTER 19

Gwyn called a last thank you after her departing neighbor, closed the door, and turned to face her sullen daughter. Job day had not gone well.

She pressed fingertips against her throbbing left temple.

It would have been nice to thank Kirsten's mom for babysitting so I could come to your class today." She kept her voice even, wanting to find out what was behind Katie's mood rather than start a fight.

With a shrug, Katie kicked the hiking boots off her feet and onto the closet floor.

Gwyn tried again. "The kids had lots of questions for me. I think they liked the models I brought in."

Another shrug. Katie's gloves followed her boots onto the floor. Teeth gritted, Gwyn reached past her, took the basket marked with Katie's name from the shelf, and held it out in silence.

Katie heaved a pained sigh but retrieved her gloves and dropped them in.

Gwyn replaced the basket. "I take it you didn't like my presentation."

"It was all right."

"Then maybe you'd like to explain why you're not speaking to me?"

Katie mumbled something under her breath.

"Pardon me?"

"I said I wish Gareth could have come instead." Katie glared at her, defiance in every tight line of her small body.

Even though she'd half-expected the response, Katie's words struck to Gwyn's core. She clenched her fists at her sides. Her daughter would rather have had Gareth there than her own mother...not hurtful exactly, but sobering.

Perhaps this would silence the sly *maybes* and *what ifs* that had plagued her since Gareth's departure the night before.

"I'm sorry you feel that way, but today was for parents, Katie, not friends. Gareth was very kind to offer to go, but it turned out that Mrs. Sweatman could babysit for me instead."

Katie scuffed at the ceramic tiles with her toe. "If you married Gareth," she said in a soft voice, "he'd be my daddy, and then he could come."

Feeling as if every molecule of air had just been sucked from her lungs, Gwyn struggled to compose herself. Damn. Despite her best effort, it seemed she'd waited too long after all.

"I suppose that might be true if it ever happened, but—" She spread her hands wide, at a loss for words.

"Marie-Josée's mommy married *her* boyfriend."

Gwyn scowled. *Bully for Marie-Josée's mommy.*

"Gareth is my friend, sweetie, not my boyfriend. There's a big difference."

"Don't you like him?"

"Well, yes, but—"

Her daughter's face settled into stubborn lines. "He'd make a nice daddy."

Way, way too long.

Gwyn's temples thudded unmercifully.

With a superhuman effort, she pulled herself together and injected a firm note into her voice. "I'm sure that's true," she said, "but it's not going to happen. Gareth is only visiting Ottawa, he lives a very long way away, and he has a whole other life besides us."

Katie's expression drooped. "I wish he didn't."

Me, too, baby. Me, too.

Gwyn dropped a kiss on top of Katie's smooth blond head and gave her a warm squeeze. Distraction time. For both of them.

"I think we still have peanut-butter cookies in the cupboard. Would you like me to warm some up for a snack?"

To her immense relief, Katie nodded, willing to follow the change of subject. "With milk?"

"Of course. You go change into your play clothes, and I'll fix the cookies. And, Katie?"

A trusting blue gaze met hers and Gwyn's heart contracted. Had those faint shadows always been a part of her daughter's eyes?

"I love you, sweetie," she said huskily.

"I love you too, Mommy. And I'm glad you came to my class today."

Little arms gave her a quick, fierce hug, and then Katie scampered up the stairs, only to stop half way.

"Mommy?"

"Yes, my love?"

"If Gareth *was* our daddy, he wouldn't leave us like our first one did."

Gwyn stared after her daughter for an eternity, then staggered down the hallway in search of peanut-butter cookies, her other children, pain killers, and whatever equilibrium she could hope to recover.

"*The* Gareth Connor?" Sandy's voice squealed in Gwyn's ear. "That was *the* Gareth Connor standing on your front porch yesterday, and you didn't introduce me? I can't believe you didn't introduce me!"

Gwyn cringed. Cradling the phone against her shoulder, she lifted a teary-eyed Nicholas onto the kitchen counter and settled him among their dinner leftovers. Wearily, she continued dabbing calamine lotion onto the spots covering his belly.

"How did you find out?" she asked.

"Hello? Your babysitter's mother, my office assistant? Elaine thought I already knew—and I can't believe I didn't! She was horrified when she realized, of course, and made me promise not to tell, but God, Gwyn, why didn't *you* tell me?"

Gwyn closed her eyes. Of course. Why hadn't she thought of that? She'd been the one to recommend Elaine to Sandy in the first place, when Kirsten's mom had decided to return to work part-time and Sandy's assistant had just quit.

She scowled. It was the last time she'd do any favors like that again.

"Because I knew you'd squeal like a schoolgirl," she told her friend.

"Mee-oww. Who peed in your cornflakes today?"

Gwyn sighed. "I'm sorry. I'm just a bit edgy today. I have a headache."

"Kids up again last night?"

"Hm? No," Gwyn said absently. "They actually slept through. Nicholas has a few more spots today, but it looks like he's almost done, and there's nothing new on Maggie."

But while the kids had slept through the night, she'd managed to stay awake all on her own anyway.

Very unsatisfactorily all on her own.

With only the memory of a kiss and her treacherous thoughts to keep her company.

When what she'd really wanted was -

Sandy's voice jarred her back to the conversation. "Then what? Trouble in paradise?"

"There is no paradise."

"Ah. The guy didn't live up to his screen image, huh? They never do, you know. I have a cousin who dated an actor once, and—"

A memory of Gareth, half-nude, standing in her upstairs hallway, seared through Gwyn's mind. Calamine lotion slopped onto Nicholas' pajamas.

"Sandy," she croaked.

"Mm?"

"The man is ten thousand times better than his image." She swallowed hard. "Trust me on that."

She mopped up the spilled lotion with the cotton ball in her hand and started doctoring the spots on Nicholas' face.

"Then I don't get it," said Sandy. "What's the problem?"

"The problem is he's leaving in a week and the kids are starting to get really attached to him. I don't think it's wise to let things get out of hand."

It would be even less wise to admit to her friend that things already had.

Silence met her words.

"Sand? You still there?"

"Yeah, I'm here. I'm just trying to decide whether I should smack you for being such an idiot or tell you how much I admire you for being so together."

Gwyn glanced down as Maggie arrived to lean against her leg, looking utterly forlorn. She cleared another spot on the counter, sat the little girl beside her brother, and reached into the nearby freezer for two chocolate-flavored Popsicles. Their suffering momentarily forgotten, the twins reached with pudgy little hands for the treats.

She returned her attention to Sandy. "And?"

"I'll let you know when I decide. God, no wonder you're edgy. Have you told him yet?"

"Last night."

Gwyn tugged Nicholas' pajama top down over his belly, lifted Maggie's, and started on her daughter's spots.

"What did he say?"

"Well..."

"What? What?"

Gwyn pictured her friend almost dancing in anticipation of a response. She sighed again. "He wouldn't agree not to see me again."

Silence met her words. Then, her voice subdued, Sandy said, "Oh. My. God."

Her response couldn't have been more unnerving if she'd tried.

Setting the calamine bottle on the counter, Gwyn took a steadying breath and tried to settle her quivering insides. It didn't work. "Sandy—"

"What are you going to do? I mean, you're going to see him again, right?"

Gwyn's hold on the cotton ball tightened. Pink lotion oozed between her fingers. "Of course not!"

"Are you nuts?"

"Thanks a lot."

"I'm sorry, and I know it's your decision, but—"

"But what?"

"Don't you think you're being a little hasty? Maybe he's a really nice guy."

Blindly, Gwyn slopped more lotion onto the cotton ball she'd wrung dry. She couldn't believe her ears. Sandy was normally such a cynic. The last thing Gwyn had expected was for her to take the side of an impossible fantasy.

And the last thing she *needed* was help second-guessing herself.

"He *is* a really nice guy," she said. "But he's a really nice guy who lives in another country, remember? In a life so far removed from mine that it might as well be in another universe."

"Yes, but—" Sandy broke off and sighed. "Are you sure it wouldn't work? I mean, stranger things have happened, you know. And besides, you can't protect your kids forever, sweetie. People are going to come and go all their lives. It happens."

"Maybe, but I can still protect them now. I'm *supposed* to protect them."

"Fine. Then what if you just see him on the side, away from the kids?"

Fighting her sense of betrayal, Gwyn demanded, "Sandra Masters, since when did you become such a romantic? You're supposed to tell me you can't believe I got involved in the first place, and that I had no business doing so, and that it's a good thing I've come to my senses and made the right decision, and—"

"Gwyn, darling," Sandy drawled.

Gwyn stared at the pale pink splotches decorating the counter and floor from the bottle she'd been waving around, and then at her children's astonished faces. A tear trickled down her cheek. She sniffled. "What?"

"Well, it just seems that if you thought you'd made the right decision, you wouldn't need me to tell you so."

CHAPTER 20

Gareth lifted his hair free and straightened the collar of his shirt.

"You know, there's a really great barber just down the street," Sean's voice drawled.

Giving the collar a final twitch, Gareth met his cousin's gaze in the mirror. With his own head kept close-cropped, Sean had given him a hard time about his hair for as long as he could remember.

"I'll keep that in mind," he replied, "if I ever need one."

Sean shook his head. "You know what cops think when they see guys who look like you?"

"That they'd like to ask for my autograph?"

Rolling his eyes, his cousin leaned a uniformed shoulder against the door frame. "So did you get hold of Catherine yet?"

"Not yet. I think she's having too much fun making me suffer. I left her another message."

"Then I'm guessing that's not who you're going out to meet right now."

Gareth wrapped the cord around his shaver and tucked it inside the black leather bag on the counter. "No."

"Playing nurse again?"

"I'm going over to Gwyn's, if that's what you mean," he said, refusing to rise to the bait.

"The kids must be getting used to having you around." Jaw flexing, Sean crossed his arms. "Maybe they'll let you watch Saturday morning cartoons with them."

Gareth reached for the coat he'd hung on the hook behind the door. He didn't bother responding.

"Did you think about what I said the other night?" Sean prodded.

"No."

"Why not?"

Tipping his head to one side, Gareth pretended to consider the question for a second. "Because I'm a big boy?"

His cousin scowled at him. "Funny."

Shrugging into the coat, Gareth sighed. "Look, Sean, I understand your concern, but have a little faith, will you? I'm not a complete idiot. I know what kind of damage can be done, and you know me better than to think I'd just walk out on anyone's kids. Satisfied?"

"No."

Gareth faced his cousin. "Why not? What more can I do?"

"You can leave them alone, damn it. I have a great deal of respect for you, Gareth, and I'd like to keep it that way. But playing daddy to someone else's kids isn't as easy as you think, and good intentions aren't worth squat if those kids get seriously attached to you and you blow it."

Gareth's jaw tightened. "I'm not playing. I happen to like Gwyn. A lot."

"Bull. This isn't about Gwyn, it's about her kids."

"Excuse me?"

As soon as he spoke the question, Gareth remembered the theory Sean had wanted to share with him Thursday night. He pushed past his cousin and stalked down the hallway, but it was too late.

"Think about it." Sean followed him into the living room. "You're here to meet the daughter whose entire life you've missed out on. You'd have to be made of stone not to feel just a bit nostalgic about the whole situation. Then along comes Gwen—Gwyn—with her kids. She's kinda cute, her kids are kinda nice, and before you know it, you're up to your neck in the one role you've always wanted, but never had."

If Sean had been anyone but his kid-brother-type cousin, Gareth would have decked him on the spot—uniform or no uniform. As it was, he curled his hands into fists and stared at the standard, apartment-issue white front door for a long moment before he trusted himself to turn around. He glared at the other man.

"You have one hell of a nerve, McKittrick."

"Just calling it the way I see it." Sean shrugged, choosing another wall to lean against and shifting his sidearm to a more comfortable position.

"Then get glasses." Gareth felt for the door handle behind him, closed his fingers over the knob, and tugged the door open, signaling an end to the conversation.

Sean ignored the signal.

"You're telling me you don't feel like you've missed out on something?"

"I've known I was missing out on something every single day since I let Amy go," Gareth growled. "I didn't need Gwyn or her kids to point it out."

"So if it's not a misguided desire to play daddy, then you keep seeing this Gwyn person because—?"

Before Gareth could reply—or better yet, tell Sean to simply kiss off—a female voice demanded,

"Who's playing daddy, who is Gwyn, and why haven't you returned my calls?"

Gareth's head snapped around and he stared at the svelte, fiftyish woman in the doorway. "Angela?" he croaked.

Fingers laced behind his head, Gareth stood at the sliding glass doors, staring out at the Ottawa River far below. If he looked to the west, he could just make out a scattering of houses that marked the town on the Quebec side where Gwyn lived.

Would she wondering why he hadn't called yet? Think he'd given up? Be relieved? His mouth twisted.

In view of Sean's theory, maybe she *should* be relieved. Because no matter how much Gareth wanted to deny his cousin's words, he couldn't help but wonder if there might be a grain of truth in them.

Leather squeaked behind him as Angela shifted her weight on the sofa. She cleared her throat.

"Well?"

"Well, what?"

"Well, say something."

He sighed. "What would you like me to say? Of course, Angela, I'm thrilled to give up my holiday with no notice of any kind and fly back to fix Damon's screw-up?"

"If you'd bothered to listen to my messages or call me back, you would have known about this three days ago," his agent pointed out, her voice distinctly testy. "I really do have better things to do with my weekends than chase after you, you know."

Gareth glowered at his faint reflection. As if three days would have made a difference. Swinging around to face the woman on the sofa, he dropped his hands to his hips. "Damn it, Ange, this is a really bad time for me. Can't it wait for a couple of weeks?"

His agent stared at him. "You're visiting your cousin, and we're talking about going back for a week. How bad can that be?"

If she only knew. Bloody hell, he and Catherine were still playing telephone tag, he had no idea when Amy was returning, and he didn't even want to think about the effect leaving would have on his relationship with Gwyn.

If they *had* a relationship.

Or should have one.

"The film is already behind schedule, Gareth," Angela reminded him, "and your contract says—"

"I know what my—" He broke off mid-growl. Inhaled. Exhaled. Tried again. "I know what my contract says."

"Then you'll go."

"Do I have a choice?" What the hell, maybe a little time and distance would give him a fresh perspective.

Standing, Angela smoothed her skirt.

"Good," she said briskly, her tone adding *it's about time.* "You pack what you need and I'll take you out for lunch. It's only noon now, and we're booked on the eight o'clock flight, so we have plenty of time."

"No." He shook his head. "Not today. I have some business here I need to see to first."

Putting time and distance between him and Gwyn was one thing, leaving without saying goodbye was quite another.

"Damon wants you in the studio first thing Monday morning."

"I'll take the red-eye tomorrow night."

"And go to work straight from the airport?" Angela raised a skeptical eyebrow.

"I've done it before."

"When you were twenty, maybe."

"I can handle it, Angela."

She eyed him for a moment, then sighed. "Fine, I'll change your flight. Then *you* can buy *me* lunch to make up for dragging me all this way just because you couldn't return a phone call."

The corner of Gareth's mouth twitched. "Deal. You can call from the kitchen. It's quiet there."

Angela looked around the room, empty but for the two of them. One slender eyebrow rose. "The kitchen," she echoed. She shrugged. "That's where I'll be, then."

But she turned at the doorway, catching him with his cell phone already in his hand, and looked pointedly at the instrument. "Is that the reason this trip is so inconvenient?"

"Maybe."

"Are you going to tell me about her over lunch?"

"No."

Chapter 21

The phone rang, shattering what little concentration Gwyn had managed to scrape together. She reached for the receiver on the fourth ring.

"Hello?"

"You sound tired."

The voice she'd been hoping not to hear, though the leap of her heart would indicate otherwise. She removed her glasses and dropped them onto the desk beside her keyboard. "Gareth. I didn't expect..."

"Gave up on me, did you?"

"Yes—I mean no." Gwyn dropped her forehead into her palm and rested her elbow on her desk. Who was she kidding? She didn't know what she meant anymore. But she could fake it.

"Of course not," she said firmly. "I hadn't really thought about it."

The word *liar* hung so heavily in the air between them, she wouldn't have been surprised to find it had been spoken aloud. Or that she'd done the speaking.

"Did I catch you at a bad time?"

"Not really. I'm trying to get in a bit of work while it's quiet, but it's not going very well." Gwyn pushed away the sketches that had so far refused to translate themselves into anything coherent in her CAD program.

"How did you manage time for work? Did you lock them all in their rooms?"

"Nothing so drastic, although I'll admit the idea has crossed my mind. Kirsten was able to come over for a few hours to keep them occupied for me. They're reading stories."

"And here I was starting to think I was indispensable."

You are.

Gwyn forced a light note into her voice to match his teasing. "'Fraid not'. But you were a great help, if that makes you feel any better."

"Marginally." A pause, then he cleared his throat. "I wanted to see you today."

The shift in topic squeezed the air from her lungs in a little hiss.

Gareth continued as if he hadn't heard the sound. "Unfortunately I have company until later this evening. My agent flew in with a message for me, and her flight doesn't leave again until eight."

Her flight?

Gwyn gave her green-eyed devil a mental whack on the head. "Your agent hand delivers your messages?"

"Only when I don't return her phone calls," he said wryly. "Anyway, the point is that I have to go back to L.A. for a few days. The sound on some of the scenes got fouled up and they need me to do some dubbing for them."

Squeezing her eyes shut, she cast about for a more suitable response than the desperate *please don't go* that hovered on her lips. Nothing. She had nothing. She bit her lip and waited.

"I leave tomorrow night," Gareth said. "I want to see you before I go."

"I—I—"

"I don't know what time I'll get back from taking Angela to the airport, so tomorrow might be better than tonight. May I come for lunch?"

It took forever to work the words past the lump in her throat. "I don't think—"

"Actually, you think too much," he interrupted gruffly. "It's only lunch, Gwyn. You, me, the kids...friends, I promise."

Friends? Was that possible?

"I—" she tried again.

"I know you don't like fast food for the kids, but I can bring something a little healthier. Pizza?"

If you married Gareth, he'd be my daddy...

"No."

Silence met the harsh, strangled word.

"No pizza, or—?"

"I can't, Gareth."

"All right, then. Dinner. Without the kids."

She shook her head for several seconds before she remembered he couldn't see her. "I can't," she whispered again.

Gareth's sigh bespoke his frustration. "You're a stubborn woman, Gwyn Jacobs. Fine. You win for now, but only because I don't have time to argue with you. I'll call you before I leave tomorrow. And, Gwyn?"

"Yes?" She covered her mouth with her free hand. Had she really just squeaked?

"If you don't answer the phone, I'll come and see you in person."

CHAPTER 22

Gareth jolted awake as something thudded onto his torso. "What the—?"

He propped himself up on one elbow and stared at the newspaper sitting on him. The cordless phone joined it. He looked up at Sean, standing bleary-eyed beside the bed.

"Just for the record, you might tell her that it's Sunday, it's six a.m., and it's my bloody day off," his cousin muttered, shuffling back towards the bedroom door.

Gareth rubbed a hand over his eyes, wiping away the remains of sleep. "Tell who?"

"Catherine. She's on the phone. And apparently you're on the front page."

The door slammed behind Sean with a force that made Gareth wince. He dropped his head onto the pillow again, closed his eyes, and drew a long, bolstering breath. His ex-wife at six a.m. on Sunday. Oh, joy.

He fitted the receiver to his ear. "Good morning, Catherine."

"We had a deal." Her voice, unusually husky for a woman, might have been beautiful if it didn't have that constant edge to it.

"Which one?" he asked dryly. To call Catherine demanding was a definite understatement, and at this point she'd extracted so many promises from him—most of which he'd come to regret—that he honestly needed specifics.

She ignored his question. "Have you seen today's paper?"

He peered at the newspaper, still sitting where Sean had dropped it. "I'm looking at it now."

"You weren't supposed to let anyone know you were here."

Gareth levered himself upright and stuffed a second pillow behind his bare shoulders. He held the receiver against his ear with his shoulder, unfolded the paper, and scanned the front page. "I was bound to be seen by someone," he pointed out. "What did you expect me to do, hide in Sean's apartment until you deigned to let me meet Amy? Our deal was for me to keep a low profile, not turn invisible."

There it was. A tiny corner story at the bottom, all of a dozen lines long. He almost choked. "For God's sake, Catherine, if you blinked, you'd miss it."

"It's still there."

"Right. *Rumor has it that actor Gareth Connor is in town,*'" he read aloud. "'*The actor has been spotted in two area restaurants this week, accompanied by an unknown woman*'...give me a bloody break. There's nothing concrete here—they even came right out and said it was a rumor!"

"It will still have the entire city watching for you, and you know it."

"If you think you're going to use this as an excuse—" he growled.

"Given the chance, I certainly would," she snapped back. "Unfortunately, it's not my decision."

"What do you mean?"

"I talked to Amy. She wants to meet you."

Gareth clenched the newspaper in his fist. A dozen emotions swept through him and settled in his gut. He fought past the tangle they formed. "She knows?"

"Of course."

"You told her over the phone?"

"Well, I couldn't very well demand she come home from Europe to meet a strange man without some kind of explanation, could I?" Catherine responded sourly. "She'll be home a week Tuesday."

Still digesting the realization his daughter knew about him, Gareth scowled. He had to wait more than another week? He'd be done by Friday, Angela had told him, which put him back here on Saturday at the latest. He'd have the whole weekend to—

A vision of auburn hair and dancing blue eyes floated to mind and he bit back an oath of surprise. Damn, but thoughts of Gwyn surfaced easily. He forced his attention back to his ex.

"What time does she arrive?"

"She'll let me know when her flight is booked. I'll call you then."

At her own convenience, no doubt.

"Please do. Was there anything else, or can I go back to sleep now?"

"Still a late riser, are you?"

Catherine had always risen at five in the morning. In the course of their short marriage, she'd done her level best to convert him, claiming that sleeping past that hour was akin to sloth. It had been one of the many bones of contention between them.

"As lazy as ever." He didn't bother to stifle a yawn. "It's probably why my career's never amounted to much."

His ex-wife gave a pained sigh. "Very amusing, Gareth. There is one more thing."

"What?"

"She wants to talk to you. Today. She's going to call my cell phone at lunch."

Amy wanted to talk to him?

But he wasn't ready.

Gareth's heart stuttered. Sixteen years he'd been preparing for this moment, and he was nowhere *near* ready.

Catherine cleared her throat.

Keep it together, Connor. You can panic when you're off the phone.

He didn't dare let Catherine see—or hear—the slightest hint of uncertainty. She'd only find some way to use it against him. He frowned.

"Why can't she call me here?"

"Is that how you want to play the game now? You've broken one promise, so you think you can toss all the others aside, too?"

He gritted his teeth. Right. He'd agreed to have Catherine present the first time he talked to Amy. Another promise made, and another regretted. He sighed.

"I'm not playing games, Catherine. If it's that important to you, fine. Where do you want to meet?"

"Well, now that you've made sure everyone knows you're in town, I suppose we'd best meet somewhere out of the way. There's a restaurant in a little town called Chelsea on the Quebec side of the river. It's called L'orée du—"

"Ruisseau," Gareth finished. Of course it was.

"You know it?"

In an instant, he sat across from Gwyn again, hair tumbled about her shoulders in a wild disarray that begged a man to become entangled in it; her red dress, modestly cut but sexier than any strapless number he'd ever laid eyes on...

"I said, do you know it?"

He closed his eyes. "I know it."

"I'll make reservations for noon."

Without saying goodbye, Gareth disconnected. He dropped the receiver onto the floor beside the bed and rolled over. He'd barely closed his eyes again—and hadn't even begun to sort through the hundred million thoughts bouncing about his brain—when a pillow whacked into the back of his head.

"Coffee's on," Sean informed him from the doorway.

"I thought you were going back to sleep."

"After talking to your ex? I'd have nightmares. What did she want?"

"Other than to give me hell about all four square inches of newspaper article? Amy's agreed to meet me."

A long pause ensued. Then, "I'll see you in the kitchen."

CHAPTER 23

Gareth slumped into a kitchen chair as Sean set a mug before him. Taking a swig of the bitter black brew that could only loosely be called coffee, he grimaced. His cousin's innards had to be made of cast iron to tolerate this stuff.

"So she finally caved to temptation, did she?" Sean dropped into a chair opposite him. "Do I get to say I told you so?"

Gareth rubbed both his hands over his face. He'd had what, three hours' sleep over the last two nights combined, and that was supposed to make sense?

"I suppose it depends what you're talking about."

"Your girlfriend going public."

Nope. He still needed more. He raised an eyebrow.

"The newspaper story?" Sean prompted.

Ah. He reached for the sugar bowl. "It wasn't Gwyn."

"Right. And you know that because—?"

"Because she wouldn't."

"Then how did they find out?"

"Gee, I don't know. Between coffee and dinner, there were only about three or four dozen people who saw me," Gareth growled. "I guess I should have asked them all to sign confidentiality agreements."

Sean eyed him, toying with his spoon. He shrugged. "Have it your way," he said. "How ticked is Catherine?"

"Ticked would be a definite understatement."

"Do you think it'll affect how things go with Amy?"

"Amy doesn't know me from a hole in the ground. Catherine, on the other hand, has been the center of her entire life," Gareth said with a sigh. "What do you think?"

"Maybe it won't be that bad."

Gareth snorted his disbelief. "We're talking about Catherine, remember? If anything, it'll be worse."

"Does she really hate you that much?"

"Not me, per se. Just the idea of not being in control. I'm an unknown quantity in Amy's life."

"What's she afraid of? That you'll turn Amy against her?"

"Not that she'll ever admit it, but yes."

"You've spent sixteen years giving in to her way of doing things for Amy's sake—if you'd wanted to stir up that kind of trouble, you'd have done it long before now." Sean picked up the sugar bowl Gareth set aside. "I've always wondered how you put up with that woman's demands."

"It was either that or watch my daughter be dragged through every court in two countries—and across the front page of every tabloid in existence. Amy was the innocent one."

"Beats the heck out of me how you've managed to avoid the tabloids on this in the first place."

Stirring his coffee, Gareth offered his cousin a ghost of a smile. "I wasn't on their radar when all this started, remember? They don't give two hoots about the struggling wannabes. By the time I made a name for myself, Amy was already four and living with Catherine and Lance in Canada."

"True enough." Sean grinned. "And if I remember correctly, you were giving the paparazzi plenty of other things to write about you."

"Don't remind me."

His cousin turned serious again. "You really think she'd have done it? Fought you, I mean?"

Gareth thought of his ex-wife, standing in the doorway of her new home when he'd gone to reason with her all those years ago, to tell her he'd changed his mind about letting go of his daughter. He remembered the tight, bitter line of her mouth and the cold, sea-green eyes. He'd already destroyed her illusion of a perfect life once. She hadn't been about to let him do so again.

He nodded. "Oh, she'd have done it, all right."

"Still, sixteen years of hiring private detectives just to keep track of your own kid?"

Gareth recognized his defensiveness and the guilt that triggered it, but he couldn't help bristling just the same. "You'd have done things differently, I suppose?"

Sean grimaced. "I'd like to say I would've, but with what you had at stake..." He trailed off with a sigh and took a swallow from his cup. "Honestly? I think I would have done everything that you did. But I would have been royally pissed about it."

"Join the club."

"And yet you're still letting her call the shots."

"It's only for a few more days. I don't know what she's told Amy so far, and I don't want to give her any fuel. She could still mess things up for me."

"I take it that means you haven't told Gwyn."

Gwyn. A whole other complication he hadn't decided how to deal with. Gareth turned sideways on the kitchen chair, leaned against the wall, and drew one knee up to support his forearm. He stared at the mug in his grasp.

"No, I haven't told her," he answered Sean.

"But you're going to."

"That depends."

"On?"

"Gwyn."

Perplexity etched itself into the lines between Sean's sandy eyebrows. "May I remind you that it's not just past a.m. on a Sunday morning? In my book, that's a tad early for guessing games. Humor me with a few more details."

"Gwyn suggested it might best if I don't visit any more."

Sean choked on his coffee. "Excuse me?"

"She's afraid the kids are getting too attached to me."

"Well. I'm impressed. I didn't think any woman had it in her to blow off the famous Gareth Connor in favor of family commitments." Sean's gaze narrowed. "You're going to listen to her, right?"

"Up until yesterday, the answer would've been no. Now I'm not sure."

"What changed your mind?"

"A certain theory someone shared with me."

"Ah. You think I'm right."

"Honestly? No. But with all that's going on in my life at the moment, my judgment might not be at its best," Gareth allowed. "And if there's even the slightest chance you're right, I'm not sure I want to risk hurting Gwyn like that. Or her kids."

Another silence. He watched the digital clock on the stove as the green display changed to reflect the passing of another minute.

"So what're you going to do?" Sean asked finally.

"I don't know. Think about it while I'm in L.A., I suppose. Maybe having some time and space—" He raked his hand through his hair. "I don't know."

"You really have a thing for her, don't you?"

Gareth reflected on the permanent knot that had replaced his stomach these days. "Oh, yeah."

"Then tell her."

"Tell her what? That I have a thing for her?"

"About Amy."

"Right." Gareth snorted. "Even if I hadn't promised Catherine I wouldn't tell a soul, can you imagine the conversation? 'Pardon me, Gwyn, I think I'm developing feelings for you, but I have this daughter I haven't seen in sixteen years, and I'm not sure if what I feel is real or part of a huge guilt complex. Do you mind if I stick around while I figure it out?'"

Sean looked him straight in the eye. "'Hey, Gwyn,'" he mimicked, "'now that I've led you and your kids on until you're all crazy about me, did I happen to mention I've been keeping this secret from you? Nothing big, only the fact that I have a daughter I abandoned when she was a baby, kinda like someone else you once knew.'"

Gareth's gut snarled tighter. "Touché." He sighed. "Bloody hell, no matter what I do, she'll get hurt."

"So minimize the damage." Sean stood up and strolled across the kitchen to place his mug in the sink.

"And how would you suggest I do that?"

"Do what she asked. Stay the hell away from her."

CHAPTER 24

Gwyn waded into the argument between her children and scooped up the game they'd been playing on the living room floor. Aptly named *Trouble*, it had been at the center of growing dissent for the last fifteen minutes, and tempers had neared boiling point. Maggie and Nicholas tugged on her blue jeans, tears cascading down their faces, howling for the return of their game. A mutinous Katie scowled up at her from the living room floor, knees tucked under chin and arms wrapped around them.

With grim determination, Gwyn held onto her fraying temper. She was sick to death of the squabbling, sick of trying to work when her creativity seemed to have taken a leave of absence without telling her, sick of sick kids, sick of pretending that Gareth Connor had no effect on her...

She cast about in her mind for an alternative to locking herself in the bathroom. It was like swimming uphill through mud. Ever since Gareth's call last night, she hadn't been able to pull two consecutive thoughts together—probably because she'd been so preoccupied with the unnerving desire to call him back and recant everything she'd said. It had taken every ounce of willpower she possessed not to do just that.

Her nerves weren't going to take much more.

Inspiration finally struck.

"I have an idea," she said, slipping the game board back into its box. "Why don't we get out of the house for a while? It's a beautiful morning. We can go for a drive up to Mackenzie King Estate, maybe take a walk down to the lake..."

Peevish tears turned to excitement. After five days of confinement for Maggie and almost four for Nicholas, the idea of an outing held instant appeal. The twins still looked horrific with their faces scabbed over, but neither had sprouted any new spots overnight, so they were safely out of the contagious period.

As for Katie, well, after being cooped up most of the weekend with sick siblings, she'd be happy just to have a change of scenery.

Half an hour later, Gwyn turned her face to the unseasonably warm sunshine as the kids combed the paths, amassing pine cones, pebbles, and fallen twigs for crafts. The day was perfect for a walk. One of those rare golden afternoons to be treasured this late in the fall. The kind of day that might make it possible, even if only for a little while, to forget the empty ache that had settled in the center of her breast.

Maybe.

Nicholas ran up with a fistful of tiny pinecones. Gwyn dutifully pocketed them and he scampered off again with a whoop. Oh, yes. It was good for all of them to be out of the house.

They walked for well over an hour. First down to the lakeshore, then through the maple forest to the tea house, once the summer home of Canada's tenth prime minister and closed now for the season. They met several other families along the path, most of whom gave them a wide berth because of the twins' still-visible spots. Gwyn was just as glad they did, because seeing women arm-in-arm with their husbands didn't make it any easier to put aside her romantic difficulties.

Sunshine or no sunshine, putting Gareth out of her mind for more than three consecutive seconds at a stretch was proving impossible.

For the first time since Jack's departure, no matter how hard she tried, she just couldn't convince herself she was happier without a man in her life. Neither could she convince herself that it wasn't Gareth she wanted to fill the suddenly yawning hole.

She kicked at a pinecone lying on the path and watched Nicholas dive to recover the abused item from the fallen leaves at the side of the path. Having Sandy's words from Friday come back to haunt her at every turn didn't help.

"Are you sure it wouldn't work?"

Of course she was sure it wouldn't work. She'd never expected it to. Not when the first breathless flutters had stirred in her when he'd invited her for coffee, not when the invitation had expanded to include dinner...

Nicholas galloped up to display his find. Gwyn summoned the expected smile, stored the pinecone for him, and watched him run off again. She sighed.

She didn't know where Sandy's sudden romantic streak sprang from, but she herself knew the difference between fantasy and reality. And as she'd told Gareth, she knew better than to believe in fairy tales.

Which left her scowling over why, then, she kept wanting to let this particular Prince Charming back into her life.

Gareth arrived at the restaurant at twenty minutes past twelve. Catherine was already seated, menu in manicured hands and a barely touched wine spritzer on the table before her. She looked up at his arrival, her sea green eyes regarding him with unveiled hostility.

Gareth braced himself.

"You're late."

"I got lost." He pulled out his chair, signaled a waiter, and sat down across from his ex-wife.

"I thought you said you knew where it was."

"I did." Gareth tightened his jaw. "It was dark when I drove out the last time."

And he may have had to overcome a small psychological barrier to being here again without Gwyn.

"Hm. Well, you're here now, I suppose." Catherine set aside her menu and raised an arched eyebrow. "Are you planning to order lunch?"

He shook his head. He doubted his stomach could tolerate food just now. "I'm not hungry."

The waiter arrived at their table side. Catherine ordered a small garden salad with a plain, broiled chicken breast and no dressing, testament to the somewhat gaunt look she'd always favored and still maintained.

Gareth ordered coffee.

"When is she calling?" he asked, the moment the waiter took the menus and moved beyond hearing.

Catherine swept back a long strand of ash blond hair and plucked at a bit of fluff on her dark green suit jacket. "Sometime after one. I thought we should talk first."

No, she thought she should read him the riot act first. He took a swallow of ice water and waited, damned if he'd make it easy for her.

After a moment, she cleared her throat. "I'd like to know what you plan to tell my daughter."

"*Our* daughter."

Her eyes sparked. "Our daughter."

"That depends on what she asks."

"Lance and Amy and I are a family, Gareth," Catherine said, her voice hard. "We've been a family for as long as she can remember. She loves him."

"I'm sure she does."

"As a father."

Funny how painful breathing could be.

"I won't let anything destroy what they have," his ex added tightly.

Gareth sighed. If she wasn't so damned annoying, he might actually feel sorry for her. Clinging to this image of perfection had to be difficult.

"I've waited sixteen years, Catherine," he pointed out. "If I'd wanted to hurt Lance—or your precious family—I could have done so a long time ago."

"So you won't tell her, then?"

"Tell her what?"

Catherine looked away. For the first time in Gareth's memory, an air of vulnerability surrounded her.

"That I prevented you from being part of her life."

Gareth leaned back in his chair, toying with the knife beside his water glass. He considered his response.

"I'm not a vindictive person," he said at last. "I would never volunteer that kind of information." He heard a tiny explosion of air from the other side of the table and lifted his gaze to Catherine's. "But if she asks, I won't lie to her."

"What kind of answer is that?"

"An honest one. I have enough to answer for when I explain why I agreed to let her go in the first place. I'm damned if I'll take responsibility for your mistakes too."

His ex-wife's chin lifted. "I never considered it a mistake to keep you away. She barely knew you. When Lance came into my life, it seemed only natural that he should take over being her father. Her *real* father."

"And I'm sure he was wonderful to her." The words weren't as difficult to say as they might have been. He'd met Catherine's husband twice before they had moved back to Canada. Both times he'd been struck by the man's quiet self-assurance and genuine warmth. He'd never doubted that Lance Carlson would be anything but wonderful to Amy.

But he still wouldn't lie to his daughter.

"You agreed with me at the time," Catherine reminded him, warming to her argument. "You agreed Lance would provide stability in her life; that it was the most important thing. My God, Gareth, you'd only seen her a dozen times since she was born."

"That was your choice," he grated, "not mine. You're the one who ran back to mummy and daddy, taking Amy to the other side of the country with you."

"And you could have followed. My father offered you a job."

"I had a job."

"You were playing in some second-class production in a seedy theater. What kind of job was that when we had a new baby?"

"One that led to where I am today," he snapped. "Like it or not, Catherine, I'm not the loser you keep trying to make me out to be."

"I wasn't cut out to be an actor's wife, Gareth."

"And I wasn't cut out to work for your father."

Catherine huffed. "Fine. We both know we weren't suited. That's not the point."

"Then what is the point?"

"You signed the adoption papers. You agreed to give up your claim to Amy."

"I also changed my mind less than a week after I signed those bloody papers, which is when you threatened to drag me—and our daughter—through every court in the land," he snarled in response. "Every photo I've ever had of her has been taken by a damned stranger—a private investigator I had to hire so I'd know what she looked like. You returned every birthday gift I ever sent her, every Christmas card—and now you're asking me to make *your* life easier?"

"I'm asking you to make your daughter's life easier."

"That's what I thought I'd been doing for the last sixteen years," he said. Before he'd met Gwyn and her kids. Before he'd seen his lack of participation in his own daughter's life in an entirely different light. "It turns out I may have been wrong."

The cell phone at Catherine's elbow rang. She made no move to answer it. On its third trill, he looked at it pointedly. "Like it or not, I'm talking to her today."

Without a word, she handed the phone across to him. He thumbed the answer icon, put the phone to his ear, and closed his eyes. No stage fright, not even in his earliest career, had ever tied his gut in knots quite like this.

"Hello?" he said gruffly.

"Is she driving you nuts yet?" a cheerful female voice asked, with a trace of huskiness reminiscent of her mother.

He smiled. "You must be Amy."

"And you would be my long-lost father."

He had to clear his throat to get the word out. "Yes."

"I'm glad to finally meet you, figuratively speaking. Are you enjoying your lunch with Mom?"

Gareth swallowed a snort. "Of course."

"Liar." Laughter tinkled at the other end of the line, reaching out to warm him from—

He frowned. He didn't even know where Amy was. He said so.

"Didn't Mom tell you?"

He refrained from saying that 'Mom' hadn't told him much of anything. "No, we hadn't talked about it."

"I'm in Wales."

"Wales?" he echoed.

"Mmhm. But Mom doesn't know why. Would you like to know?" A mischievous delight threaded through Amy's voice.

Gareth found himself grinning in response. And he found himself liking this daughter he had yet to meet.

"All right."

"Can you keep a straight face?" she asked, and then answered her own question, "Of course you can. You're an actor. Brace yourself, then—I came here to meet you."

Gareth's gaze flew to meet Catherine's as he fought to hang on to the most difficult straight face he'd ever been asked to maintain. "I see," he said.

CHAPTER 25

At one-thirty, Gwyn packed three happily exhausted kids back into the car for the ride home. With a raucous round of *There's a Hole in the Bottom of the Sea* taking place in the back seat, she drove the winding back road through the Gatineau Hills towards Chelsea and the promised hot-chocolate stop. Sunshine or no, the November air still had enough nip in it to chill fingers and toes.

Not until she drove down the last hill into the little Outaouais town did she realize their route took them past L'orée du Ruisseau, where she and Gareth had dined. Her foot lifted from the gas pedal, slowing the car. Masochistic it might be, but a part of her needed to see again the restaurant where the line between fantasy and reality had blurred for the first time. To relive those magical—

"Look, Mommy!" Katie exclaimed, her voice high-pitched with excitement. "It's Gareth!"

Gwyn's heart leapt into her throat even as her stomach lurched to her toes. Dear God, Katie was right. It was Gareth. Standing in the restaurant parking lot, the breeze lifting his thick, dark hair off his collar...

And his hands resting on the shoulders of a woman whose face was turned up to his.

Magic vanished into thin air, bringing reality sharply back into focus.

Before she could draw enough air to voice an objection, Katie had rolled down her window and all three kids were yelling at the top of their lungs, "Gareth! Gareth! Over here, Gareth!"

Gwyn's swift prayer that he wouldn't hear them went unanswered.

He looked toward the road, his dark brows meeting over his nose, and for a split second—one that felt just as she imagined eternity must—their gazes locked. Then, her face hot and her children still yelling out from the back seat, Gwyn turned her attention back to the road and pushed down on the accelerator, leaving him behind.

Along with a shattered part of herself.

Gareth stared after Gwyn's disappearing car, shock sitting cold and hollow in his gut. *Damnation.*

"Someone you know?" Catherine enquired, stepping back from the brief, polite kiss she'd bestowed on his cheek and straightening the line of buttons on her coat.

"What?" Gareth frowned at Catherine, still reeling from the impossible odds that Gwyn would drive by just now—and from the almost physical impact of her stunned gaze. Just when he'd thought life couldn't possibly get any more complicated.

"I said, someone you know?"

"Yes. A friend."

Friend. What an inadequate word. Shaking off its shock, his mind began functioning again. He had to get to Gwyn's—had to explain...what? Bloody hell, what a mess.

"I have to go," he muttered in Catherine's direction. He had no idea what he'd tell Gwyn, but trusted he'd come up with something on the way. Anything to take away the bottomless hurt he'd glimpsed in her eyes.

"You're joking."

Catherine's drawl stopped him in his tracks. Keys in hand, he looked over his shoulder.

"About what?"

"You've come all this way to meet your daughter, and now you're going to chase off after a skirt? She must really be something if you're willing to put her ahead of Amy."

"What she is," he growled, "is none of your business. And you know bloody well I'm not putting anyone before Amy. How could I? You've managed to make sure that there *is* no Amy for another week, remember?"

Catherine lifted her chin, her already cold eyes becoming frosty. "And I'm not above making that absence as permanent as possible if you're having difficulty keeping your priorities—and your promises—straight."

But Catherine's words were hollower than she could ever know.

"I know more than Mom thinks," his daughter had said across the thousands of miles, *"and I have questions I want you to answer, not her."*

With one hand on the open car door and the other resting on the roof, Gareth shook his head at his ex-wife. "Give it up, Catherine. We both know you can't stop this from happening anymore. Amy is eighteen now, old enough to make her own decisions. Like it or not, one of those decisions is to meet me."

Bitter fear twisted deep in Catherine's eyes. Her mouth tightened. "You're enjoying this, aren't you?"

"Hardly."

"You won't win, you know. No matter how hard you try, you'll never win." She lifted her chin, her voice fierce. "You may have fathered her, but she's *my* daughter, Gareth. Mine. And I won't let you take her away from me."

Without responding—how the hell *did* one respond to an accusation like that?—Gareth slid behind the steering wheel and started the engine. So. She'd finally admitted her darkest fear. He grimaced and shifted into gear, then pulled past his ex-wife's rigid form. Poor Catherine. She had no idea what was in store.

"I'm arriving on Monday, not Tuesday," Amy had told him. *"I'd like you to meet me at the airport if you can. But please don't say anything to anyone. Especially not Mom. I love her, and I know she means well, but—well, we can't really talk if she's there."*

A week from tomorrow. Gareth checked for oncoming traffic, then pulled out onto the road. Seven days to think about what he would say to his daughter, and wonder what she would say to him...

And to figure out what the hell to do about Gwyn, because given his reaction to her just now, it seemed Sean's theory might be flawed after all. What he felt for Gwyn had nothing to do with her children, or nostalgia, or anything other than—

Well. He had a week to figure that out, too.

CHAPTER 26

Gwyn saw Gareth the instant she pulled onto her street.

He sat on the top step of her porch, elbows balanced on knees and sunglasses shielding his eyes from her. Briefly, she toyed with the idea of driving past, but the kids were tired and hungry—and besides, judging by the grim set of Gareth's jaw, there would be little point to the maneuver. Whether she returned an hour or a day from now, instinct told her he'd still be waiting.

She turned the car into the driveway and slipped the gear shift into park, then twisted in her seat to unbuckle Maggie and Nicholas with unsteady fingers. The kids flew ahead of her, across the lawn and up the stairs, clamoring for Gareth's attention, showing him the treasures from their walk. Gwyn followed at a pace made slower by dragging feet—and by a serious lack of oxygen.

She climbed the stairs to the porch. Gareth stood by her front door, Maggie in one arm and Nicholas swinging from the other while Katie chattered non-stop at his side about their adventure. His sunglasses remained in place.

She sorted through her cluster of keys, searching for the one for the house. The entire bunch thudded to the porch floor.

Katie swooped down, snatched up the keys, and handed them back to her without missing a beat in her tale about the red squirrel that had climbed her leg to get a peanut. Gwyn clutched, missed, and closed her eyes as the keys dropped a second time.

"Mommy!" Katie's voice was exasperated.

"Here, Katie," Gareth's deep tones said, "I'll open the door for your mum."

Gwyn him turn the key, push the door inward, and herd her children inside. He turned to her.

"Are you coming?" he asked, with that familiar, faint trace of humor.

I haven't decided yet. She moistened parched lips with the tip of her tongue—and immediately regretted the action when a muscle in Gareth's jaw tightened and flickered.

"Gareth, come see my pinecone!" Nicholas demanded, reappearing in the doorway and tugging at Gareth's arm. "I found the biggest one!"

"Did not!" Maggie's muffled voice denied from inside the house.

"Did too! Gareth, are you having supper with us? Mommy's making Goldfish soup."

A dark eyebrow rose above sunglasses. "Goldfish soup?"

With a mighty effort, Gwyn regained her voice. "Tomato soup with cheese crackers shaped like fish."

"Ah." He squatted down in front of the little boy, removing his sunglasses—finally—and tucking them into his inside jacket pocket. "Tell you what," he said, "I need to talk to your mum for a bit, and then I'll come see your pinecone, all right?"

"And mine?" Maggie's hopeful face appeared in the open doorway over his shoulder.

Gareth reached around and poked at her belly with his finger. "And yours," he promised. "But you have to let me and your mum talk first."

They both nodded and disappeared back into the house. Katie arrived next in the doorway.

"Can I have—"

"May I have," Gwyn corrected automatically.

Katie heaved a pained sigh. "May I have a glass of milk? Please," she added quickly.

Gwyn nodded. "Pour some for your brother and sister, too, please."

Three sets of feet thundered toward the kitchen at the back of the house, leaving the two of them alone. His eyes no more readable now than they'd been behind his sunglasses, Gareth stepped back in a silent invitation for her to precede him inside. As he followed her and closed the door, she removed her coat and hung it in the closet, then began picking up the items strewn about the hall floor by her children.

Any other day she would have called them back to do the work themselves, but for now, with the tension building in the front entry the way it was, the task kept her hands busy. Unfortunately, it did nothing to keep her mind off the image of Gareth standing next to another woman, her face turned up to his...

Gareth cleared his throat.

Maggie's hat fluttered to the floor.

"Gwyn—"

Panic prodded her to speech. She whirled to face him.

"I'm sorry, I'm being rude," she said. "Would you like a cup of tea or coffee or something? You must be frozen after sitting on that porch."

A faint smile curved his lips. He leaned back against the door, his fingertips tucked into the front pockets of his jeans; his leather jacket opened to reveal the same snowy fisherman's knit sweater he'd worn when they first met; his hair loose, the way it had been the last time they'd stood in this hallway together...

Gwyn gulped. If the tension didn't do her in, the memories very well could.

"I'm fine, thanks," he said.

Gwyn picked up Maggie's hat a second time. "Are you sure? It's no trouble, because I was going to make myself something anyway."

"Gwyn, we need to talk."

She tucked the hat into Maggie's wicker basket on the closet shelf. She tried to take a deep breath, but it lodged in her chest, forming a painful lump that pressed against her breastbone. She stooped to collect Nicholas' mittens.

Gareth shifted his weight against the door. Her heart hammered against her ribcage.

"Did you hear me?" he asked quietly.

Her children's voices floated down the hallway to her. She hesitated, tuning in to the sound. Absorbing it. Letting it fill her, ground her. Then she steeled herself and turned to face Gareth, lifting her chin.

"We've already said everything that matters." Fierce pride stabbed through her at the firmness she heard in her own voice.

Gareth straightened from his post, shaking his head. "I don't think we have," he said, "because it matters that you saw me with Catherine today, and we haven't talked about that yet."

Catherine...knowing the woman's name didn't make the hurt any less. Nor did it change what Gwyn needed to do. Had to do, not just for the kids, but for her own sake. She bolstered her resolve and lifted her chin.

"Who you take to a restaurant is your own business."

"I didn't *take* anyone to L'orée du Ruisseau except you. Catherine is my ex-wife. We had some...business to discuss, and she suggested the place because it's out of the way. The local paper has caught wind that I'm in town, and Catherine isn't fond of the media."

Gwyn forced herself through the flood of relief brought on by the words *ex-wife*. The woman's identity was none of her concern. And neither was that oblique reference to *business*. "You don't have to tell me this."

"I wanted to explain."

She turned to the closet and stuffed Nicholas' mittens into the nearest basket, her labeling system forgotten. "Friends don't need explanations."

Silence followed her words.

"Friends," Gareth repeated, his voice low. Gruff. "Is that what you want us to be?"

Gwyn couldn't have forced a reply through her constricted throat if she'd tried, and so she contented herself with a nod—an affirmation of a lie. Her back still to Gareth, she closed her eyes and concentrated on not diving headlong into the closet in a desperate attempt to escape.

His voice dropped an impossible octave lower. "And what if I don't want to be just friends, Gwynneth with two n's? What if I want more?"

Her eyes shot open. She heard him move, felt the heat of his body behind her, the warmth of his breath stirring her hair. Oh, dear God.

"Are you finished talking yet?" Nicholas demanded.

Gwyn sensed Gareth's sudden, coiled tautness, heard his sharp inhale. For the life of her, she couldn't turn around.

"Not yet, buddy," he said.

"Then can we watch a movie?"

"Gwyn?"

The word caressed the nape of her neck. She jerked her head up and down, hoping he would interpret the movement as the agreement for which it was intended.

"Your mum says yes," he informed her son.

"Mommy says we can watch a movie!" Nicholas bellowed, thudding into the living room behind them.

Katie and Maggie's footsteps sounded in the hallway, headed toward them from the kitchen. Gareth muttered a curse behind her and she smothered a giggle—Lord, hysteria was the last thing she needed right now. The kids' footsteps moved into the adjacent living room. She took a deep, steadying breath and sidled sideways, edging out of the closet and away from Gareth's overwhelming nearness.

"That won't work, you know," Gareth's voice rumbled.

She shot him a quick look over her shoulder.

"Running away," he elaborated.

She stopped sidling and turned to face him, wiping her sweaty palms against her jeans. The closet door frame nudged between her shoulder blades. "I'm not running away."

But she'd like to.

"Good." His hands still in his pockets, Gareth studied the tile floor. "I didn't come just to explain about Catherine, Gwyn."

Gwyn's heart thudded against its confines.

"I meant what I said on the phone. I really do want to see you again. And not just today."

"B-but you're leaving—"

He smiled. "And coming back. Friday, I hope."

That hadn't been the leaving to which she referred, but try as she might, she could put together neither protest nor explanation. She stared at him, seeing the tension in his shoulders, the muscle flickering in his jaw, the outline of hands curled into fists in his pockets. Her belly quivered.

You're a consenting adult, Gwyn Jacobs. A grown woman. If your very own private fantasy is this insistent...

Gareth raised his gaze to hers, eyes dark with intensity, determination, desire. Memories of motherhood scattered to the four winds. The hollowness beneath her ribcage settled lower in her belly, becoming an ache. A hunger.

A woman's need.

"Gwyn?" The rough sound of her name carried a multitude of questions.

She closed her eyes. Enough. She was a mother, yes, but she was also human. She could take no more...could deny no more. As long as she kept Katie and Maggie and Nicholas out of it—

"All right," she whispered.

"I know you're concerned about your kids, and I respect that, but—" Gareth's voice broke off. "What did you say?"

Her voice still husky, but louder this time, she repeated, "I said all right."

"You'll see me again?"

"Yes."

"I'm not talking about being friends."

She opened her eyes. Lifted her chin. Met his gaze with a steady one of her own. There would be consequences, she knew, but heaven help her, she just couldn't care anymore. "I know."

He took a single step towards her. Locking her knees into place to keep herself upright, she wrapped her fingers around the door frame at her back for extra support.

"As much as I like your kids," Gareth continued softly, "this has nothing to do with them."

She nodded. Her fingertips lost all feeling.

He took another step. "This is just you and me."

Gwyn inhaled his warmth. It mingled with the clean, sharp scent of his aftershave. Intoxicating. Devastating. His breath fanned her cheek. Her own strangled in her throat. She lifted her chin, closed her eyes...

"Are you guys kissing?"

Gareth's jaw clenched. Gwyn released the air from her lungs in a tortured rush. She opened her eyes again. *Lord, Nicholas...*

Gareth dropped his chin onto his chest, sighed, and looked sideways and down at her son. "Not yet," he told Nicholas, "but that was the general idea."

"Gross."

Gareth smothered a surprised laugh with a cough. "You wanted something?" he reminded Nicholas.

"Katie can't get the movie to work."

"Would you like to handle this, or shall I?" Gareth asked Gwyn. Despite the wry amusement dancing in his eyes, heat still glowed in the dark depths.

She tightened her numb fingers around their anchor. "Be my guest," she said, not bothering to mention that she didn't dare move from her post for fear of falling flat on her face.

Gareth moved off to help her children, and Gwyn sagged against the door frame. A hot wave of shame swept over her. He would have kissed her if Nicholas hadn't interrupted just now, she thought. Kissed her the way he had the other night and she wouldn't have done anything to stop him. Stop him? Dear Lord, she would have encouraged him...

With her children here. She bit back a groan. So much for keeping them out of it. What kind of mother was she?

Gareth strolled into the front hall, his eyes dancing. He held up a DVD case.

"They wanted to see this," he said, "but I made a judgment call and vetoed the idea. I hope you don't mind."

She blushed. It was one that Sandy had brought over the week before. One of his. And definitely unsuitable for the kids.

"You never told me you were a fan," he teased, tossing the case onto the hall bench.

"I'm not—I mean, I am, but I—"

"Mommy watches all your movies," Katie called from the living room.

The heat in Gwyn's cheeks intensified—and began to spread.

"Does she, now?"

"Her and Auntie Sandy," Nicholas added. "But they won't let us."

Not to be outdone, Maggie piped up, "Auntie Sandy says you're a hunk. What's a hunk?"

Gwyn found a semblance of a voice. "Never mind. Watch your movie."

Crossing his arms, Gareth leaned against the living room doorway, near enough that she had no trouble seeing the wicked glint in his eyes.

"And what does your mum say about me?" he asked the three traitors in front of the television set.

She closed her eyes, certain even her toes were blushing now, and wished fervently to be transported far away...

"She says you're a god," Katie replied. "And she growls."

...*very* far away...

Peeking through her lashes, Gwyn found Gareth doubled over in silent, helpless laughter. She opened her eyes and scowled at him. "Are you having fun?" she asked crossly.

"Oh, Gwynneth," he gasped, hands resting on knees, "you have no idea!"

In spite of her mortification, the corners of her mouth twitched in response. She clamped her lips together, refusing to give in to the impulse to laugh. "That was dirty pool."

"I know. And I'm sorry. Really."

The apology lost something in the shaking of his shoulders.

She waited for Gareth to pull himself together. Nicholas padded out to join them again.

"Did I miss it?" he asked.

"Miss what, sweetie?" Gwyn asked. She rolled her eyes at Gareth's exaggerated attempt at being serious, and then gave in to her reluctant grin. Well, at least as a tension breaker, Katie's words had certainly been effective.

"The kiss."

Her smile dropped into oblivion.

Gareth stepped into her stunned silence. "I thought you said kissing was gross."

"That's what Katie says," Nicholas informed him. "I wanted to see for myself."

"I see." Gareth quirked an amused eyebrow at Gwyn, waiting for her response.

"I don't think you need to see anything except your movie right now, Nicholas," Gwyn managed in spite of the strangulation going on in her throat. "Off you go."

Nicholas' feet dragged with reluctance, but he did as instructed. In the silence of the little boy's departure, Gareth cleared his throat.

"So," he said. "You growl, do you?"

Gwyn's toes blushed again.

CHAPTER 27

Gwyn dropped a kiss on top of Katie's head, tucked the covers around her, and tiptoed from the room. She paused to listen at Maggie and Nicholas' door for a moment, satisfying herself that the breathing within was deep and even, and then sat down on the top stair to debate her next move.

Next move? Who was she trying to kid? She hadn't recovered from her last one. Gareth's blunt announcement that he wanted more than friendship, while not completely unexpected, had been shocking enough, but her agreement—her instant, unguarded, unequivocal agreement...

She dropped her face into her hands and stifled a moan. Damn Sandy and her romantic ideas. What had she been thinking? Nothing had changed since Thursday night. If anything, the way her kids had matter-of-factly absorbed him into the family dynamics this evening had underscored, a hundred times over, the danger posed to their hearts if this continued. They were already head-over-heels about the man she'd allowed into their lives, and who could blame them? He was so good with them. Patient, fun. He was a natural.

She had to face it: even if she could carry off a casual affair with Gareth, the kids wouldn't escape entirely unscathed. Not anymore. Which meant she needed to shift into damage control mode and try to keep things from getting any—

"Are you planning to sit there all night?"

At Gareth's gentle, amused tone, Gwyn's heart missed several beats, completed a series of impossible acrobatic flips, and then began hammering so loudly that he was sure to hear.

Lord, she wouldn't have been surprised if the neighbors heard.

She left her face in her hands. "Maybe," she mumbled.

He chuckled, and the warm sound tingled through her. She peered between her fingers. He stood at the bottom of the stairs, watching her in amusement, sweater and well-worn jeans molding to contours that tugged her imagination in tantalizing directions...

And jacket in hand.

Surprise made her hands drop to her lap. "You're leaving?"

Gareth laid the jacket across the rail beside him and leaned against the wall. "I have a plane to catch," he reminded her.

Of course. She grappled with a tiny wash of relief—and a tidal wave of disappointment.

"But that's not the only reason."

It wasn't?

His lips quirked. "Well?"

"What?"

"Don't you want to know what the other reason is?"

She shook her head. He chuckled.

"Will you at least come and say goodnight?"

Not at all sure whether the note underlying the invitation was one of threat or promise, Gwyn grasped the banister and pulled herself to her feet. She descended toward him and, when he didn't move to let her pass, paused one stair up, eye-level with dark, smoldering fire and inches from a potent male aura. Her world tipped sideways.

"I think you should," he said.

She gripped the handrail until the ache in her knuckles remained her only link to reality. She thought she should, too, but it might be prudent to ensure they were talking about the same thing.

"Should what?"

"Ask why else I'm leaving."

She gulped for air. She absolutely didn't want to know, because it was enough that it was for the best. Reasons didn't matter. They couldn't matter. But when she tried to deny him, she managed only a thread of a whisper, a single word. "Why?"

Strong, heated fingers closed over hers, slid against them, twined with them.

"Because if I don't leave now, I won't leave at all." His thumb stroked her wrist, playing havoc with her pulse. "Because, besides missing my plane and breaking my contract, I'd still be here in the morning when your kids woke up, and you'd hate both of us if that happened. I respect you—and them—too much to do that to you."

Gwyn squeezed her eyes shut and tried to focus on his words rather than his touch. *Respect. Kids.* She felt certain the words held importance, but she couldn't seem to get past the warm, pulsing ache spreading through her body.

"Damn it, Gwynn," Gareth swore in her ear.

He'd moved closer. Close enough that his scent filled her senses to overflowing, and his hair brushed her cheek when she moved her head, and...

"You're not helping," he muttered.

Her eyes fluttered open. "Wh-what?"

"I said, *you're not helping*," he grated.

With a shock, Gwyn realized he hadn't been the one to move after all. Somehow her own feet had shuffled forward, and now she teetered on the edge of the step, her free hand resting against his shoulder for balance. Her face flamed. She dropped her hand and stepped back.

"I'm sorry—"

He shook his head, his smile made tight by the tension in his jaw. "Don't be. I'm just a bit rusty at this honorable thing. Which brings us to the next discussion."

Gwyn would have liked to retreat a few more steps before she tried to discuss anything with him, but he still held her hand captive. With his thumb continuing to travel its hypnotic path over her wrist, she couldn't muster the will to pull away. She cleared her throat. "What discussion would that be?"

"The one where we decide what we do now. You see, much as I'm enjoying Goldfish soup and doing chicken pox dot-to-dots, I'm afraid those pursuits still fall under the heading of friendship." He lifted her hand in his, turned it over in his grasp, and traced a finger across her palm. "I meant what I said about wanting more than that from you, Gwyn, and I don't know how long honor will hold out."

Nothing on earth could have persuaded her to meet his gaze at that moment.

Gareth lifted his other hand to push a strand of hair away from her face. "Come away with me."

Except maybe that.

Her startled gaze flew to his. *Yes*, she wanted to say. *Oh, yes.*

"Away?" she actually managed.

"Just for the weekend. We'll go somewhere quiet, just the two of us. Somewhere we won't be inter—"

"*Now* are you going to kiss?" Nicholas asked from above them, his voice a study in exaggerated patience.

Gareth's fingers tangled in her hair. Leaning his forehead against hers, he heaved a pained sigh.

"I rest my case," he said.

Then, before she could do more than brace herself to move away and confront her son about being out of bed, he raised his head again. Mischief danced in his eyes.

"Do you suppose if we give him what he wants, he'll be satisfied?"

The suggestion startled her. "I—I—"

"I thought so, too." His gaze holding hers, he raised his voice. "Yes, Nicholas," he said, "now we're going to kiss."

Gwyn tried her demurral again. "I—I don't think..."

Gareth ignored her. His hand slipped beneath her hair to cup her neck. She sucked in a quick breath. His thumb followed the curve of her jaw, and his focus shifted to her mouth. Protest died on her lips.

And then he kissed her. A gentle, unhurried kiss. A kiss that reached inside to touch her in astonishing ways. A kiss that deepened, hungered, and warmed every corner of her—

"It's not *that* gross!" Nicholas yelled, presumably at his sister in her bedroom. Then, in a cheerful, only somewhat quieter voice, he called over the upstairs railing, "Thanks, Gareth. You can stop now."

Bare feet slapped against the wood floor as he headed back to bed.

Gareth's mouth went still against Gwyn's. It compressed. His shoulders began to shake under her hands, and she choked back a slightly hysterical, answering giggle. Pulling back, he rested his forehead against hers once more.

"And on that note," he said, his voice vibrating with laughter, "I think I'd better leave."

It took a concentrated effort to release her grip on the thick knit of his sweater, but Gwyn nodded, stepping away and folding her arms across herself. Gareth caught her hands and drew her down from her step to stand in front of him on the landing.

"Will you think about it?" he asked, his voice gruff.

Gwyn didn't need to ask him what he meant. And she figured it was a pretty safe bet that she would think of little else. She nodded again.

A tiny smile tugged at the corner of Gareth's mouth. "Lost your voice, have you?"

And her sanity, too, apparently.

A chuckle rumbled through him. "I'll take that as a yes—and as a compliment." He released her hands and picked up his coat from the rail. "I'll call you from L.A."

CHAPTER 28

He called on Wednesday.

It was two-thirty in the morning, and Gwyn had been tossing and turning for the last three hours without achieving anything that neared a sleep-like state. Not that she really expected to, given her recent track record. She scowled at the clock beside her bed, flounced onto her back, and debated the idea of doing the laundry—or maybe scrubbing the kitchen floor. Either activity would be infinitely more productive than continuing to pretend she might rest.

The phone's sudden shrill nearly had her clinging to the ceiling. She rolled over and grabbed for the instrument.

"Hello?"

"It's me. Did I wake you?" Rich, dark tones washed over her, velvet-smooth.

Gwyn clutched at the duvet and dragged it up to her chin. Her heart thudded against its confines. She swallowed. Cleared her throat. Managed a barely coherent, "No. I was awake."

"Me too."

Silence.

She wiped sweaty palms against the duvet, one at a time.

"I miss you," he said.

She squeezed her eyes shut and coached herself through the forgotten art of breathing. *Inhale...exhale...*

Gareth's voice deepened, roughened. "Tell me you're suffering as much as I am."

"I—uh—"

"The truth."

The ache that had started in her belly spread relentlessly outward. He wanted the truth. But how could she tell him something she still hadn't come to terms with?

"Gwyn?" the deep voice prompted. The edge to it startled her, its rawness echoing her own state.

"I'm here."

"And?"

She exhaled shakily and tightened her fingers around the receiver. "And I'm suffering, too," she whispered.

He muttered something she didn't catch.

"Pardon?"

"I said *good*. No one should have to go through this kind of misery alone."

She heard him take a deep breath, and imagined him running an impatient hand through his dark hair. The ache inside her softened and warmed. Lord, she'd never get to sleep now.

"I've wanted to call you both nights I've been here," Gareth said, "but I've been getting back to the hotel after midnight, and I didn't want to wake you by calling so late."

"And tonight?"

"I couldn't wait anymore. Should I apologize?"

"No."

"Good. I'm pushing Damon to finish things up as fast as possible so I can catch the red eye on Thursday night." He paused. "Have you thought about the weekend?"

Every waking minute.

"Yes."

"Yes, you've thought about it, or—?"

She twisted a fistful of duvet in her free hand. "Sandy's coming over after work on Friday. I told her I'd be back Sunday afternoon."

Silence met her words, lasting so long she began to wonder if their connection had failed. Then Gareth cleared his throat.

"It's probably a good thing we have thousands of miles between us right now, you know."

She smothered her nervous giggle with a fistful of duvet. "Probably," she mumbled.

"But I wish we didn't."

Gwyn's entire body flushed hot. Dear God, did the man have any idea how potent he could be—even long distance? Even if she'd been able to think of a reply, she couldn't have uttered it.

Thankfully, Gareth didn't wait for one. "Until Friday, then," he said. "Sleep well."

As if.

Gareth linked his fingers beneath his head and stared up at the ceiling. She'd said yes. Yes to an entire weekend with him. Just the two of them, unhurried, uninterrupted...

He sucked in a ragged breath, his body catching fire at the very thought of what lay ahead. Bloody hell, forty-two years old and he felt like a kid facing his first date—right down to the nerves and the conviction that the next two days were an absolute eternity stretched before him.

He rubbed his hands over his face and scowled. The shortest eternity ever, maybe. He not only had to finish dubbing the film in those two days—after convincing the director that a week's worth of work could be done in less than forty-eight hours—he also had to find somewhere he could take Gwyn. Somewhere private, where they wouldn't be seen, and he wouldn't be recognized.

He'd have to wait until morning for Damon, but the location…

He reached for the phone again.

Seconds later, his cousin's groggy voice responded, "Yeah."

"It's Gareth."

Silence. Then, "Are you dying?"

"I hope not."

"Is anyone we know dying?"

"No."

"Then call back in the morning."

"I'll make it quick, I promise."

Sean sighed heavily. "What?"

"Do we still own that cabin you talked me into buying with you a few years ago? Out near someplace that starts with a *p*?"

"Perth. And it's a cottage, not a cabin," Sean corrected. "And why the hell do you want to know about it at—" He paused. "It's almost three a.m. here, for chrissake."

"Just answer the question and you can go back to sleep."

"Yes, we still own it."

"Can it be used at this time of year?"

"The water's turned off for the season, and it gets damned cold if the wood stove goes out, but there's still electricity and yeah, I've used it during the winter."

"What does it look like?"

"*Excuse me*? You want me to describe a building to you at three in the—" Sean muttered something violent under his breath. "What the hell is this about, Gareth? And what time is it there anyway? Shouldn't you be sleeping?"

"It's late here too. Look, just humor me, will you? Is the place a dump or what?"

"*No,* it's not a dump. It's—I don't know—casual, I guess you'd call it."

"But nice?"

"Yes, it's nice."

"Guy nice or girl nice?"

"Have you been drinking?" Sean asked suspiciously.

"No."

"Then what—" Sean broke off. "This wouldn't have anything to do with Gwyn, would it?"

"It would."

"She'll love it, you can blame me if she doesn't, I still think you're an idiot, and now you can kiss off and let me go back to sleep."

With his ear ringing from Sean's none-too-gentle hanging up, Gareth grinned with satisfaction and returned the receiver to its cradle. Location solved, dubbing to go.

And only two days until Gwyn.

CHAPTER 29

Gwyn swung her duffle bag onto the passenger seat and slammed the door shut. She turned to her friend. "Well, I guess that's it. Any questions?"

"Yes. Are you sure you want to do this?"

"I meant about the kids."

"You didn't specify."

"I'm specifying now."

"The kids will be fine," Sandy said. "Rob will be fine. I'll be fine. It's you I'm worried about. Couldn't you have done this with a normal guy instead of a Hollywood superstar?"

Gwyn huddled into the thick warmth of her oversized cotton pullover. She scowled at the redhead. "Would you kindly make up your mind? A few days ago you were the one telling me I should give this a chance."

Sandy pounced on her words. "Then you think it does have a chance?"

"That's not what I meant." Gwyn sighed. "Your romantic streak is all very nice, Sand, but I'm too much of a realist to see this as anything more than it is."

"A two-night fling?"

"Something like that."

"And am I the only one who sees something wrong with this picture? Jack left four years ago, sweetheart. Maybe if you'd done this once or twice since then, it wouldn't seem so serious."

"It isn't serious. It's a weekend away and I'm a big enough girl to handle it."

"So when Sunday rolls around, you'll just come home to your kids and pick up where you left off, is that it?" Sandy crossed her arms and returned her scowl. "Damn it, Gwyn, if you insist on going through with this, at least be honest with yourself."

Gwyn stared at her friend in silence for a long moment, and then she walked around the car and opened the driver's door.

"The kids' health cards are on my desk," she said. She slid behind the steering wheel, closed the door, and rolled down the window. "I'll have my cell phone with me, but if something comes up and you can't reach me, call Gareth's cousin. His name is Sean and his number is on the fridge. Any questions?"

Sandy shook her head, and Gwyn reached for the ignition.

Her friend's soft voice stopped her. "Hey."

Gwyn braced herself, not sure she could take another lecture.

"I'm wrong, aren't I?" Sandy asked. She tilted her head to one side. A half-smile curved her lips, but it didn't ease the concern in her eyes. "You've already been honest with yourself."

Gwyn thought of the hours she'd engaged in an internal debate over the wisdom—or idiocy—of meeting Gareth like this. She thought of the ache she'd lived with for days now, and of how the very sound of his voice across thousands of miles could erase all the stresses of a day as if they'd never happened.

She no longer doubted that she was in over her head. When—not if, but when—she and Gareth went their separate ways at the end of the weekend, she would suffer greatly. Her mind flinched from the pain contained in that thought. In the end, her final decision about the weekend had been simply based: if she had to suffer anyway, at least she'd have this one time.

So had she been honest with herself?

She gave Sandy a little smile. "Brutally," she said. "See you Sunday."

Gareth moved the vase of flowers from the coffee table to the kitchen table, glowered at it, then picked it up and carried it to the bureau facing the cottage's front door. Would she like the mixed bouquet? Maybe he should have gone with roses instead. Every woman he'd ever met liked roses.

But Gwyn wasn't every woman.

Maybe he should have skipped the flowers altogether.

"I mean really, Connor, how lame can you get?" he muttered aloud.

He grabbed the vase and marched it back into the living area, setting it with a thump beside the wine glasses he'd already laid out. Sighing, he rubbed a palm over his freshly shaven jaw line. Flowers, wine, music. All the makings of a first-class seduction, which was not what he wanted the weekend to be.

Well, not entirely, anyway.

He had no doubt both he and Gwyn had certain expectations of their time together. Hell, he'd barely been able to contain the fire roaming his body ever since she'd agreed to the weekend, but he didn't want her laboring any longer under the mistaken impression he wanted only the physical from her. Not now that he'd decided Sean and his theory were both as far out in left field as they could get.

Two days away from Gwyn—away from the lightness her smile brought and the ease of just being with her—had convinced him he had finally, after forty-two years, stumbled onto the real thing. The head-over-heels, without-a-doubt, once-in-a-lifetime kind of love that had nothing to do with his guilt-ridden past, and nothing at all to do with fulfilling some kind of fantasy role.

His lips quirked at the absurdity of the last thought. If he *had* been looking to play out a father-fantasy, he doubted it would have included spotted kids, overflowing bathtubs, or Goldfish soup.

No, despite what Sean thought, this was no fantasy. It was real, almost unbearably precious, and...

His amusement faded.

And as Sean had pointed out a few days ago, unspeakably fragile because of his continued deception.

He scowled at the flowers. He loved her, but how the hell did he tell her. More precisely, when? If he told her before she found out about Amy, her hurt and betrayal could go so deep that they would outweigh everything else. But if he confessed his secret first, he risked the chance she wouldn't listen to his declaration of love at all.

Talk about damned if he did, damned if he didn't.

Bloody hell.

About to seize the flowers yet again, if only to give himself something to do besides brood, he paused at the sound of tires crunching over gravel. An engine purred into the driveway and fell silent. A car door slammed.

Gwyn had arrived.

He'd have to wing this as best he could.

CHAPTER 30

She'd arrived.

Somehow Gwyn managed to park her own car beside Gareth's, remove her keys from her ignition, and climb from the vehicle—all, she was certain, without conscious participation. But not even auto-pilot could move her feet away from the car and toward the cottage.

Her fingernails bit into her palms.

Now what?

She watched a lazy wisp of smoke drift from the chimney and across the paling blue of the late afternoon sky. The distinct chatter of an irate red squirrel sounded somewhere in the distance, the only sound other than the thud of her own heart in her ears. She drew a shaky breath. Her gaze roved over the cottage, a small, cedar-sided box tucked in beneath soaring pines and naked maples. A lake shimmered behind it. An immense stack of firewood sat on the deck against the building, running most of the length and height of the wall, stopping short of the single window and screen door.

Cozy and rustic, it was the perfect place for a weekend away. A weekend with—

The screen door squeaked open. Gareth stood in the doorway, wearing faded jeans and a thick, black turtleneck that deepened his eyes to unreadable shadows. Propping the door open with his foot, he folded his arms across his chest and rested his shoulder against the frame, waiting.

For her.

Gwyn tucked her trembling hands behind her. She leaned against the sun-warmed fender.

"So." Gareth's mouth quirked into a wry smile. "Are you planning to stand there all day?"

His words summoned a flash of *déjà-vu*. She remembered their last parting, when she'd sat on the stairs, too tangled up inside to face him. Just as she'd done then, she replied, "Maybe."

The shadows in his eyes softened. Warmed. His voice took on a husky resonance. "Will you at least come and say hello?"

She stuffed her hands inside her pockets to hide their shaking and forced herself upright from the vehicle. But when she began walking around her car to retrieve her bag, Gareth's gruff command stopped her.

"Leave it," he said. "I'll get it for you later."

Gwyn turned. Her nerve faltered once again. Gareth held the door wide for her in invitation. She stared at him. She'd told Sandy she could handle this, but what if she was wrong? If she left this man now, before anything had really happened between them, she would already face an unfillable hole in her life. But after a weekend in his arms? She drew a jagged breath as anticipated anguish flooded her soul.

How would she survive?

Gareth held out his hand to her in silence. In the same silence, she walked toward him, no more able to deny him than a river could turn away from the ocean that would swallow it.

He took her hand when she reached him, and his fingers threaded with hers, strong and warm.

"I wasn't sure you'd come," he said.

"Neither was I," she admitted.

"I'm glad you did." He lifted her hand to his mouth and brushed his lips across her knuckles, then turned her hand over and pressed another kiss to her palm.

Gwyn's insides began a slow, sinuous melt.

Gareth lips grazed the inside of her wrist. A tiny gasp escaped her. His grasp tightened. He untangled his fingers from hers and slid his hand up her arm...over her shoulder... around the nape of her neck. His thumb traced the curve of her ear.

She tried to pull back, just enough to recapture the sanity she felt slipping away from her, but Gareth held her fast, his gaze traveling over her face with a nearly physical touch. Slow heat trailed in its wake.

"Do you have any idea how much I've wanted to do this?" he muttered. "How many nights I've lain awake imagining..."

His lips brushed her forehead. "Wanting..."

He feathered kisses along her jaw line. "Aching..."

She thought she might go mad with the tension building inside her. "Gareth."

"Ssh." The sound whispered against her hair as he tugged her inexorably closer. Panic fluttered in her breast.

Too fast, she thought. *Too soon.* But the hands she put up to brace against him betrayed her, clinging to his thick, soft sweater instead of pushing away. Then his mouth covered hers, and his need exploded into her own. Caution vanished like shadows before sudden bright light.

Abandoning her grip, she slid her fingers up to tangle in his glorious hair—and to pull him recklessly, desperately closer. She barely registered the slam of the screen door behind them when he stepped back, tugging her with him.

As long as his mouth didn't leave hers, as long as his hands continued their exploration of her neck, her shoulders, her spine...

His fingers splayed across her hips and tugged her closer yet. Hardness met her belly. Gwyn gasped, her mouth breaking free of his, and then bit back a groan when his lips targeted the hollow of her collar bone. His hands slipped beneath her sweater and curved over her bare ribcage, thumbs teasing the undersides of her breasts. With a sudden surge of courage—and a lack of inhibition she vaguely supposed should shock her—she let her own hands glide over his chest and down to his stomach, glorying in the sharp contraction of muscles beneath her touch. Gareth went rigid, his groan muffled in her hair.

"God, Gwyn, this isn't what I intended," he muttered, his breathing harsh. "I wanted to kiss you, yes—and hold you—but not attack you the second you walked in the door."

Gwyn squeezed her eyes shut and rested her forehead against him. Her fingers dug into the cable knit of his sweater. She struggled, through a haze of want, to make sense of his words.

Kiss her? Hold her? She might have expected that to begin with, but now that a thousand fevered sensations coursed through her body? Dear Lord, the man couldn't be serious.

Not when it took every atom of willpower she possessed just to remain upright instead of sinking to the floor, taking him with her.

But Gareth's hands had closed on her shoulders, and he'd actually taken a step back. A step away from her. Gwyn bit back a protest and then, ashamed of her need but shameless in her desperation, skimmed her hands under his turtleneck and across his chest. His nipples pebbled under her palms.

Swearing softly, he held her away.

"Behave," he said hoarsely. "I'm trying to apologize."

From arms' length, Gwyn pushed the bottom of his turtleneck out of her way and drew her fingernail down the vertical line of hair bisecting his muscled diaphragm.

"I didn't ask for an apology."

Determined hands grasped hers and held them wide, away from their path.

"Fine," he growled. "Then I'm trying to convince at least one of us I'm not some kind of Neanderthal."

"I don't think you're a Neanderthal."

"No?"

"No." Giving up her fight against his hold, she twined her fingers with his. Strong, lean hands closed over hers with a gentleness that belied the almost palpable hunger between them. She imagined their bodies tangling together the way their hands did. Heat flared deep in her belly. She drew an uneven breath, the tang of wood smoke tickling her nose, mingling with the musky scent of Gareth.

"No," she said again, "but I do think that if you leave me like this, I might come apart at the seams."

Gareth swallowed audibly. His hands tightened on hers. "You're not playing fair. We're supposed to have candles, and music, and wine. I want to do this right, damn it—"

"But this is right." Her gaze left their linked hands and traveled slowly up his length. It slid along his tense, muscled thighs, so powerfully defined by soft, faded denim; touched oh-so-briefly on the hardness that, for a fleeting instant, had held unparalleled promise; rested in unashamed admiration on the sculpted abdomen that she herself had uncovered...

The fire in her belly became molten.

Gareth's grip on her hands tightened.

She lifted her eyes to meet his, struck by the simple truth of her own words. She whispered them again. "This is right."

His iron hold on her hands loosened.

"I suppose we could have candles later," he said unevenly.

Her heart leapt.

"And music," she agreed, pulling her fingers free.

"And wine."

His knuckles grazed her jaw, then his hand traveled lower... lower...she tilted her head back and felt her breath catch in her throat.

"And then we could do it right," she whispered.

"Twice," he promised.

He took possession of her lips with a hunger that sent reality spinning into oblivion. She met him kiss for kiss, touch for touch. His fingers encountered the bottom edge of her sweater, fumbled with it, thrust it out of his way. Hers slid beneath his turtleneck and dug into the coiled tension of his shoulders.

He tugged her sweater over her head, and it whispered past her back as it slid from his hands. The feel of a carpet beneath her feet told her that they'd moved further into the cottage, but the realization was fleeting, and when the cool air grazed her belly, unimportant. From a long way off, she marveled at her own boldness when she pulled impatiently at his turtleneck, and then, when he paused to strip it off, at the way her hands strayed to the waistband of his jeans.

A fraction of a second later, his hands spanned her waist, followed by the warmth of his mouth.

Need became her world, defined only by Gareth's lips, his hands, his body. She ached for him in ways she was sure she'd never known; hungered for him in places that were dark, and moist, and secret. Her touch became frenetic. She wanted, needed, to discover him—all of him—before the last shreds of coherence vanished.

Her bra gave way, spilling her breasts, unconfined, into his welcoming hold. Crisp, curling hairs scraped against her skin, taking sensitivity to a new level.

She kicked aside her shoes, and thought she might die of sheer, exquisite torment when Gareth slowly—dear Lord, so slowly—slid her jeans down, over her hips and legs, until she could step out of them. Her panties followed. Torment stepped up to torture when he pinned her hands in one of his and followed the garment's route with tiny, barely-there kisses.

She crumpled to the floor beside him. She tried to say his name—to beg him to do something, anything, to ease her distress—but he folded her into his arms and buried his face in her neck, and her throat closed on her words.

Gareth lowered her to the carpet, its fibers rough—but not unpleasantly so—beneath her bared skin. He rested himself on one elbow and pushed back her hair.

"You are so beautiful, Gwynneth with two n's," he whispered. "So very, very beautiful."

Gwyn couldn't have responded if she'd tried, for his fingers had left her face and began a slow, insistent exploration, trailing here, darting there, pausing to incite, tease, inspire. Existence blurred into sensation and sound and insatiable, unquenchable thirst. Thirst for his hot mouth, for the taste of his skin, for what she could no longer stop—or deny.

Reality threatened to intrude once, when his warmth left her, but he stilled her protests with a murmur and a promising touch. She did little more than register the sound of something tearing open before he returned, lowering his length along hers once more. She wriggled to meet his touch.

"Open your eyes."

The sheer unexpectedness of the command made her obey. "What?"

"Open your eyes," he repeated, nuzzling her ear. "I want to see you."

The request took her breath away. "S-see me?"

"When I do this," he said, his voice low. Rough.

His hand slid over her belly and down her thighs, then trailed upward again. Gwyn parted beneath his touch, her breathing harsh and uneven in her own ears. The dark intensity of his eyes held her captive.

"And when I do this."

His fingertip grazed her. Electricity jolted through her belly, wringing a startled moan from her.

"And this," he growled, shifting his weight to cover her, nudging against her.

Arching beneath him, she squeezed her eyes closed against the myriad of sensations threatening to overwhelm her. Her lips parted in a soft, almost silent inhalation.

"Open your eyes, Gwyn," Gareth ordered again.

She bit back a moan. She couldn't...

He moved against her, teasing, tormenting. Something wondrous stirred inside her. Her eyes shot open.

"Yes," Gareth murmured. "Like that."

Balancing himself on his elbows, he cupped her face in his hands—and then slid into her. Once, twice, again.

Her eyes widened. "G-Gareth—?"

"Go with it, love," he urged. He moved again, faster now. "I'm right here."

Her fingers raked his shoulders, seeking an anchor as her world rocked beneath her. Her breath quickened. Her lashes drifted down...

"Look at me, sweetheart." His voice, thick and ragged, held a note of urgency she couldn't deny.

She spiraled upward in ever-faster circles, her gaze fastened desperately to his, sensation washing over her in vast, incessant waves. Sheer, mindless need lifted her hips from the floor to meet his every thrust, and his eyes darkened an impossible shade more.

"God, Gwyn—" he rasped.

She shattered then, her cry mingling with his, into a thousand splinters of color and heat and light—and an ecstasy so exquisite that she knew, in a moment of pure and absolute clarity, that she would never be the same again.

Not ever.

CHAPTER 31

Gwyn woke on Saturday morning to bright sunshine, the smell of freshly brewed coffee, and a man whistling a lively tune. None of which held any familiarity for her. She blinked at the unpainted, wood-planked ceiling above her.

In her world, she rose before the sun, didn't smell coffee unless she made it herself, and was the only one in the house who knew how to whistle.

She stretched her arms over her head, basking in the sheer pleasure of sleeping in and being waited upon, then winced at another unfamiliarity: the kind of intimate tenderness she hadn't experienced in a long time. With a rueful grimace, she eased herself into a more comfortable position.

Her movements stirred the bed linens, releasing Gareth's clean, male scent and letting it mingle with her own. Vivid memories stirred of how the tenderness had come about.

An involuntary, muffled gasp escaped her.

The whistling stopped.

Gareth's dark head appeared in the bedroom doorway.

Okay, so maybe not such a muffled gasp.

"Good morning." Gareth looked rested, relaxed, and satisfied enough to cause her face to heat. "I thought you might sleep away the entire morning."

"What time is it, or don't I want to know?"

"It's not that bad. Only nine-thirty."

"Not bad? That's awful. You should have woken me."

"I tried. Twice. You're very unfriendly when you're tired."

"Really?"

"Something about how I should go away and get my own cereal."

She would have apologized, but Gareth chose that moment to lean against the door frame and cross his arms. Her gaze reflexively followed the movement, settling on the torso she had—

She gulped.

Gareth regarded her with a lazy, knowing grin that turned her internal thermostat up several more degrees. "Sleep well?" he asked.

She nodded, trying discretely to ensure that the covers hid as many inches of her as possible. "You?"

His grin widened. "Very."

Gwyn bit her lip and looked away, searching for something to say and coming up frustratingly short.

"Well?" he asked. "Are you getting up or not?"

She clutched the down duvet a little tighter, supremely conscious of her nakedness beneath it. Mischief sparked in Gareth's eyes, assuring her he was aware of her predicament—and that he derived a great deal of enjoyment from it.

She screwed up some of the directness he claimed to like about her. "Of course," she said. "But not with you in the room."

He chuckled. "Fair enough. I'll pour coffee."

She waited until she heard the clink of cups being taken from a cupboard, then she pushed aside the duvet and swung her legs over the edge of the bed. A new dilemma presented itself. With her clothes from yesterday presumably still decorating the living room floor and her overnight bag in the car, she hadn't a stitch to wear.

She weighed her options. Asking Gareth was the most obvious solution, but that mischievous amusement in his eyes pretty much guaranteed at least some kind of comment to add to her discomfort. And parading out into the living room clad in the duvet would almost certainly engender a similar reaction.

Her gaze fell on Gareth's open suitcase atop the wooden bench at the foot of the bed. She dismissed the notion out of hand. It was way too forward.

Or maybe it's just the sort of thing a confident, worldly woman would do in the same situation, her inner voice countered. A woman self-assured enough to drive two hours out into the country to spend a casual weekend with a man. One who was capable of that kind of fling, and who knew how to behave on a morning after.

She drew up her knees and dropped her forehead onto them. Therein lay the real trouble. Clothes—or the lack thereof—weren't the problem at all, nor were they likely to make much difference to the real issue.

The issue of exactly how one should behave on the morning after, when the very concept of a fling was foreign...

"I didn't think to bring cream," Gareth called out to her. "Will milk do?"

Gwyn lifted her head. Much as she wished otherwise, she couldn't hide under the covers all day.

"Milk is fine," she called back, forcing a lightness into her voice that, combined with a tension she couldn't quite disguise, made her sound a little like Tweety Bird.

Rousing herself to actual motion, she picked up the thick, cable-knit turtleneck Gareth had worn the day they met. Not because of any sentimental reasons, but because it seemed to offer the most coverage. Then, semi-clad, she strolled out to the kitchen with a hard-won casualness she hoped would hide her mass of seething nerves. A casualness that fled the instant Gareth's eyes raked over her and settled, glowing, on the sweater's edge a scant few inches down her thighs, putting to rest any illusion of coverage.

She tugged, with a complete ineffectiveness, at the bottom of the turtleneck. "I couldn't find—I didn't have—" she stumbled. Fiery heat flamed over her cheeks.

Way to keep your cool, Gwyn.

"I don't mind," he assured her. "I was just thinking it looks considerably better on you than it ever did on me."

She recalled how the sweater's snowy whiteness had emphasized his dark good looks and magnetism in the shadowed theater. Remembered her initial reaction to that magnetism. And seriously doubted his observation.

She kept her thoughts, however, to herself.

Gareth held out a cup of coffee to her. She made herself step forward as if she drank coffee half-naked every morning and weekend affairs were a regular occurrence in her life.

When she reached to take the mug, however, he held it fast and imprisoned her free hand in his. Her heart stopped mid-beat, shuddered, then resumed its life-giving force with adrenaline-powered beats.

Gareth lowered his lips to the curve of her neck. "Now I can say a proper good morning," he murmured against her skin.

Her coffee-cup hand jerked. Scalding heat barely registered before Gareth muttered a curse and leapt away. He took the mug from her hand, caught up a dish cloth from the counter, and mopped the dripping fluid from her fingers.

"Are you all right?"

She nodded, biting down hard on her lip. How unbelievably stupid...

She snatched the cloth from him and rubbed her hand vigorously.

"I'm fine," she said. "I'm so sorry. Did I burn you?"

She turned her attention to mopping up the puddle on the floor, all the while excruciatingly aware of Gareth's nearness as he leaned against the counter and watched her. Aware, too, of his silence in the face of her non-stop verbosity.

"I can't believe I was so clumsy. Do you need a first-aid kit? I didn't think to bring one, but maybe your cousin—"

"Gwyn."

She finished her mop-up in silence. She stood and dropped the soiled cloth into the sink. Then she faced Gareth, her fingers clutching the turtleneck's hem.

Dark eyes studied her. "What's going on?"

"I don't know what you mean."

"I mean, you're behaving like a scared rabbit. What's going on?"

"Nothing." She forced a bright smile but couldn't meet his gaze. "Nothing."

"Regrets?" he asked quietly.

"No!" Startled out of her discomfort, she raised her eyes to the shadowed, almost pained reserve in his. "No, it's not that, honest."

"Then what?"

"I don't know..." She sighed. "Yes, I do. It's this." She glanced around herself. "All of this."

Gareth followed her gaze but didn't appear enlightened. "All of what?"

"This. Being here. You. Everything."

"Gwyn—"

"It's the whole morning-after thing," she muttered, feeling renewed heat creep into her cheeks. "I haven't done a morning-after thing for fifteen years, Gareth." She looked away, gnawing on her lip again. "I'm not very—I don't usually—I've never—" She stopped and heaved a sigh. "Oh, hell," she muttered. "I'm sorry."

"For what, being honest?"

"For being so—so—" She hugged her arms to herself and sought a word that would describe her emotional quagmire—and allow her to complete a sentence. Inexperienced? Unworldly? Gauche? All of the above?

"Gwyn."

She started, realizing that Gareth had moved to join her. His wide shoulders filled her field of vision, and his hand lifted to smooth back a strand of hair from her face.

"Will you please stop tying yourself in unnecessary knots?"

She blinked. "I don't know what you mean."

"Do you really think this is just a weekend fling?" he asked, tracing her jaw line with the back of one finger, infinitely gentle.

She tried to untangle her tongue to tell him she'd never wanted more, but the lie refused to be spoken.

"That's all I expected," she finally managed, her voice husky. *All that I let myself expect.*

Gareth tipped her chin up. "It's not all I expected."

She stiffened. "Gareth, I don't—"

He put a single finger against her lips. "We can't keep pretending—*you* can't keep pretending—that what's happening between us can be resolved with a one- or two-night stand."

She took his hand from her mouth. "We talked about thi—"

"Not all men are like Jack." His voice was quiet. Flat.

"No," she agreed, knowing—and not liking—where the conversation was headed. "But some are a higher risk than others."

She referred to his high-profile, unconventional lifestyle, but as she watched his jaw clench she felt on some deep, instinctive level that she'd once again unwittingly touched a nerve of some kind. She refused to probe, however, because it didn't matter. Couldn't matter.

Frustration played across brooding features. "Damn it, Gwyn, it's been four years," he said, his voice rough. "I'm the first man you've let close in all that time. Doesn't that count for anything?"

"I told you before, I don't believe in fairy tales."

"Good," he retorted, "because believe me, I'm no Prince Charming and I've never once thought of you as a damsel in distress."

She couldn't help but think of spilled pencils, dead car batteries, and sludge-filled bathtubs. As if he'd read her mind, Gareth's mouth curved wryly.

"Well, maybe once or twice," he conceded, "but never for very long." He took her face in his hands, his thumbs caressing her cheekbones, tracing her jaw line. His gaze was penetrating, serious...loving?

"I know you're scared," Gareth continued, "and I know you're worried about your kids. But I also know that what we have between us is too big to walk away from. I'm forty-two years old, Gwyn, and I have never felt about anyone the way I feel about you."

His hands were so warm, so strong, so gentle. Gwyn's breath strangled deep in her throat. It took every ounce of her resolve not to close her eyes and melt into his touch.

"Don't," she croaked. "Please don't."

Catching the arms she tried to cross over herself, he held them at her sides. "Why not? You can't tell me you don't feel anything."

"I'm not. I mean, I do, but I can't." She gestured impatiently, her movements hampered by his grip. She stilled herself, then inhaled deeply. She could do this. She had to do this, because she couldn't survive another Jack. None of them could.

"I'm not saying I don't feel anything," she said, her voice quiet and measured. "I'm saying I don't want it to go any further. If two ordinary people like Jack and me couldn't make it work, then—"

"Then what, Gwyn? Then no one else deserves a chance? Or just I don't?"

She blinked in surprise at the bitterness underlying the question. She hadn't meant it that way at all. "Lord, Gareth, it's not about you—" she began.

"Actually, it's more about me than you know," he muttered.

CHAPTER 32

Releasing his grasp on her, Gareth turned away to pace the small kitchen. His secret loomed huge in his mind, and he wondered yet again how he had managed to make his life so very complicated. How he would ever redeem himself while keeping Gwyn's heart—and his own—intact. He turned to face her.

I love you, he wanted to say. *I love you more than I thought I was capable of loving a woman. More than I ever dreamed any man* could *love a woman.* But the words jammed in his throat, tangling with all the other things that his conscience told him should be said first.

"God, Gwyn, there's so much I want to tell you," he growled. "I owe you so many explanations."

On the other side of the room, Gwyn retreated behind the table, avoiding his eyes. "I told you before, friends don't need explanations."

Frustration surged in him, edging his voice. "Are we back to that again? Friends?"

She lifted her chin a defiant inch. "We never passed it," she said. "Not really."

"Bull."

"I won't deny that there's a potential for something more," she continued as if he hadn't spoken, "but I meant what I said about needing to protect my kids."

She hesitated. He waited, sensing more to come. She sighed.

"Gareth, we have a weekend together...a wonderful, uninterrupted weekend. Can't we please just leave it at that?"

"No."

Her startled gaze flicked back to him. "What?"

"I said no. I won't settle for being friends when we both know we have a chance at so much more."

She went still. He wrestled with his conscience one final time, then made his decision. While he couldn't break his word to his daughter, at least Gwyn would know how he felt when she learned his secret. He'd just have to trust her to be strong enough to handle it.

"I love you," he said softly. "I think I fell in love with you the first time I saw you in that theater, and again over coffee in that little café, and over building blocks on your living room floor, and over dinner and tuna casserole and spotted kids and late-night phone calls. I fall in love with you each and every time I see you, or speak to you, or think of you, and an entire lifetime will never be enough to show you how much. And unless I'm very much mistaken, you feel the same."

Across the room, entirely too far away, Gwyn blinked away a shine of tears. She shook her head. "We're too different. Our lives—"

"Do you love me?"

"That's not the point."

"It's exactly the point."

"You live on the other side of the world, and—"

"Do you love me?"

"And you're famous, and I'm just an ordinary person, and—"

Gareth could think of a thousand ways to rebut that statement, but he made himself stick to the issue.

"Do you love me?" he repeated yet again.

He watched the woman he loved steel herself, then whisper her denial.

"No."

He smiled. "Liar."

Her tears spilled over at last, making her blue eyes shimmer, her lashes go spiky. "Damn it, Gareth—aren't you listening to anything I say?" she demanded.

"No," he said simply. "Because none of it matters. Distance, jobs, lifestyle—those are just details. We're both old enough, experienced enough, to work those things out."

"And what if we can't?" she asked, dashing away her tears with the sleeve of his sweater. "What then? You walk out on my kids the way their father did? Leave me to pick up the pieces of their lives a second time?"

He gritted his teeth and battled the guilt over a promise that wouldn't let him give her a direct answer; wouldn't let him assure her that he had learned that particular lesson the hard way and had no intention of repeating his mistake. Until Gwyn knew about Amy, simple reassurance would, at least to him, feel all too hollow.

Best to deal instead with all the other issues. He crossed his arms and leaned back against the counter.

"Fine, let's sort it out now."

"Wh-what?"

"Let's sort it out now. What's your first concern?"

"It's not that simple."

"Humor me."

She stared at him for a moment, then said quietly, "All right. We live thousands of miles apart, and the kids' lives are here."

That was easy.

"I'll move."

"Here? But your job—"

"My job takes me all over the world as it is. It doesn't matter where my base is, it matters where you and the kids are."

"You'd move in with us? Into our house?"

"Yes."

"But you're used to something so much bigger. Fancier."

"I love your home, and I'll only love it more if you allow me to share it with you. Next problem."

"You do so much traveling."

Easier still.

"Yes, and planes travel both ways. I can afford to cut back and be more selective about the roles I take. I'll come home every chance I have, and you and the kids can visit the sets whenever possible. And when I do have to be away, I'll call you every day—at least once a day. Other families make it work, and we can, too. Next?"

"My kids..."

Easiest of all.

"I fell in love with them over the blocks, too," he said.

He watched her slender throat convulse. Balling his hands into fists in his pockets, he made himself remain where he was, knowing she needed her space right now, needed to wrestle her demons by herself.

"You're so often in the spotlight," she offered now. "And I live so privately. The thought of having to be in the public eye—or my kids being there—"

He'd have to partially concede that point.

"I can't promise you the same level of anonymity you have now," he said, "but I can promise I'll do my level best to keep my private life private. There will be some interest at first, of course, but the media has a short attention span. As soon as something more interesting comes along, we'll be forgotten."

"And the parties and premieres and publicity events?"

"Only if you want to."

"And your friends—"

"Will love you."

"You don't know that."

"Yes," he said. "I do."

Gwyn chewed her lip so fiercely that he feared for its survival. Fresh tears threatened.

"What if you get bored with us?" she whispered.

He very nearly laughed aloud. "With your three? I have trouble imagining that."

"You know what I mean."

"Sweetheart, all I know is that boredom is the very last thing you should worry about. From the moment I walked into your home, I felt as though I was meant to be there. As if I'd been waiting for you and your kids my whole life. I belong with you, Gwyn. I belong with them. I *fit*."

Her internal war raged on, conflict clearly written across her features in the disbelief, hope, apprehension, and other emotions that passed too swiftly for him to even identify. Gareth allowed himself to straighten away from the counter and stroll toward her.

She watched him through tear-bright eyes.

He stopped in front of her.

"I love you," he whispered.

She closed her eyes and drew a breath that shuddered through her entire frame.

"A weekend would be so much easier," she said.

"Probably," Gareth agreed.

"I always tell the kids that not everything in life is easy."

"Very wise."

She stayed silent for a moment. Then she opened her eyes. Her level, steady gaze locked with his, a tremulous hope forming in their depths as he watched.

"Those must be quite the building blocks."

"Oh?" Gareth suddenly found breathing difficult.

"I think they did it for me, too."

CHAPTER 33

"You're worrying again," Gareth's resigned voice broke into Gwyn's reverie.

She turned from the patio window where she'd been pretending to watch the few, drifting, late-afternoon snowflakes, while in reality doing just what Gareth accused her of. Worrying. Again.

She accepted the cup of tea that he offered and smiled an apology. "Sorry, I can't help thinking."

Gareth shook his head at her. "Haven't you run out of problems yet?" he asked, but amusement tinged the exasperation in his voice, and Gwyn knew that he wasn't really annoyed.

Not yet, anyway.

After having been down this particular road several times over the course of the day, however, she wouldn't blame him a bit for beginning to lose patience. And they still had all of tomorrow ahead of them.

Gareth parked himself beside her. He leaned a shoulder against the door frame, lifting his cup to sip his tea.

"Out with it," he said.

"It's nothing, really."

"If it's bothering you, it's something. Out with it."

"It's a little thing, I know, but do you like camping?" she asked. "I take the kids every summer, but if you don't want to—"

"I love camping," he assured her, then went on to list some of the many other objections she'd managed to raise so far. "I love biking, I love swimming, and I love hockey. I haven't played baseball since Sean and I were kids, but I'm sure I can remember how, and what is this really about, Gwyn?"

She opened her mouth to deny an ulterior motive to her concerns, then snapped it shut again. There did seem to be an underlying theme, didn't there? Camping, sports...all the kinds of things that—what?

That a father would do.

Oh.

"Gwyn?" Gareth prompted. "What is it, love?"

A little thrill ran through her at the sound of the endearment, threatening to sidetrack her—not unwillingly—into a whole other contemplation of the weekend's unexpected turn of events. *Gareth loves me. He's not leaving. He's staying and—*

She pulled herself firmly to heel. And what?

"Are you sure you've thought this through?" she asked him now. "I mean, really through. All the way through."

The corner of his mouth twitched, deepening the laugh lines there. "I'll bite," he said. "How through is through?"

"My kids are still young. They've never really had a man in their lives—especially Nicholas and Maggie. They're going to want—they're going to think—are you sure you want to be—" She broke off, unable to put her children's needs, her own deepest desire, into actual words.

She didn't need to.

"A father?" Gareth asked softly. He reached out and tipped up her chin until their eyes met. Warm understanding and absolute certainty gazed back at her. "You have no idea how sure I am, darling Gwyn, or how much I've thought it through, over and over again." Almost as an aside, he added in a mutter, "Believe me, I've been ready to take on this role for sixteen very long years."

Relief swelled in her and she turned her face into his hand, pressing her lips to his palm. "It just seems like such a lot to ask."

He chuckled and, not for the first time in their acquaintance, replied, "You didn't ask, remember? I offered."

She smiled back at him and, with a new-found confidence and comfortable daring, moved in to nestle against him. "You'll have to watch those offers," she teased. "You may have noticed I'm accepting them more often. If you're not careful, you'll be in over your head."

"Sweetheart, I was in over my head the moment you sat down beside me in that theater," he said dryly. He took the cup from her and set it with his on the nearby fireplace mantel. "But if you're in the mood to accept offers..."

He fitted his lean length against her, his hands possessive, his intent unmistakable. Gwyn's body cooperatively turned to molten lava.

Part of her, however, held back. Something niggled at the edges of her consciousness.

"Why sixteen years?" she asked.

Gareth pushed aside her hair and pursued a trail with his lips along her shoulder, up her neck, to the base of her ear.

"What?" he murmured against her skin.

Shivering, she made a belated effort to pull back. His arms tightened, holding her to him. She pushed harder, leaning back to regard him.

"Gareth, I'm serious. You said you've been ready to take on fatherhood for sixteen years. Why that number?"

His body went still against hers.

"Did I say that?" he asked lightly. Evasively.

Alarm bells sounded in her brain, clamoring for her attention. Something wasn't right. She pushed harder and almost stumbled when he released her without warning, without a fight.

"You know you did. What's going on?"

Faster than she would have imagined possible, Gareth's eyes turned bleak. He leaned against the patio door frame again, his arms crossed, one fist raised to cover his mouth. Pain slashed across his features.

Dark premonition loomed over Gwyn like some kind of vulture.

She waited.

Gareth's arms ached for the feel of Gwyn's body within their circle again, but he didn't dare reach for her. The way she'd pulled away had left a gaping wound he would have sworn he could feel bleeding. He couldn't bear to feel her recoil like that a second time.

And she would if he tried to touch her right now. He saw it in her eyes, buried just beneath the slowly splintering trust in lake-blue depths. He drew a ragged breath. Deprived of her touch and faced with the demons of his own creation, his faith in their ability to weather the truth seemed suddenly, sickeningly naïve. Maybe if they'd had more time first; if they'd talked more, made love more…

But like this?

It's too soon. We're too new…we won't survive this. Not yet. Not now.

But a single, careless, offhand remark had left him with no other choice.

He steeled himself. Tightened his fist. Ignored the heat that radiated from Gwyn's body in stark contrast to his own icy core.

"Gwyn, there's something I haven't told you—"

The trill of a cell phone cut him off and made them both jump. Gareth sent a black look in the direction of the sound.

"That's mine," he said. "Sean's the only one who has the number. He wouldn't call without a reason."

Gwyn nodded. Not a flicker of expression gave away her thoughts, but her careful stillness alone spoke volumes. His cousin's timing could not have been worse.

The phone shrilled again.

"It might be about one of the kids."

Gwyn nodded again.

Gareth strode across the kitchen to where he'd left his phone beside the sink. Lifting the offending instrument, he jabbed the talk button in mid-ring.

"This had better be good," he grated.

"Oh, it's good, all right," Sean's voice drawled in return. "Amy's here."

CHAPTER 34

Gareth faced three challenges following his cousin's words: breathing, comprehension, and incapacitating disbelief. He found himself clutching the countertop, not for support, but for a lifeline to reality—a physical reassurance that he was still somehow connected to earth.

"Say that again?" he said hoarsely.

"Amy is here."

"Here where? In Ottawa?"

"Here in my apartment."

"Right now?"

"I'm looking at her as we speak, cuz." Sean paused, then added, "And it gets better."

Gareth suppressed a groan. "Catherine?"

"The paparazzi."

"Bloody hell."

"My sentiments exactly. And probably most of my neighbors'. And airport security's."

Gareth released his grip on the table and rubbed his hand over his eyes. "Is she all right?"

"She's shaken up, but I think she'll survive. Those guys really are a bunch of sharks, aren't they?"

"Tell me about it." He'd always taken the paparazzi pretty much in stride, careful to protect his privacy while recognizing they were an unfortunate part of the world in which he'd chosen to live, but the thought of those locusts swarming his unsuspecting and unprepared daughter...

His daughter. He passed his hand over his jaw and tried to force his mind past stunned and into functioning again. His daughter was here. Less than two hours away. He inhaled deeply and turned, mustering his thoughts.

Gwyn stared back at him.

The wind left his lungs with an audible hiss for the second time. *Gwyn.*

Her eyes held his, filled with questions that made his gut clench. Bloody hell.

"You still there?" Sean asked.

Oh, what tangled webs we weave...

Setting his jaw, he resolutely turned away from the gaze he could no longer bear to hold. "Yeah," he said. "I'm here. Tell me what happened."

"Amy let slip some details to a friend in the hostel where she was staying in Cardiff. Turns out he wasn't much of a friend. When the local press started nosing around, she decided to clear out while she could. She managed to catch an earlier flight, figuring she'd just surprise you, but the paparazzi beat her here. I got a call from airport security about an hour ago—" Sean broke off as Gwyn's cell phone, still on the counter beside Gareth, began its own musical trill. "Is that another phone?"

Gareth scooped up the offending instrument and held it out to Gwyn in silence. She took it, careful not to let her fingers touch his. His mouth compressed.

"It was Gwyn's," he said to Sean, turning away. *One disaster at a time.* "She has it now. Go on."

"So anyway, a couple of my buddies from work picked her up and—" Sean stopped again. "Did you say Gwyn answered her cell?"

"Yes, why?"

"If you can get it away from her, you might want to try," his cousin suggested, an unfamiliar note of quiet in his voice. "You just made the local evening news."

Gareth's gaze flicked to where Gwyn stood by the patio doors again, her phone held against her ear with whitened knuckles, her face as still as marble.

"Gareth? You still there? Did you hear me?"

"I heard you," he said. "It's too late."

Gwyn watched as Gareth, little more than a shadow among shadows, locked the cottage door and pocketed the key. A snowflake drifted through the fading daylight to settle on her cheek. It lingered there for a second, its tiny coolness reflecting the frost that had claimed her heart. More flakes come to rest on the deck at her feet.

How fitting that the world and her soul should turn to ice at the same time.

Gareth turned to her. Her gaze flicked up at the movement, then shifted away again, coming to rest on the faint shimmer of the lake, visible through the bare trees. She scrunched her hands into fists inside her pockets.

Gareth cleared his throat.

"Are you sure you're all right driving home in the snow? I really wish you'd stay overnight and go back in the daylight."

A note of concern roughened his voice. She still didn't look at him. Couldn't bring herself to meet the eyes she knew searched her face, any more than she could stay alone in the cottage where she and Gareth had—

She hunched her shoulders against a chill that had nothing to do with drifting snowflakes. They'd had this discussion already. In the cottage after they had both ended their phone calls, and the unbearable silence had been broken by Gareth's quiet, *I have to go.*

After she had nodded but stayed silent, because words seemed inappropriate. Inadequate. Empty.

She hadn't needed an explanation. Not after the details Sandy had provided—details from the newscast that aired as they spoke. She hadn't even wanted an explanation. Not really. She was too stunned, too numb, too shattered to have listened to anything that Gareth might have said then. And he, seeming to sense that, had resorted to banalities. *Would you like a coffee before we go? Do you have your toothbrush? Your sweater? Are you sure you're not hungry? The roads could get bad with this snow—are you sure you're okay to drive?*

Yes, they'd had this discussion already, but maybe repeating it would be better than the wordless chasm that would stand between them otherwise.

And so she answered.

"I'll be fine. I have winter tires on the car, and I'll take my time."

"At least follow me back so you don't get lost in the dark."

A new suggestion. One she instinctively wanted to refuse but made her hesitate. The last thing she needed now was to get turned around on dark, unfamiliar country roads—something all too possible in her present state of mind.

"Only to Perth," she compromised. "I'll probably stop there for a coffee. I'll be fine after that."

She sensed, rather than saw, his capitulation. A change in his shadow's stance, perhaps, or the controlled quiet of an expelled breath.

"All right," he said. "We should get going."

His fingers closed over her elbow, but the tiny jolt of electricity that accompanied his touch seemed to travel through a stranger's body, unconnected to her own. She let him guide her off the deck and across the gravel driveway to her car. Removing her hand from her pocket, she reached for the driver's door handle.

Gareth's warm fingers closed over hers.

She couldn't pretend this touch had no effect.

Pain sliced through her, threatening to cleave her heart in two. In the blink of an eye, white-hot need heated her frozen soul to its core, making her desperate to be held, to be reassured, to be told that this was nothing more than a twisted, horrific nightmare.

Breathing became a torment.

"God, Gwyn, I am so sorry," Gareth muttered above her head. Agony laced his voice. "I owe you so very many explanations."

Her heart squeezed inside her. "Don't," she whispered. She didn't know how to deal with her own pain right now. She couldn't possibly bear his as well.

"Your daught—" she couldn't finish the word. "Amy needs you, and it's a long drive."

His fingers tightened on her hand.

"And you, Gwyn?" he asked. "Do you need me?"

She pulled free. "We'd better go."

He let her get into her car then, silently handing her overnight case to her when she was settled behind the steering wheel.

"Follow me out," he reminded her when she reached for the door handle. "And call me when you get home."

"I don't think—"

"I need to know you're safe," he growled. "Call me, or I'll call you. And if you don't answer, I'll be on your doorstep."

She knew he meant the threat. Knew, too, that she couldn't see him again. Not tonight. Maybe not—

No. She wouldn't decide that now. Not yet.

"I'll call," she said. Then she turned the key in the ignition, and Gareth closed the door.

CHAPTER 35

Gareth glanced into the rear view mirror as he maneuvered past the massive trucks sanding Perth's main street. The headlights that had followed him for the last half hour had dropped back, and a signal light had come on to indicate Gwyn's intent to stop, as she'd said she would, for a coffee. Her vehicle turned into the brightly lit parking lot of a donut shop.

Lifting his foot from the accelerator, Gareth hesitated, the two halves of his life wrenching at him. Gwyn behind him, Amy before him. Both suffering. Both in need. But only one, he knew, who would let him try—in all his clumsiness—to help right now.

He pushed down on the gas pedal again, leaving Perth and Gwyn behind. Trying to ignore the certainty that an invisible thread connecting them stretched tighter with every mile, nearing its endurance, threatening to snap.

When he pulled into the visitor parking lot of Sean's apartment building an hour later, a dozen paparazzi swarmed his car. He shoved open his car door against the tide and shouldered his way through with none of his normal patience for what he considered a hazard of the job.

Locusts, he thought again. They might be a part of the world he'd chosen to live in, but Amy hadn't been given any such choice. Scowling, he made no apology for treading on an unknown foot.

Given the chaos they'd created in his life this evening, they were damned lucky he didn't do more than step on toes.

He lengthened his stride, ignoring the clamor of voices and the microphones and cameras shoved into his face. In a matter of seconds he reached the safety of the apartment building where a uniformed Ottawa police officer guarded the glass-door entrance. Sean must have called in reinforcements.

Swinging the door open at his approach, the cop grinned at him.

"Normally I'd ask for proof of residence," he said, "but I suspect you're the cause of the entire ruckus." He pulled the door shut behind Gareth and added, "Things should calm down soon. We're waiting for a court order to move the sharks back a hundred meters and prohibit entry to the building."

In the face of everything else, a court order seemed too trivial for words, but Gareth forced a smile he hoped at least looked grateful.

"Thanks," he said. "I appreciate it."

The cop looked like he might like to continue the conversation, but Gareth was in no mood for pleasantries. He focused on the elevators at the other side of the lobby and made himself look stressed. No great stretch under the circumstances. "If you'll excuse me—"

"Of course. Go!" The cop waved him on without hesitation. "And, Mr. Connor—good luck. She's a beautiful girl."

Gareth paused in mid-stride and turned back, looking at the other man properly for the first time. Obviously brought up to speed by Sean at some point, the officer looked to be in his late forties. He probably had kids of his own around Amy's age. That would explain the understanding in his eyes, the unspoken connection between one father and another.

"Thank you," Gareth said again, and this time he meant it. The smile, too.

The ride in the lift took forever, giving him far more time to reflect than he would have liked. Time to wonder when Gwyn would arrive home, and if she would keep her word about calling him. Time to wonder if his agent had begun damage control yet. Whether Catherine had seen the news, and how she'd reacted. What his first words to his daughter would be. How he would explain to her...how he would explain to Gwyn...

If he would ever get the chance to do the latter.

At last the lift opened onto the empty corridor leading to Sean's apartment. He stood for a long moment with his hand holding the door to one side. He'd walked down this hallway fifty times or more since he'd arrived in Ottawa. How had he never noticed how long it was? Stepping into the hall, he let the lift door swish shut behind him.

This was it.

Placing one foot ahead of the other, he began the walk toward his daughter. By the time he arrived at the brass "1021" tacked to Sean's door, his palms were slick and his belly hollow. Sixteen years of waiting for this day, and now look at him. He'd rehearsed more for this moment than any role he'd ever played, but he'd never felt less prepared.

Of all the many things he'd expected from this overdue foray into fatherhood, a serious humbling hadn't been one of them.

Sliding the key into the deadbolt with one hand, he turned the door knob with the other.

CHAPTER 36

Gwyn sat in a corner of the donut shop, fingers wrapped around the cooled ceramic cup and its less-than-appealing contents. She hadn't even tasted the coffee she'd ordered. Just sat and stared at the brown-paper-bag colored fluid until the steam stopped rising from its surface, and the cream began to congeal around the edges.

Sat, stared, and waited.

But for what? The numbness to subside? Hurt to take over? Anger? She had every right to feel both, she knew. That Gareth could have deceived her in that way—and the magnitude of the deception still took away her breath—knowing her history, *knowing* what Jack had done to her...

Instead, she felt nothing but a sense of loss that went too deep for words. Too deep for feelings. Very nearly too deep for her to function at all.

Sudden musical tones jolted her out of her melancholy. She dug into her coat pocket and pulled out her cell phone, glancing at the call display before she answered. Home.

"Hi, Sand," she answered.

"Hey, kiddo. How're you doing?"

"I'm okay."

"Sure you are." Bottomless sympathy echoed in Sandy's words. "You almost home?"

Gwyn closed her eyes. "Actually, no. I'm staring at a cup of cold coffee in Perth."

"Perth? I see. Just how cold is this coffee?"

She stuck her finger into the brown murk and grimaced. "Ice."

"Ah." A long few seconds passed. Sandy cleared her throat. "Sweetie, you can't sit in Perth for the rest of your life."

"I know."

"Are you all right to drive home tonight? You can always camp out in a hotel until morning."

"No. I'm fine. Really. I'm just—" She trailed off, having no idea how to finish. How to describe her current state.

Sandy's tone became brisk, her advice practical. "Well, your kids are hoping you'll tuck them in, so why don't you buy yourself a fresh coffee to go? I'll let them watch a movie until you get here, and then I'll help you get them into bed."

Gwyn nodded. Then she remembered Sandy couldn't see her. "All right," she said. "I'll do that."

"Good. And, Gwyn," Sandy's voice turned fierce, "you'll be okay, you know."

Gwyn closed her cell phone. Wishing she could share her friend's certainty, she brushed away a tear.

Gareth stared at the willowy young woman who had risen from the couch at his entrance. Dark eyes, so like the ones he saw in his own mirror every day, stared back at him, uncertain, questioning, shining with a mix of the same thousand emotions that milled within him. A tremulous smile curved a mouth indisputably inherited from Catherine. Nervous hands tugged the folds of a blanket closer around slender shoulders; one reached up to tuck a strand of long, dark hair behind an ear.

He swallowed, encountered a lump, cleared his throat.

"Hey," he said. The first word he'd spoken to his daughter's face since she was two years old.

"Hey," she replied, and without warning, she burst into tears.

A half-box of tissues later, they sat facing each other on the couch while Amy sniffled her way through the last of her watery explanation. "So anyway, they were already here when I landed. The paparazzi, I mean. I didn't know what to do—they kept yelling questions at me, and their cameras were flashing, and—"

Gareth plucked the soggy tissue from her fingers and handed her a fresh one. "You did the right thing," he assured her, despite knowing from a brief conversation with Sean that, in hysterics, she had assailed an unsuspecting airport security officer and nearly gotten herself arrested before things had been straightened out. Minor details.

She giggled through her tears. "Hardly," she said. "But thank you for saying so."

She blew her nose, added the tissue to the growing pile on Sean's coffee table, and sat back to regard him ruefully. "I guess I really blew it, huh? And after Mom asked you to keep the secret—"

Gareth shook his head. "It's nothing we can't handle," he said. "In a day or so, I'll have my agent arrange an interview with someone, we'll give enough details to get the sharks off our backs, and it will all be over."

Amy looked skeptical. "It's really that easy?"

He smiled. "No. But if we can hang tight for a few days, some other personality is bound to do something that will take the spotlight off us." He gave Amy's hand, resting in her lap, a gentle squeeze. "A month from now they'll have forgotten all about you."

She grimaced. "I'm not sure Mom's nerves will hold up that long."

Neither was Gareth. "Speaking of your mother, does she know where you are?"

"I called her when I got here. She wanted to come and get me, but Sean managed to talk her out of it." Dark eyes sparking with the faint mischief Gareth had encountered in their only phone conversation, she added, "Thank God."

He mentally echoed the sentiment, but said, "I should call her too."

Amy put a hand on his arm. "Don't. Not tonight. She's put you through enough. Let me handle this tomorrow, when she picks me up."

He didn't know how to respond. Or what to think.

His daughter smiled. "Mom means well, but she's a little... controlling. You may have noticed."

A snort escaped him before he could catch it back. Amy laughed.

"I thought so. Anyway, remember when I told you I knew more than Mom thought I did? Well, I found out about you when I was fifteen. I went to Lance and he told me everything, on condition that I not speak to Mom about it, or try to contact you until I turned eighteen. He even told me about all the rules she'd imposed on you for our first meeting."

Amy looked a little teary again, and Gareth reached for another tissue.

"That's why I went to Wales to find you," she continued, her voice wobbling as she accepted the tissue and dabbed at her eyes with it. "I wanted it to be just me and you, and instead I got an airhead travel companion and a dozen paparazzi."

Gareth hastened to head off another full-blown meltdown. "How did you first find out? About me, I mean."

"Apart from the suspicions I'd had my entire life because Mom developed a migraine every time I asked who I resembled in the family? You sent me a birthday gift that year. A pair of Celtic-cross earrings."

The only gift that hadn't been returned to him. He'd spent an entire year thinking that Catherine had begun to soften at last, only to have the sixteenth birthday present come back as if the fifteenth had never happened. At the time, he'd assumed the gift had just gone astray. He'd never dreamed—

"Speaking of birthdays," he said, "I have something for you. I'll be back in a minute."

He went to his room and returned with the suitcase that had stood unopened in the corner since his arrival. He set it on the coffee table and smiled at the question in Amy's eyes.

"Go ahead," he said. "Open it."

Then he watched while his daughter caught up on a lifetime of missed birthday gifts and lost opportunities. Watched, passed tissues as needed, and, in a separate part of himself, counted the minutes ticking by as he waited for word from Gwyn.

CHAPTER 37

Tucking the duvet around Katie's shoulders, Gwyn leaned over to kiss her forehead. Her daughter, already more than half-asleep, smiled without opening her eyes.

"I love you, Mommy," she whispered.

"I love you, too, sweetie," Gwyn returned softly. She brushed a lock of hair back from the still baby-smooth cheek. "Sleep well."

She tiptoed from the room, turning off the desk lamp on her way, and pulled the door shut behind her. As was her routine, she paused outside Nicholas and Maggie's door and listened for a moment to their breathing, deep and even in their sleep.

A stab of guilt twisted inside her. All three had insisted on waiting up until she'd arrived home at nearly midnight, hours past their normal bedtime. They would be so tired tomorrow...

All because of a cold, congealed cup of coffee that she might as well have foregone, for all the good it had done her.

She started toward the stairs. The stop in Perth had been a complete waste of time. It had given her neither the benefit of a caffeine boost nor the ability, as she'd hoped, to come to terms with any of what had transpired at the cottage. She'd left the coffee shop and driven the entire way home in exactly the same fog in which she'd operated since hearing Sandy's words over the phone: *"Gwyn, sweetie, I'm watching the evening news and—well, I just wondered—I thought you'd want to know—unless maybe you already do, but I figured you'd have at least mentioned it—Gwyn, did Gareth ever tell you that he had a daughter?"*

A silhouette loomed at the foot of the stairs, interrupting the mental replay of her fateful conversation with her friend. Gwyn's heart gave a leap. For a moment, her treacherous mind placed Gareth on the bottom landing, waiting for her as he'd done before. Then her new reality took over, slicing through any lingering haze with a ruthlessness that quite literally took away her breath. Her knees buckled.

Not Gareth. Sandy. Sandy waiting to comfort her with empty words, because Gareth—

Because Gareth—

She sat down on the top step with a thump. Her arms crossed over her knees, she buried her face against them.

Because Gareth had lied to her. He had systematically torn down every wall she'd erected to protect herself and her family—worn down every objection, countered every argument, taken over her judgment, her heart, her soul...

...and she had let him.

"Gwyn? Sweetie?" Sandy's soft voice broke through her pain. "I made some tea. Come and sit."

Gwyn raised her head. "How could he?" she asked.

Sandy shrugged, helplessness in her blue gaze. "I don't know what to say."

"He told me he loved me."

"Oh, Gwyn."

"He said we could work everything out. He said—" She gulped against the knife in her throat. "He said—God, Sand,

I should've known better. I *did* know better, but I didn't want to listen to myself."

"Honey, you can't possibly blame yourself!"

Scowling, Gwyn dashed away an escaped tear. "I'm the one who let him in. I have no one to blame for that *but* myself."

Sandy's face tightened into lines of disagreement, but she shrugged, keeping her arguments to herself. "We can debate that another time," she said. "Right now, how about that tea?"

"I have to call Gareth first—he wanted to know when I got home."

"Do you want me to do it?"

Gwyn shook her head. No matter how tempting the offer, she wouldn't put it past her very loyal friend to add a few choice words to any conversation with Gareth. "Thanks, but I can manage. Really."

"Then I'll pour the tea."

Gareth held up the teapot and looked askance at his daughter, who shook her dark head.

"Thanks, but I think my back teeth might start floating if I drink any more." Amy tilted her head to one side, her arms wrapped around a large, brown plush teddy bear—her fourth-year birthday present—and studied him from her place at one end of the couch. "So? I have to ask. Am I what you expected?"

He set the pot back on the glass-topped coffee table. "No. And yes. I really wasn't sure what to expect, I suppose.

I'd seen your photos, of course." He paused. In deference to Catherine, he hadn't yet confessed his private investigator to Amy. After a moment, he continued. "So you were what I'd expected in that way, but I think you're more grown up than I'd imagined."

"Having missed so many years must have been hard for you."

"I have to ask you something, too." He stared down at his hands. "Are you really as forgiving as you sound? I dropped out of your life when you were still a baby, and—"

Amy reached over to cover his hand with hers. "Lance was a good dad," she said. "He still is. From what he told me, you would have been too, if you'd been given a chance."

"Exactly how much *do* you know?" he asked, regarding his daughter narrowly.

"Like I told you before, more than Mom thinks. A lot more. I know you changed your mind, and that you tried to get Mom to change hers."

Thank God.

"I've never regretted anything so much in all my life," he said.

"Lance told me."

Gareth made a mental note to buy Lance a case of the best Scotch he could get his hands on. "You're really okay with everything, then."

"I really am." Amy's eyes danced. "Of course, if you'd asked me when I was fifteen, it might have been a different story, but I've grown up a lot since then."

The phone on the table beside Gareth rang, cutting off his reply. He withdrew his hand from beneath Amy's, twisting in his seat, and then paused as he heard Sean's deep voice answer in the kitchen. His hand hovered above the receiver. He listened to his cousin's murmured responses, then to the distinct click that ended the call.

Only when Sean appeared in the kitchen doorway did he let his hand drift back to his side.

"Gwyn?"

Sean nodded, his gaze flicking towards Amy. "She said to tell you she's home."

"But she didn't want to talk to me." Which was why she'd called Sean's apartment number and not his cell phone.

His cousin shook his head. "No."

"Right. Thanks."

Amy *ahemmed* discreetly. "I take it this Gwyn is someone special?"

"Very."

"Tell me about her."

It was late, Gareth thought. He should probably insist Amy get to bed, but given the time-altering effects of a trans-Atlantic flight, she most likely wouldn't sleep just yet anyway. And given his own royally screwed-up life, neither would he.

He poured himself another cup of tea and sat back on the sofa. "Her name is Gwynneth," he said. "With two n's."

CHAPTER 38

"May I have some more milk, please?" Maggie inquired, holding out her glass to Gwyn.

Gwyn gritted her teeth at the little girl's careful formality, typical of the way all her children had treated her since this morning. Reaching across the lunch table, she took the glass from her daughter. She'd strived since waking to maintain a note of normalcy in the household, but seemed instead to have made the atmosphere ever more brittle with her efforts. She forced a smile.

"That was very polite, Maggie, thank you."

Maggie's solemn expression didn't change. "You're welcome."

Gwyn sighed and picked up the nearby milk carton. Her eyes drifted to the bold-faced kitchen clock. Only twelve-fifteen. Could this day possibly drag by any slower? She tipped the carton toward Maggie's glass.

A sudden shrill from the telephone jolted through the oppressive silence, causing her to jump and send a stream of milk across the table.

"Damn it!"

Three pairs of startled, accusing eyes stared at her. Maggie's bottom lip quivered. The phone rang again and Gwyn bit back a second, choicer phrase.

Katie pushed back from the table and retrieved the dishcloth from the kitchen sink. She set it beside Gwyn's plate.

The phone warbled a third time.

"Should I—?" Katie asked, her gaze locking onto the intrusive instrument.

"No!" Gwyn drew a deep breath and attempted to soften her response. "Thank you, sweetie, but we're having lunch and the machine will take a message."

No one pointed out that the machine had been taking messages all morning. Fifteen of them, to be exact. As if on cue, a loud click interrupted the telephone's fourth ring. They sat, waiting for the greeting to end, and for the voice they'd come to expect to follow.

"Please leave a message after the tone and we'll be happy to return your call," her voice said from the machine.

Beep.

"Damn it, Gwyn, you can't avoid me forever," Gareth's deep tones growled through the kitchen. "We have to talk. We *need* to talk."

The raw frustration in his voice sliced deep into Gwyn's belly. Clamping her teeth over her lower lip, she coiled her fingers around the chair's seat, battling the desire to spring up and grab for the receiver.

Not while the kids are up. She'd made that decision at some point during her sleepless night and, unlike all her other resolutions where Gareth was concerned, she was determined to stick to this one.

"Gwyn, *please,*" Gareth's voice dropped lower, roughened. "I know you're hurt, and I know I've messed up, but I really can explain if you'll just give me a chance." A small silence ended with a sigh. "Fine, have it your way for now. But just so we're clear on this, I hope you understand that I'm going to keep trying until you talk to me. And that I meant what I told you yesterday. All of it."

Silence fell over the kitchen once again, broken by a second loud click from the answering machine.

"Mommy?"

Gwyn pried her fingernails out of the wooden chair seat beneath her. She picked up the dishcloth and set it in the middle of the milk puddle. "Yes, Nicky?"

"Did you and Gareth have a fight?"

If only it had been that simple.

"Kind of, I suppose."

"Madame Lucie says that when friends fight, they should talk about it."

Gwyn made herself smile and keep her present opinion to herself regarding the kindergarten teacher's playground peace tactics.

"Are you and Gareth still friends?" Nicholas methodically stabbed his fork into the macaroni in his bowl.

"I won't settle for being friends..."

Gwyn inhaled a shaky breath. She looked at each of her children in turn, seeing their uncertainty, feeling their confusion. It would be so easy to spout platitudes, to give them the reassurance they wanted. But she wouldn't lie to them. Not on top of everything else.

"I don't know," she said.

Katie stared at her plate, saying nothing. Nicholas nodded solemnly. Maggie sniffled.

In a devastating moment of clarity, she saw the full impact of her actions on her children. The parallels to Jack she'd sworn would never happen.

Despite all her declarations to the contrary—her empty, meaningless assertions—she had put her own desires above the welfare of her kids. Taken a calculated risk that had placed three innocents in the direct path of the same kind of hurt their father had once inflicted on them. Gambled, and lost.

Knowing that this could happen.

She shoved back her chair and stumbled to the counter. Fighting back a wave of nausea, she dropped the milk-sodden cloth into the sink, then turned on the tap and splashed cold water over her face and the back of her neck. The nausea slowly receded.

The knife in her heart remained.

She straightened up from the sink and reached for a dry tea towel. Turning, she stared at the sad little group at the table. Lord, how had she ever messed up their lives so thoroughly? And how did she even begin to make it better?

The elusive specter of "normal" hovered before her once more.

"Come on, guys," she said, adopting a brittle note of cheer, "let's finish lunch and then find a game to play, all right? Who's up for Hungry Hippos?"

No one answered.

Nicholas looked up at her with a fierce scowl. "Mommy?"

"What, Nicky?"

"If talking doesn't work..."

"Yes?"

"I can punch him in the nose for you."

CHAPTER 39

The day did eventually end, but it took a very long time to do so. While the phone had stayed silent for the remainder of the afternoon, Gwyn's nerves had jangled unmercifully at the thought of the looming conversation.

She found herself inventing and discarding a hundred different reasons she wouldn't be able to call Gareth once the kids were tucked into bed, but even if she'd managed to find one plausible enough to suit her, she knew she had no choice but to talk to him. He'd been quite serious in his last message about not giving up. She wouldn't put it past him to show up on her doorstep if she continued to ignore him—a situation that would just compound the whole mess, because saying what she had to say by phone would be hard enough.

It crippled her breathing just to think about having to do so in person.

And so, when she had turned out the last bedroom light, fetched the last glass of water, and kissed the last cheek, she returned to the kitchen to deal with the inevitable.

She found Gareth's cell phone number still scrawled across the refrigerator whiteboard, and before she could reconsider yet again, she punched the digits into the phone.

Gareth answered on the first ring.

Gwyn squeezed her eyes shut and sat down on the floor with her back against the fridge. "It's me," she said.

"I was getting ready to come over there."

"I thought you might be."

"You don't want me to."

"No."

"Gwyn—"

"You lied to me."

There. It was out. A single, tidy little phrase that encompassed it all: truth, accusation, and unbearable hurt.

Starkly underlined by Gareth's ragged, indrawn breath.

"I never meant to hurt you, Gwyn, I swear. I wanted to tell you. You have no idea how much I wanted to tell you."

She imagined him running an impatient hand through his hair the way he did when he was frustrated or upset. Then she wiped the familiarity of the thought from her mind.

"But you didn't."

"I couldn't. I'd made a promise—" Gareth broke off with a curse. "I need to start at the beginning for you to understand. Will you listen?"

No, she wanted to say, because it wouldn't matter to the final outcome. To what she knew she needed to do for the sake of her kids.

"Yes," she said, because she wasn't yet ready.

And she did listen. She listened, and heard the pain of what he had been through during the years without his daughter, and even understood his reasons for having kept Amy—that entire part of his life—a secret from her.

When he was done, she let herself absorb his words for a moment, wondering if they might somehow make a difference.

They didn't. His explanation may have alleviated the hurt and betrayal, but it didn't change the certainty she'd been right all along. She should never, ever have opened up herself—or her children—to the possibility of this kind of hurt in the first place. And she would never do so again.

"Are you serious?" Gareth asked hoarsely when she told him as much.

Gwyn closed her eyes against a prickle of tears. "I'm serious. I do understand why you didn't tell me about Amy, really I do. But it's not about that."

"Then what is it about?"

"Me. I can't—I don't—"

"You don't trust me."

"I don't trust anyone." Bracing her elbow on her upraised knee, she dropped her forehead into her hand. "Especially me. I knew something wasn't right—I knew there was something you weren't telling me. Damn it, Gareth, I knew better all along than to get involved with you."

"It seems to me we're more than just *involved*."

She bit her lip. "Fine. Then I knew better than to fall in love with you."

"But you did."

"Yes."

"And I fell in love with you."

"Gareth, don't. Please."

"I will apologize a hundred thousand times for hurting you," he continued as if she hadn't spoken, "but not for loving. Never for loving you."

She steeled her heart against the frustration in his voice. "Then I'll apologize for it," she said, "because I'm the one who knew we should never have gone as far as we did. I could have stopped it and saved us both—saved us *all*—a lot of pain."

"Damn it, Gwyn, there doesn't have to *be* this much pain. I'm not Jack. I'm not running out on anyone."

"Maybe not now, but you and I both know there are no guarantees in life, Gareth. Who's to say we wouldn't split up somewhere down the road? In a year, or two, or ten?"

Gareth's impatience snarled across the phone line. "Even if we did split up—and understand I'm following *your* line of thought here, not mine—I would never just drop out of their lives the way Jack did."

"You wouldn't have to," Gwyn said, "because they'd still be hurt, and I would still be responsible. I'm sorry, Gareth, but I can't take that chance. I won't."

CHAPTER 40

"So what now?" Sandy asked when Gwyn finished telling her the tale on the phone the next morning.

Gwyn sat back in her office chair, resting her head against the padded leather. "Now I get on with life. I get up in the morning and make breakfast, I take the kids to school, I get caught up on all the work I've let slide..."

And I wait for a very, very long time for the pain to go away.

"Do you think he'll just let it go like this?"

"Maybe not right away, but eventually he'll have no choice. My mind is made up, Sandy. I'm doing the right thing."

"Are you?"

Gwyn lifted her glasses up slightly and pinched the bridge of her nose between her thumb and forefinger. Was that the start of a headache? After two sleepless nights and counting, she supposed she shouldn't be surprised.

"What's that supposed to mean?"

Her friend sighed. "I don't know. I mean, *I* think you're doing the right thing—I know I'd certainly do the same in your shoes, but—ah, hell, Gwyn, you don't need me second-guessing you on this, do you?"

"Not really."

"As long as you're sure you'll be able to hold out against him. He seems pretty persistent."

"I'm sure." Most of the time, anyway. As long as she remained focused on how this was best not just for her, but for the kids too, her determination stayed pretty steady. In weaker moments, however...

She shored up her resolve for the hundredth time that morning. "He has to leave eventually. He has his work, his life. All I have to do is hold out long enough and—"

"Theoretically," Sandy's dry voice interrupted.

Gwyn sighed. "Theoretically," she agreed.

"This isn't going to be easy, Gwyn. You know that."

"I know. I also know I have no choice. I can't put the kids through a second family break-up."

"You didn't put them through the first. Jack did."

"Whatever. I can still make damned certain there isn't another."

"Who's to say there'd be another? You and Gareth might—"

The phone beeped in Gwyn's ear, signaling another call waiting. Only too happy to cut the conversation short, she said, "Sorry, Sand—I have to go. I have another call coming in."

"What if it's him?"

"Then I'll make polite conversation about the weather and tell him to have a nice day," Gwyn lied, thinking it far more likely she'd hang up out of sheer panic. "It's probably just a client anyway."

"Call me later?"

"Of course." She held the receiver button down for an instant, prepared herself as best she could for the possibility it might be

Gareth after all, then answered with her professional daytime, "Gwyn Jacobs Architecture and Design."

"Ms. Jacobs? It's Nicole at the school. Can you come over here? I'm afraid we have a situation."

CHAPTER 41

"Holy shit, it's like running a gauntlet out there!" Sandy panted, slamming the door shut behind her and looking more frazzled than usual. She clapped a hand over her mouth and pulled a face at a giggling Maggie. "Forget Auntie Sandy said that, okay, Magpie? Hey, how about putting my purse in the kitchen for me?"

Still giggling, Maggie ran to do as she was bid, and Sandy turned to envelop Gwyn in a hug.

"You poor thing," she said. "On top of everything else..."

Gwyn gave a quick squeeze back but felt no need to remain in the embrace. She was too damned angry to need Sandy's—or anyone's—sympathy. She pulled away, calling out a reminder to Nicholas as she did, "Away from the windows, Nicky."

Her son obediently bobbed his head back down from where he'd been sneaking a peek through the blinds at the gathered paparazzi. He returned to his Lego-building.

"How did they find out?" Sandy asked, trailing after her into the kitchen.

"Katie did some bragging on the playground last week. One of the lunch monitors apparently overheard her and, when the news came out about Gareth this weekend, decided to make a few extra bucks." Gwyn held up a hand to forestall her friend's wrath. "She's already been suspended."

Undeterred, Sandy growled, "She should be fired. Or drawn and quartered!"

"That could still be arranged." Digging through a kitchen drawer, Gwyn unearthed the community telephone book and slammed it onto the counter. "Anyway, when the kids went out at recess, the paparazzi were waiting. They scared the living daylights out of poor Maggie."

"And *they* should be—" Sandy shot a sideways look at the avidly listening *poor Maggie* and finished, "Well, never mind. You get my drift. What about Nicholas and Katie?"

"Katie's on a field trip for the day, thank heavens. The teachers will keep her inside the school until I pick her up. And Nicholas—" Her fist closed spasmodically on a page in the phonebook, tearing it from its binding.

Sandy looked alarmed. "Are you okay?"

Gwyn made herself release the paper. She smoothed it out again as best she could, then continued turning the pages.

"I'm fine," she said, "but one of the photographers is probably limping. Nicky laid into him and landed a half-dozen good kicks on the shin before the teachers pulled him off and got him inside."

"Seriously?"

"Nich'las was pertecting me," Maggie said proudly.

"I'm sure he was," Sandy told her, admiration for her "nephew" ringing in her voice. Quiet concern underlined her next question, however. "They were close enough for him to kick one of them?"

"They were close enough to be talking to both of them on the playground at recess. That's been dealt with, too." Gwyn realized she'd passed what she was looking for. She swore and flipped backwards through the pages.

"Maggie," said Sandy, "Why don't you go and help Nicholas with the Lego and I'll make us all some popcorn—would you like that?"

"'Kay," Maggie said agreeably. "Can we have hot chocolate too?"

"Of course."

Maggie trotted off to join her brother. Sandy took the phone-book away from Gwyn.

"Take a deep breath and tell me what you're looking for," she said. "I'll find it for you."

Gwyn took the suggested deep breath, then another. And then she began to shake. "Damn it to hell and back, Sandy, those—those—"

She gritted her teeth against the uncharacteristic language that threatened to spill over and filled her lungs for a third time. "Maggie was in hysterics. They wouldn't stop taking pictures even while she was crying. Half the playground was in an uproar."

With no similar compunctions regarding language, Sandy quite succinctly described what Gwyn herself thought of the paparazzi lying in wait outside her front door. When she had finished, she remained silent for a moment, then asked, "What are you going to do?"

"I'm calling the cops. That's the number I was trying to find, by the way. Non-emergency."

Her friend flipped to the front of the book and located the listing within the first few pages. She took a green highlighter from the drawer and drew a line over the number. "Have you considered calling—"

"No."

"But he might be able to—"

"No. Apart from the fact that it would give those leeches another reason to hang around my front door, I'm perfectly capable of handling this on my own." Gwyn took the book from Sandy and lifted the cordless phone from its base. "I used to manage just fine before Gareth arrived in our lives, remember? I'm sure I still can."

"Would that be me or you you're trying to convince?"

Gwyn declined to answer and headed instead for the hallway. "I'm going to call from upstairs where the kids can't hear. Do you mind watching them for me?"

Sandy's raised voice followed her out of the kitchen. "He'd want to know about this, Gwyn. There's such a thing as *too* independent sometimes, you know!"

Gareth prowled the perimeter of Sean's living room, his mind and heart so hopelessly enmeshed, that he could no longer separate raw emotion from rational thought. Not the best state in which to attempt solving a problem that seemed insurmountable in the first place.

He stopped at the balcony doors and scowled across the river. He should just go over there and—what? Try to talk to her through her front door? Because he was fairly certain that's what he'd be doing. She'd already stopped taking or returning his calls, so his chances of getting inside her house seemed nothing short of impossible.

Which left him at the same point he'd been when she'd hung up on him last night: exactly nowhere.

Bloody hell, there had to be *something* he could do. Some way to get through to her, make her listen, make her give him—*them*—another chance.

He resumed his pacing.

"Keep that up and you'll wear a hole through my carpet," Sean's voice observed from the kitchen doorway.

"I'll buy you a new one."

His cousin crossed the room and held out a glass to him. "That wasn't the point."

Gareth took the glass and sniffed suspiciously at its contents. He raised an eyebrow. "Whiskey? It's a little early in the day, don't you think?"

Sean lifted his shoulders in a lazy shrug. "You look like you could use it. Besides, it's not like you'll be driving anywhere soon."

"Rub it in, why don't you?" Gareth handed the glass back to him. "Thanks but no thanks. My head is messed up enough as it is."

Resting his shoulder against the wall, one hand tucked into his jeans pocket, Sean swirled the glass in slow, thoughtful circles.

Gareth heaved a pained, exaggerated sigh. "What?"

"Maybe she just needs a little time. This was an awful lot to be hit with, after all."

"Finding out about Amy, you mean?"

Sean nodded. "And the whole secret thing. That had to have hurt."

"It did," Gareth said grimly. "But Amy's not the problem."

"What, then?"

"Jack."

"Her son?"

"Her ex. She's determined not to put the kids at risk of another break-up."

"So much so that she's causing the break-up herself?"

"Something about it being better to do so now, before the kids get more involved, because there are no guarantees that we'd make it as a couple."

Sean frowned, mulling over the information, then grunted. "Damned if that doesn't make sense," he muttered, "in a twisted-logic kind of way."

Gareth laughed, a short, humorless bark of sound, and resumed his trek around the apartment. "Tell me about it. I'm still trying to figure out an argument." He glanced over his shoulder as the phone rang. "Unless that's Amy, I'm not in."

Stopping at the balcony doors again, he listened to his cousin answer the phone and ask who was calling. He gave a start of surprise when Sean tapped him on the shoulder with the instrument.

He turned. "Amy?" he asked.

Sean shook his head.

"I told you—"

"It's someone named Sandra Masters. She says she's a friend of Gwyn's and it's urgent."

CHAPTER 42

Gwyn peeled off her coat and unwound the scarf from her neck. She dropped them onto the hall bench with a huge sigh of relief and not a trace of guilt about violating her own *put it away* rule. Glancing into the living room, she saw Nicholas and Maggie cuddled up on the couch to listen to their favorite audio book. Katie's excited voice drifted down the hall from the kitchen where she'd run to tell Sandy about their brush with fame. As if the camera flashes in the school yard and the police escort home had all been just one big adventure.

Heaving a sigh, Gwyn stooped to undo her boots. The creak of a floorboard heralded the approach of someone down the hallway, and she flashed a sideways smile at Sandy.

"Mission accomplished," she told her friend with satisfaction. "The cops were great. I can't do anything about those creeps hanging around in the street, but they've been read the riot act about coming anywhere near the kids again, and now I know how to go about laying a complaint if I need to."

Boots removed, she straightened up again. In the kitchen, Katie's voice reached a high note of excitement and Gwyn shook her head wryly. Oh, to be seven again.

Wait. Katie's voice was continuing? Why?

She strained to eavesdrop on her eldest daughter for a moment. Yes, she was definitely telling the story. To someone on the phone?

Sandy cleared her throat, looking guilty. Gwyn's heart missed a beat.

"Sand? What's going on?"

"I was worried!" Sandy burst out. "You, the kids—you don't need this paparazzi crap, Gwyn!"

"I know. That's why I went to the police," she said, the words slow as she struggled to say them without betraying the panic rising in her. Sandy wouldn't have. She couldn't have.

"I know. And it was a great idea, but I just wanted to be sure—I wanted you to be safe. I even called Rob and he agreed it was the best thing to do."

And then Gwyn knew who listened to Katie's story. Knew who waited for her in her kitchen. She sagged against the wall.

"Oh, God, Sandy, why?"

"Hear me out before you get mad, okay? Please? He only wants to help. He knows how to handle those jerks. And besides, having a bodyguard is only temporary."

"A *what*?"

"A—a—" Sandy looked pale and miserable as she twisted her hands together. "A bodyguard. A temporary one."

For a long moment, Gwyn didn't respond. She didn't know how. Staring past her friend, down the corridor to where Gareth sat listening to Katie's story, she waited for the panic to overtake her, to mar her thought processes the way it always seemed to when he was involved. She'd had no time to prepare, no time to shore up her defenses or assemble her arguments or plan her strategy.

Had, really, every right to be an absolute wreck.

But instead, calm infused her—the kind of calm she hadn't known since before she first sat down in a theater box on a rainy Sunday afternoon and had her world turned upside down.

"Enough," she said.

"What?" asked Sandy.

Gwyn straightened up from the wall. "I said enough. I can't do this anymore."

"Do what, the paparazzi? Gareth said it wouldn't last long."

"Any of it. I can't do any of it anymore."

Sandy sidestepped hastily as she strode down the hallway. "Gwyn? Sweetie, are you all right?"

Ignoring her, Gwyn focused with single-minded determination on her destination—and her purpose. Her momentum carried her to the middle of the kitchen, where she pulled up short beside the table and faced down Gareth Connor without so much as the flicker of an eyelid.

"I don't want a bodyguard," she announced, "and I don't need your help."

Gareth regarded the auburn-haired, whirlwind presence with a wary eye, taking in the determined set of her jaw, the coolness of her blue gaze. As far as conversational openings went, a simple hello would have been a great deal more promising.

Pushing back from the table, he rose to his feet. At least he'd made it through her front door, even if it hadn't been by Gwyn's own invitation. All he had to do now was keep from blowing his chances. He began by pitching his voice to a low-keyed calm of his own.

"I know it's hard, but they'll lose interest soon. I've already arranged to appear on a talk show next week with Amy. Once the whole story comes out, the tabloids will move on to more exciting things. In the meantime, this is Guy Armand, a friend of Sean's." He indicated the man at the end of the table. "If it's all right with you, I've asked him to make sure the wolves keep their distance from you and the kids."

Sean's friend, a former cop turned professional bodyguard and an absolute ox of a man, stood up. Ignoring his outstretched hand, Gwyn eyed his bulk from head to toe with a cool assessment that had Gareth admiring her sheer nerve.

"No offense to Monsieur Armand, but it's *not* all right with me. I don't want a bodyguard, temporary or otherwise. I've already called the police and dealt with the matter."

Armand began gathering up his briefcase and papers.

"I'll wait in the other room," he said. "You can let me know when you're ready for me."

"We'll join you," Sandy volunteered, shepherding a solemn Katie from the kitchen.

With the room empty but for the two of them, Gareth tucked his hands into his front pockets and tried again. "Gwyn—"

She cut him off, and again he felt that unfamiliar edge to her.

"I mean it, Gareth. No bodyguards and no help. Sandy shouldn't have called you."

"The press can be pretty rough when you're not used to them. The kids—"

"The press will go away when you do."

Gareth felt as if she'd slapped him. He balled his hands into fists inside his pockets.

"Damn it, Gwyn, if you'd just let me—"

"No." Gwyn lifted her chin. "It's over, Gareth. I want my life back. I want to start sleeping again and stop jumping every time the telephone rings. I want to take my children to school without running a gauntlet to get there, and I want let them play in the front yard without a bodyguard. I want to be normal again. I want—" she paused and took a deep, shaky breath. "I want you to go home. Go back to the world where you belong, get to know your daughter, take the paparazzi with you. It's time to let me and the kids start healing before any more damage is done."

Gareth turned from her, struggling with a sense of overwhelming futility. She spoke with such conviction, such certainty. How did he even begin to argue with a determination like that?

He stared around Gwyn's kitchen. His gaze lingered on the counter where a polka-dotted Maggie and her brother had negotiated with him for French fries; the stool where a tearful Katie had turned to him for comfort over a job-day gone awry; the place where he'd stood watch over Gwyn while she slept, exhausted from the demands of a life he wanted only to ease.

Futility began to mesh with overwhelming loss.

He closed his eyes.

"You're sure this is what you want."

"I'm positive."

"Because this is best?" he asked. "Or just safest?"

"Don't you understand?" she whispered. "From where my kids stand, there's no difference."

CHAPTER 43

"So that's it, then?" Sean asked as Gareth hung up the phone.

"That's it," said Gareth. "Six a.m. tomorrow. It was the earliest I could get."

"Will you let her know?"

"Yeah. Just so she can stop worrying about the paparazzi."

And so she'd know the exact moment she could begin rebuilding her life without him in it.

"What about the kids? Will you say goodbye to them?"

The unseen fist that resided in Gareth's chest these days gave his heart a cruel little squeeze. He thought about the moments in Gwyn's front hall when he had faced the three small people who had become such a huge part of him. Maggie, who wrapped her arms around his neck and pressed her cool, juice-sticky lips to his cheek; Katie who solemnly offered him a hand in her most grown-up manner; Nicholas who stood aside and glowered, refusing to look at him.

He remembered the way his gaze had locked with Gwyn's over their heads; remembered the agonized, accusing *I told you so* in her tear-bright eyes. Remembered how his own anguish had filled him so completely that nothing else in the world existed while he gathered his coat, stepped onto the familiar front porch for the last time, and heard the door close behind him.

The fist in his chest tightened some more.

"No," he answered Sean. "I already said goodbye at Gwyn's."

"He called, didn't he?" Sandy said before Gwyn had fully articulated her *hello*.

"Yes, but how—"

"Your voice sounds different. Did you talk to him?"

"He left a message. He's leaving on the 6:00 a.m. flight tomorrow." Gwyn wasn't surprised to hear she sounded different. No one could have died as much inside as she had and not be changed.

"So that's it then," Sandy said. "It's really over."

Closing her eyes, Gwyn bit down on her lip to keep back the tears. She lifted her hand and absently massaged at the space where her heart had once resided. In her mind, Gareth's last message played again.

"I wanted to let you know I'm leaving."

"Yeah," she said. "It's really over."

"Are you all right? Do you want some company?"

"Thanks, but I'm fine."

"Do you think—will you call him to say goodbye?"

"If you want to call me back, I'd like to at least say goodbye."

"It's better if I don't."

"What about a number in L.A. if you need to reach him for anything?"

"I won't need to reach him."

"No. I suppose not. I just thought—you know, if maybe—"

A harsh intake of breath. A muttered expletive. "Damn it, Gwyn, I don't want to do this."

"I'm doing the right thing, Sandy."

Ever loyal, her friend responded with quick stoutness, "Of course you are, sweetie. You're absolutely doing the right thing."

"Nothing that hurts this much can be right."

"I just wondered, that's all. In case you ever decided you wanted to talk to him..." Sandy's voice trailed into a wistfulness that made Gwyn's hand twist into a fist over her heart.

"Call me, Gwyn. Talk to me. Please."

Gwyn's hard-won resolve began a slow crumple. She stood, sending her office chair rolling into the wall behind her. "Um, Sand? I have to go—I hear one of the kids up."

Sandy would hear the lie in her voice, but she couldn't remain any longer on the phone with her well-meaning friend. Not if she was going to survive this.

"I'll call you in the morning, all right?"

A pause, then Sandy's sympathy reached out to her through the line. "Sure, sweetie, I understand. And Gwyn?"

"Yes?" her voice had dropped to a strangled whisper.

"Try to get some sleep, okay? You're almost there."

CHAPTER 44

Sleep turned out not to be much of an issue, however. In fact, it became a complete *non*-issue around eleven, when Gwyn gave up on the idea after a mere half-hour of lying in bed with Gareth's message replaying on an unending audio-loop in her head.

Faced with the entire night ahead—and seven and a half hours until Gareth's plane left, not that she was counting—she did the only sane thing she could.

She cleaned. The entire house. From top to bottom, with the exception of the bedrooms where, to her immense relief, her children slumbered peacefully despite her frenzied attempts to avoid thinking or feeling or imagining...

And when she finished with the routine chores such as bathrooms and dusting and mopping, she cleaned cupboards, closets, her office, and the fridge. She wiped, sorted, polished, discarded, and in general did whatever was necessary to keep Gareth's voice out of her head and her own traitorous misgivings tightly locked away.

"*You're almost there,*" Sandy's voice reminded her.

She clung to the reassurance in the words. She *was* almost there. A few more hours and she would have what she wanted: her life back. Gareth would be gone, her family could return to normal, and—

Gareth would be gone.

Gwyn paused in mid wipe-down of the top fridge shelf. She waited for her heart to climb out of her toes and into its proper place again. Almost there? Normal? Who did she think she was kidding? She'd never been further from normal in her life. Not even when Jack had left her with three children to raise on her own.

Bloody hell, to coin a phrase.

She sat back on her heels, took a firm grip on her wayward heart, and returned to her cleaning. *Small steps, Gwyn. Make it until six—*

When Gareth would be gone.

—and then deal with the next thing. Like the rest of your life without him.

Bloody hell.

She ran out of nooks, crannies, and dust-bunnies at three-thirty a.m., with two and a half hours remaining before Gareth's departure. Pushing back a sweat-dampened lock of hair, she stared at the kitchen clock. Now what? She considered the idea of sleep again, but a brief inventory of her energy level told her she'd worked herself past that magical moment of fatigue and into the kind of wired over-exhaustion that guaranteed several more wakeful hours.

She returned to her contemplation of *now what?* She glanced again at the clock. Three thirty-five. Two hours and twenty-five—

Stop it. You're just making it worse.

She looked around the kitchen. Raindrops drummed against the kitchen window. There had to be something—her eye fell on the half-open door to the laundry room, and she groaned. God, no. She couldn't possibly be that desperate, could she?

Her gaze strayed back to the clock. Three thirty-seven.

Or maybe she could.

She crossed the kitchen and pushed open the laundry room door. A basket sat on the counter, overflowing filled with items of clothing that most of them had forgotten they even owned. She swore it existed solely to torment her.

Shoring up her resolve, she stalked across the freshly cleaned floor and reached up to the cupboard above the basket for the iron.

She set up the board in the living room where she could have the dual distraction of television in addition to the detested chore. Settling on a re-run of an old sitcom, she tugged the first piece of clothing from the tangle in the basket. A few minutes later she had Katie's favorite dress neatly hung from the doorway molding.

One item down and approximately thirty to go.

With luck, that would be enough to keep her occupied until take-off.

Wind gusted against the house. Gwyn glanced out the window at the rain-drenched night. Would his flight even leave on time in this weather? Regardless, he'd have to be at the airport early to get through security for an international flight.

Which means he'll be up by now, if you want to call.

The traitorous thought rocked her back on her heels. Lord, could her extremely annoying inner voice not give her the least bit of rest? Of course she didn't want to call. That would only prolong the agony—for both of them.

She plucked another item from the basket and blindly spread it out on the ironing board. They'd already said the necessary goodbyes. Another conversation at this point would be nothing more than a rehash of what had already been covered. It would change nothing. It couldn't, because she wouldn't allow a repeat of Jack in their lives.

She swiped the iron over the fabric on the board. Stopped. Stared.

She was ironing Gareth's shirt. The denim one he'd worn when he'd cleaned out the bathtub. The one she'd watched him take off ever so slowly in her upstairs hallway while her toes curled into the carpet and her heart—

The smell of superheated fabric singed her nostrils. She yanked the iron off the shirt and set it upright with a shaking hand.

And then stood helpless before a flood of other images that refused to be stopped.

Gareth's dark head thrown back in a delighted laugh. His gentle arms cradling her sick daughter. His gaze, nearly black in its intensity, pinning her to the wall like a captured butterfly. His body wedged into a rocking chair with her son for story-telling. His capable hands making short work of cleaning a kitchen. Those same capable hands intent on another purpose altogether...

And then his voice, speaking words that she had refused to listen to, hadn't wanted to hear. *"Damn it, Gwyn, there doesn't have to be this much pain. I'm not Jack. I'm not running out on anyone."*

Gwyn put a quivering hand to her mouth.

Gareth wasn't Jack.

And he wasn't running out on them.

This wasn't about him at all. It was about her. Her need— because she'd been so wrong about a man once—not to repeat her error now. Dear heaven, out of sheer desperation, she'd forced the very break-up she'd sworn to avoid.

The illumination was nearly blinding.

"Gwynneth Jacobs," her own muffled voice said to the accompaniment of the sitcom's canned laugh-track, "you idiot!"

A sudden shadow loomed over her mind.

Gareth. The plane.

Oh, God.

She looked at her watch. Twelve minutes after four. He'd be getting ready to leave for the airport. She had to stop him.

She unplugged the iron and bolted for the kitchen. Shaking fingers dialed Gareth's cell-phone number, committed to memory in spite of herself when she'd finally been able to erase it from the fridge white-board. Midway through the first ring, a tinny female voice cut in to advise that the cell phone number was no longer in use.

Gwyn pushed the call end button with a shaking hand. Of course. He would have picked up a temporary cell phone to use while he was in town, but now that he was leaving—

Now that he was leaving and she couldn't remember his cousin's phone number...God, now what?

"Think, Gwyn, think!"

Phone in hand and Kirsten's line ringing in her ear, she jogged back down the hallway. Taking the stairs two at a time, she struggled out of her soiled sweatshirt. Two rings, nothing. She darted into her bedroom and stripped off her jeans, then scrabbled in her closet for clean ones.

Halfway through the fourth ring, Kirsten's sleep-drugged voice mumbled a greeting. Gwyn pulled her head out of the closet, fresh jeans in hand.

"Kirsten, thank God you're home!"

"Gwyn?" her babysitter muttered. "What time is it? What's wrong?"

"It's late. Or early. Very early." Phone tucked into the crook of her shoulder, she struggled to pull on the jeans without toppling. "I need you to watch the kids for me."

"Now?"

"Five minutes ago, actually." Gwyn tried to keep the panic from her voice as she looked again at her watch. Four twenty-three. He'd be going through security in just over a half-hour. The drive to the airport would take her—she didn't want to think about how long the drive would take. She just wanted to get there.

"Kirsten, please. I don't have time to explain. Just please, please get over here. Don't even get dressed, okay?"

Finally awake, her babysitter's voice cleared. "I'm on my way."

Gwyn tossed the phone onto her bed and wrenched open a drawer in search of socks. Before she had the second one pulled on, the doorbell rang. Lord, the poor girl must not have even bothered with shoes.

She grabbed a turtleneck from another drawer and tugged it on over her head as she ran down the stairs. Opening the door with one hand, she reached for her coat with the other.

"That was fast. Thank you so much, Kirst—Sandy!" She stopped and stared at her friend. "What are you doing here at this hour?"

"I've been thinking about it and I've decided you're wrong. You're not doing the right thing." Sandy brushed past her, unbuttoning her coat. "Go get dressed. If you hurry, you can catch him before he goes through secur—wait. You *are* dressed. But how did you know I was coming?"

"I didn't." Gwyn slid her arms into her coat. "I decided I was wrong too."

"Well, it's about bloody time."

Gwyn took the keys from the hook by the closet door and picked up her purse from the bench. "Kirsten's on her way over—can you stay until she gets here?"

"Of course—but exactly how many babysitters did you call?"

Gwyn paused in her search for gloves. "One, of course. Why?"

"Because I know Kirsten, but I don't know her." Sandy pointed out the door.

Gwyn peered at the dripping wet girl on the porch. Even if her face hadn't been plastered all over the local news for the last week, she would have recognized her anywhere. With those eyes, she looked exactly like her father.

She set her purse down again. "Amy?"

"Mrs. Jacobs, I know this must be a surprise, but I've been thinking all day and all night and I can't help but feel this is all my fault and I could never forgive myself if you let Gareth go because of me and I think you'd be making a terrible mistake and won't you please go after him?"

After that number of words strung together in a single breath, Gwyn could do little more than gape in astonishment at her unexpected visitor.

"Please?" Amy whispered.

A throat cleared in the shadows beyond Amy's shoulder. Gwyn sought the source of the sound, her gaze coming to rest on a petite blonde folding down an umbrella.

"Catherine Carlson," the woman said, holding out her hand. "Amy's mother. She woke me a half-hour ago and explained everything on the way over. Apparently she holds me at least partly responsible for the mess between you and Gareth. For the record, I think she's right— both about me being responsible and about you going after him."

Gwyn automatically shook hands, unable to formulate even a murmured *hello*. Amy stumbled through an explanation of having always relied on public transport and never bothering to get her driver's license as the reason for dragging her mother into her relationship-rescue efforts. Beside her, Sandy stuck out a determined hand for her own introduction.

"Sandra Masters," she said. "Gwyn's friend. And her babysitter, if I can get her out the door."

Amy looked stricken. "But where are you going?"

"Yes," Kirsten's voice joined in with a yawn as she climbed onto the porch, shaking raindrops from her umbrella. "Where *are* you going at this ungodly hour?"

"To the airport," Sandy said briskly. She handed Gwyn's gloves and a plaid umbrella to her and steered her out the door. "The roads are awful, so drive carefully, but hurry. You'll have to catch him before he goes through security."

Gwyn glanced at her watch. Four thirty-five.

Sandy smiled reassurance. "You'll make it," she promised. "Now go."

"The kids—"

"Will be fine. If they wake up, they can join the party. Ladies, who wants coffee?"

And just like that, Gwyn found herself driving through the pouring rain to the airport with a four-thirty a.m. coffee klatch going on in her house.

CHAPTER 45

Gareth slouched against the passenger door of Sean's car, his elbow resting at the base of the window, fingers absently tracing his bottom lip. Rain sheeted against the window, distorting the view flashing past.

She hadn't called.

He hadn't really expected her to—or at least, he hadn't thought he expected it—but he had hoped. Bloody hell, how he'd hoped. Now the reality of her silence wedged like a brick beneath his ribs, making his every breath ache. He'd waited until the last possible second before leaving Sean's apartment—waited and hovered by the phone, but to no avail.

He rubbed his hand over gritty eyes. Even now, he couldn't believe it was over. Couldn't believe Gwyn had convinced him at last that this was what she wanted; that it was for the best. With every fiber of his being, he'd wanted to deny her words, to show her how very wrong she was.

But her desire for safety was so strong it overshadowed everything else in her life, including him, and her simple, unequivocal *"I want my life back"* had been his final undoing. Try as he might, he had been unable to find the elusive argument to her twisted logic.

Gareth scowled at his reflection. Perhaps he'd been attempting the impossible all along. Maybe no logic existed to counter the illogical. Maybe he was going about this the wrong way.

A soft grunt of surprise escaped him.

"Something wrong?" Sean asked from the driver's seat beside him.

"I'm not sure." Gareth re-wound his thought process and played it over again in his mind. Was it possible? Could that really be the solution? Could it be that simple?

Gareth shifted in his seat and stared at his cousin. "Sean, how do you handle a complete lack of logic?"

"In an argument, you mean?" Sean shrugged. "I don't."

"But what if you want to win the argument?"

"It depends on how important winning is, I suppose. And how sure I am that I'm right."

"You're very sure. And you need to win."

"Actions speak louder than words, cuz," Sean said matter-of-factly. "And it took you long enough to figure it out."

Gareth sighed. He really hated when Sean made those cryptic little remarks that seemed to have nothing whatsoever to do with the conversation.

"Figure what out?"

"That you won't convince her with words. Or by giving up."

Gareth glowered at his cousin. "And you didn't share these words of wisdom with me before because—?"

Sean snorted. "Let's just say Gwyn hasn't been the only one suffering from a certain amount of illogic."

Taking a deep breath, Gareth counted to ten. Then to ten again. "Turn the car around." he said. "I'm not going to the airport."

"I know."

"I—you know?"

"Mm. Another thing I was waiting for you to figure out."

Gareth peered out into the rain-lashed, still-dark morning, taking real note of his surroundings for the first time. "We're in Aylmer."

"A block from Gwyn's. I looked up her address this afternoon."

Gareth struggled with conflicting desires to both hug his cousin and slug him. Before he could decide which action to take first, Sean pulled up on the street behind two other vehicles in front of Gwyn's brightly lit house.

"Does your girlfriend always throw parties at five in the morning?" He slipped the car's gear shift into park.

"Not that I'm aware of." Gareth's gaze settled on the empty driveway and his stomach sank. "Especially when she's not home."

Sean switched off the engine. "Well, we're here now, so we might as well see what's going on."

Mayhem, thought Gareth as Gwyn's door swung open and a crowd of faces stared at him in dismay. That's what was going on.

"You can't be here!" a distraught Sandy squealed at him, very nearly dancing a jig on the spot. "You're supposed to be at the airport!"

"Gareth?" a familiar voice asked with equal distress.

"Amy?" He stared at his daughter in bewilderment. "What are you doing here?"

"I brought her," his ex-wife informed him coolly, balancing a scowling Nicholas on her hip. "The question is what are *you* doing here?"

"Catherine! What the hell is going on?"

And why was Nicholas glaring at him with such ferocity?

A cacophony of voices followed, each so loud and excited he didn't have a hope of picking out just one. He exchanged bemused looks with Sean, then held up both hands.

"Quiet!" he bellowed.

Instant silence reigned.

"Thank you." He looked around the expectant faces and pointed to one. "You. Kirsten, isn't it?"

Gwyn's babysitter nodded.

Gareth took a deep breath, did his best to rein in his growing impatience, and grated, "Where the bloody hell is Gwyn?"

Kirsten looked at the watch on her wrist and stifled a yawn. "Halfway to the airport, probably."

"Halfway—why?"

"Why do you think, you bloody dense oaf?" his ever-proper ex-wife asked. She rolled her eyes toward the ceiling. "She went to stop you from getting on the plane."

He couldn't help it. He gaped. "She what?"

"Go after her!" Amy's voice urged.

"He'll never make it," someone else said.

More voices chimed in, their volume surging again.

"Maybe he should stay here."

"What happens if he meets her halfway back?"

"We could call the airport and ask them to page her."

The voices faded to meaningless noise as Gareth struggled to absorb the news. Gwyn had gone after him. She wanted to stop him. She'd changed her mind. She was at the airport.

And he was here.

His hand shot out and grasped Sean's arm. "We have to go after her."

But his cousin shook his head. "You'll never make it. By the time we get there, she'll be on her way back. You're better off waiting for her here."

"That will take forever."

"It'll take less time than driving out to the airport and back," Sean pointed out. Then, with a mock-innocent grin, he added, "Besides, just think how fast time will pass with all these people to keep you company."

Gareth stared again at the expectant faces, now joined by Maggie and Katie. He could handle the kids, he thought, but the others?

"Maybe you'd all like to go home?" he suggested hopefully. "You could still catch some sleep..."

"And miss the outcome?" Sandy demanded. "Not on your life."

The others' heads nodded agreement. With a sigh, Gareth resigned himself to his temporary fate. A tug on his pant leg drew his attention. He looked down into Maggie's face and dropped to one knee beside her.

"Hey, Magpie, how are you doing?"

"Fine, thank you." She stuck the tip of a finger into her mouth and leaned against his shoulder, regarding him curiously.

"What?" he asked.

"Are we having a party?" she asked.

"I don't think so, sweetheart. At least, not yet. Maybe when your mum gets home we can think of something to celebrate."

She nodded, then looked around as her brother placed his lips close to her ear and whispered something. Nicholas stepped away again, arms crossed and still scowling. Maggie turned back to Gareth.

"Nich'las wants to know if he still has to punch you in the nose."

With a superhuman effort, Gareth swallowed his laughter and regarded her solemnly. "You tell Nicholas," he said, "that physical violence will no longer be necessary."

Maggie frowned in confusion at the lengthy sentence.

Gareth gave her a hug.

"No, love," he said. "He doesn't have to punch me anymore."

CHAPTER 46

She'd missed him.

All that soul-searching, all that effort, all those people in her house rooting her on...

And she'd missed him.

Gwyn stared up at the departure screen. She'd made it to the airport in what she'd thought was record time and had camped out beside the security gate, certain she'd catch him before he passed through. Before he boarded. Before he left.

She'd stood, dripping onto the polished floor, anxiously scanning the faces of the passengers, drawing suspicious looks from security staff. She'd remained when the final boarding call came for his flight, and while the last few stragglers passed through the gates and disappeared.

Gareth hadn't been among them.

Somehow, in spite of her efforts, he'd made it through the gate before she'd arrived. Disappeared into the belly of the airport where she couldn't follow, couldn't explain, couldn't tell him how wrong she'd been.

And now the departures board blinked with cool green numbers and letters that said his plane was gone. On time. In spite of the weather. And she didn't have a phone number for him, and she didn't know his cousin's last name, and she couldn't ever reach him again.

He would never know she'd changed her mind.

Gwyn paused before opening the door, bracing to meet the crowd waiting for news on the other side. She could handle the questions, but the inevitable sympathy...?

That might be another matter altogether.

Maybe they'd understand she needed some time and space. Maybe they'd look at her, instinctively grasp what had happened, and just leave without comment. Maybe.

Pushing open the door, she stepped into the front hall—and utter chaos.

"What happened?"

"Where have you been?"

"We were worried sick!"

"What took you so long?"

She stared in confusion at the faces confronting her, not one of them showing the kind of curiosity—or the compassion—that she'd expected.

"I was at the airport," she said, thinking that they needed reminding for some bizarre reason, "trying to find Gareth. But I missed him."

Saying it out loud brought a new, fresh pain and she caught her breath sharply. "I missed him," she said again, whispering this time. "He's gone."

Instead of the offered arms or condolences she'd decided might not be so bad after all, however, a fresh babble broke out among the gathered company.

And then, through the clamor of voices, her name. Softly spoken in deep, rich, unmistakable tones. Gwyn started. She stared.

One by one, the others quieted. One by one, they smiled and moved aside and departed in the direction of the kitchen, towing a protesting Nicholas with them past the figure standing halfway down the hall. Until no one stood between her and—

"Gareth?" she whispered, staring in disbelief. "But you're on a plane to L.A. I couldn't stop you."

"On the contrary, you couldn't make me go."

"I—I couldn't?"

He shook his head. "I decided you were wrong after all."

"You did?"

"I decided," he continued, beginning the slow, measured advance that always wreaked such havoc with her nervous system, "that if it takes the rest of my life, I will somehow convince you to trust me."

She took an involuntary step back, coming up against the front door someone had closed. Gareth stopped a scant few inches away. He braced his right hand against the door beside her head, his left hand on the other side. A familiar, sweet ache began low in her belly. She breathed in his scent. Minty, musky, all male.

"I'm not Jack, Gwyn."

"I know."

"Say it," he demanded.

"You're not Jack," she whispered.

Gareth's mouth, so near her own, curved with grim satisfaction. She lifted her gaze to the banked fire glowing in the depths of his eyes.

"You're Gareth Connor," she said. "The man I love. The man I trust."

Gareth drew a ragged breath.

"God—you so very nearly convinced me—"

She put her hand to his mouth, stopping his words. "I'm so sorry," she said. "I was afraid—not just for the kids, but for me, too. I couldn't face losing you."

"So you sent me away?" he asked dryly. He took her hand in one of his and pressed his lips to her palm. "I was so tied up inside over hurting you that it almost seemed logical," he admitted. "I just wanted to make it better for you."

"You did," she said. "You came back."

His gaze darkened. "And I will never, ever leave."

Gwyn shook her head. "I don't need promises, Gareth."

"Perhaps not, but I need to make them. I love you, Gwynneth with two n's, and I will *not* leave you, do you understand?"

Her breath caught in her chest. She nodded. "I understand," she whispered.

"Good," Gareth growled, tipping her face up to his. "And now that we've cleared that up—"

"Mommy?" Nicholas' voice queried politely.

Gareth went rigid against her. He sighed. "Or perhaps not."

He turned his head, dropped his chin to his chest, and regarded her son with a wry patience she admired tremendously, given her own desire to scream.

"Yes, Nicholas, we're kissing," he said. "Or trying to."

"That wasn't my question."

"Of course it wasn't." Gareth shot Gwyn a long-suffering look. Removing his hands from her hips, he stepped away with a muffled groan. Then he turned his full attention to the little boy. "Right then. How can we help you?"

"Katie says you and Mommy are in love."

Gareth quirked an eyebrow at her. "Ever notice how your eldest always seems to be the instigator behind these interruptions?"

He slid his hands into his pockets, leaned against the wall beside the living room doorway, and regarded Nicholas with utmost seriousness. "What exactly is your question, Nicholas?"

"If you *are* in love, does that mean we're getting married?"

Gwyn caught her breath, heat rising from her neck to scorch her face. "Lord, Nicholas," she groaned, "how in the world do you come up with these things?"

"Katie told me to ask!" her son replied indignantly.

Gareth chuckled and shot her an *I told you so* look, then turned his attention back to Nicholas. "Do you think we should get married?"

Nicholas eyed him. "If we do, can I have two bedtime stories and watch cartoons before school?"

She watched Gareth struggle to maintain his straight face. "Um...that would be a no."

"Man!" Nicholas heaved a heavy sigh, then gave a prosaic shrug of his shoulders. "Oh, well. We can still get married if you want."

"Nicholas—" Gwyn moved to crouch beside her son, but a strong hand on her arm stopped her and drew her back up again.

"It's not quite what I had in mind," Gareth said quietly, "but I'm learning that not much goes according to plan where your kids are involved. And besides, I do want."

Her world went very still.

Gareth smiled a slow, unhurried smile that made her toes curl against the floor. With strong, capable, infinitely gentle fingers, he brushed back the hair from her face.

"I want," he continued, "to have you beside me for the rest of my life. I want to share your home, and your family, and your heart. I want to face every day with you; to laugh with you; to lighten your load in every way I can. I want to hold you in my arms every night and make love to you every chance I get. I want, my darling Gwyn, to be your husband, if you'll have me."

"Is that a yes?" Nicholas asked, tugging at Gwyn's sweater. "Are we getting married?"

The intrusion jolted Gwyn out of a stupor that might have otherwise rendered her catatonic. She smiled down at her son, and then raised her face to Gareth.

"Yes, Nicky," she said. Sheer, unadulterated joy swelled in her, chasing away every last shred of insecurity she had ever experienced. "That's a yes. We're getting married."

Gareth's eyes locked with hers, his love an unmistakable blaze in their depths as his arms slipped around her.

"*Now* can we have a party?" Maggie demanded, wedging herself between Gwyn and the wall and gazing up expectantly.

Ignoring the new intruder, Gareth completed his enfolding of Gwyn, burying his face in her hair and wrapping her so close that no one else could possibly come between them.

"I love you," he muttered.

"I love you, too."

"And you know that I love your kids."

She sensed something more behind his words and drew back a little to raise an eyebrow. "But?"

He sighed and cast a wistful look at the crew that had assembled near their feet. "But if I'm allowed one last want," he said, "I would really like a nice, long honeymoon. Without kids."

OTHER BOOKS BY LINDA POITEVIN

Sins of the Angels (Grigori Legacy #1)
Sins of the Son (Grigori Legacy #2)
Sins of the Lost (Grigori Legacy #3)

COMING SOON

Forever Grace

ABOUT THE AUTHOR

Linda Poitevin lives near Ottawa, Canada's capital, with her husband, youngest of three daughters, one very large husky/shepherd/great Dane-cross dog, two cats, a rabbit, and a bearded dragon lizard. When she isn't writing, she can usually be found in her garden or walking her dog along the river or through the woods. She loves to hear from readers, and you can email her at *info@lindapoitevin.com* or stay in touch with her on Facebook, Twitter, and her blog for news and updates.